THE LOCK-UP

A DCI BOYD THRILLER

ALEX SCARROW

Published by GrrBooks

Dad, this is the Boyd book you never got a chance to read. I hope, if there's some kind of afterlife, you can read it over my shoulder. This one's for you. Miss you, mate. X

1

'All right, everyone! Thanks for turning up so early... but let's have some quiet in here, please!'

Colin Holmes turned away from the bellowing storage-unit manager to his friend and patted the wad of notes in his jacket pocket. 'It's this unit we want, Sid.'

Sid had a wad of notes too, clutched tightly in both hands. 'Why this one?' he asked. 'What's so special about it?'

Colin nodded at the yellow corrugated pull-up door, on which was stencilled 'Unit 37', Banksy style. 'It's one of the older ones. Look at the edges,' he said, pointed them out. 'The paint's chipped.'

From experience, Colin knew what to look out for. Frequent opening tended to chip the paint at the sides of the door and the storage company repainted them when the units became vacant.

'Means it's been used for ages. Might be full of old stuff that's worth something,' he said. He glanced at Sid. 'You sure you're okay with me doing the bidding?'

Sid nodded. It was his first auction and he'd taken a giant leap of faith in stumping up his half of the money –

five hundred quid was no small amount in these hard-pressed times. 'Sure. Just don't go mad, though.'

Colin shook his head. 'We've a ceiling bid of a grand. I promise. But we won't get anywhere close to it, mate. Trust m–'

'Quiet! *Please!*' barked the manager.

Colin shut up.

'All right, then. Here we have Unit Thirty-Seven. Its ten-year lease expired last year and I've not been able to get hold of the renter, so its contents are up for grabs now. Right then, let's start the bidding.'

This morning, Colin noticed, only a small crowd of *panners* had turned up. And most of them had gone once the previous unit's auction had run its course. That unit was so old that even the number itself had started to chip off the corrugated iron. The veteran panners had all been there for that one and the bid price had crept up to just over six hundred.

'Starting bid of fifty!' began the manager. 'Let me hear fifty.'

A hand raised beside Colin.

'Fifty, bid. One hundred, anyone?'

Colin cautiously side-eyed the other dozen or so bidders gathered there. *Not yet. Hold on. Don't look too keen.* He kept his hand down. Another hand went up. The manager asked for one fifty and the first bidder raised his hand again.

'Two hundred?' the manager called out.

Colin had managed to rally Sid into going halves with him fairly easily, because Sid's second-hand shop was starting to look pretty bare. Colin had thought that the recession would have been a boom time for Sid, but quite the opposite had happened. No one seemed to be moving house or refurbishing and thus willing to part with resaleable household items just to be rid of them. And the people who did come into his old warehouse were after silly-priced, rock-bottom bargains. Sid was desperate for some super-cheap items that he could tart up and fill the floor with again.

'Two fifty!' The manager beamed at a ruddy-faced woman with frizzy long ginger hair tumbling down over her rounded shoulders and a T-shirt that bore a caricature of Harry and Meghan and the words 'Ginge & Whinge'. 'Thank you, love. Do I hear three hundred?'

Colin chanced another glance at his fellow bidders. Interest seemed to be waning now.

'Three hundred? Anyone?'

Colin raised his hand with a show of vague interest.

'Excellent! Three fifty, folks. Do I hear any advance on three fifty?'

Frizzy Hair met Colin's gaze with a steely '*Don't even go there, sonny*' expression on her face. 'Three-fifty,' she said.

Bollocks.

'Four hundred? What d'ya say?' asked the manager, looking at Colin. Sid was staring at him too, urging him to go for it.

Easy, thought Colin. *Not too keen. Not too keen.*

He shrugged, pulled a face and began to make a show of turning away. Then, just as the manager was shifting towards the woman, Colin paused and raised a hand. 'Go on, then. Let's do four.'

The manager nodded at him. 'Four, it is. Ma'am?'

Frizzy Hair curled her lip at Colin, then shook her head.

'Four hundred! Four hundred!' The manager hesitated before saying it a third time, then nodded at Colin. 'It's yours for four hundred.'

~

It took a couple of minutes for Colin to fill in the paperwork: a GDPR form requiring him to hand over any items that might contain personal data for wiping; and a disclaimer excusing the storage business from liability of any injury sustained in clearing out the unit. He stood by Unit 37, waiting for the other panners to move on, to bid for the next auction unit. There were always loiterers, nosy buggers who wanted to get a glimpse of what they'd just missed out on.

Frizzy Hair was one of them.

'Excuse me?' said Colin. 'Are you waiting for something?'

'Just curious,' she replied testily.

Sid, though, was eager to unlock the padlock and get a look inside. 'Never mind her.'

'Yeah, well...' stalled Colin, glaring at her. 'It's *my* unit now, love. Why don't you move along?'

'Rude,' she muttered. But she turned her back and finally strode away to catch up with the others who were now at the far end of the passage.

'Come on, mate,' said Sid. 'Let's see what we've got.'

Colin released the padlock and bent down to grab the handle. 'Ready?' he said to Sid with a grin.

Sid's head bobbed frantically like a dashboard nodding dog.

'All righty, then...' said Colin. 'Let's see what treasure we've won.' He jerked the sliding door upwards with a shrill screech of unoiled castors.

He stared in silence for a few moments at the unit's contents, then finally he sighed.

'Oh... shit.'

2

Now, see... this is much better.*

There was actually room to stretch a little. Boyd had always been a restless sleeper, flipping from one side then to the other like a freshly landed tuna, as Julia had always said. In Charlotte's modest double bed, with Ozzie and Mia taking up leg room at the bottom end, he'd been boxed in and committed to picking one carefully chosen Tetris position at lights out and sticking with it for the night. It was that or cause a Mexican wave of shuffling bodies as everyone reconfigured.

His bed, however – his *king-sized* bed – afforded him the luxury of returning to his old habits with space to spare.

The gulls were loud this morning, screeching with excitement as they swooped and dive- bombed above Ashburnham Road. Boyd presumed they knew it was a Thursday and the first weekend of June was just round the corner, with all the opportunities for airborne thuggery that that entailed: stealing ice creams from unsuspecting toddlers and chips from unguarded cardboard cones. The weekend DFLs and local out-of-towners were lambs to the slaughter as far as the feathered mafia were concerned.

He checked his watch. 6.05 a.m. It was far too early to stir. But – thank you, gulls – he was wide awake now and unlikely to get back to sleep. Instead, he turned to look at Charlotte, sleeping softly, her face lost beneath dishevelled locks of auburn hair. The hair fairies had clearly had a party with her last night. He gently lifted a tress to reveal her lips and nose. He couldn't help but smile at the way her lips twitched in her sleep: pouting, then pursing, pouting, then pursing again. He wondered what she was dreaming about. Eating a Creme Egg? Counting ticket sales at the theatre?

He settled onto his back and looked up at the high ceiling. There were mornings when he promised himself he'd bring the ladder up here and dust the numerous cobwebs from the picture rail and coving. Not today, though. Today his mind was on the Stephen Knight court case. It was Day Three, and Warren was due to step up to the witness stand this morning to do his bit. Knight was likely going down for those girls he murdered and hid in his Martello tower over three decades, but the clincher would almost certainly be his attempt to gut young DC Warren with his antique Napoleonic bayonet. Knight's barrister was probably going to try to make the violent struggle look like self-defence at the hands of an overzealous and inexperienced young detective: '*The blade? Well, as my client has already said, it fell off the wall during the struggle, Your Honour, and my client was in a state of alarm after DC Warren launched his unnecessary attack.*'

Boyd smiled. *Right. Like that's going to wash.*

Warren was shitting-bricks nervous, though. It was his first ever court attendance and Boyd knew that the young DC's eyes would be frantically searching him out in the gallery for moral support – although Boyd hadn't yet decided whether or not he should actually go to the court with him. Maybe it would be better if he just waited outside in the lobby. Either way, he'd planned to go into work an hour early to review Warren's account of events with him one more time and to remind him, again, of all the witness-stand dos and don'ts.

Boyd's phone buzzed once on his side table to remind him to get up. He did so slowly, careful not to wake Charlotte. Ozzie and Mia hopped off the bed onto the floor as he pulled on his work clothes. Not the tired uniform that Sutherland insisted he wear while inhabiting his old office and temporary DSI role but a smart suit. Dark blue and actually ironed.

Ozzie woofed. A test bark. He was getting ready to shout for his breakfast. Boyd raised a finger to hush him. 'In a minute, mate,' he whispered. 'Just give me a bloody minute.'

He needed to be in work for 8 a.m. Warren would be waiting for him, his printed-out statement clasped tightly in his trembling hands. Boyd laced up his old Oxfords, dangled a burgundy tie around the collar of his unbuttoned and untucked shirt and led the dogs out of the room.

Mia and Ozzie headed along the landing, then tumbled down the stairs nosily – like a herd of bloody elephants, the pair of them – to wait for Boyd in the kitchen. He passed Emma's door and lingered for a moment, curious to know if she was having another murmured early-morning conversation on her phone with Dan.

Officially they had split up. But negotiations, it seemed, were ongoing. Looming fatherhood had scared Dan away, as Boyd had thought it might, but he wasn't *gone* gone. They were talking still, at least.

He heard nothing, so he started down the stairs, pausing

and wincing for a moment at the slight pain in his side. It was like a jogger's stitch that kept coming and going, with increasing regularity, but it tended to pass quickly. He hastened towards the kitchen to get the dogs' breakfast served up before a noisy protest kicked off and woke everyone up.

Ozzie was frantically jumping on the spot like dead weight on a bungee cord, while Mia circled Boyd's legs daintily like a cat.

'I know, I know,' he said with a sigh as he dug into the bag of kibble beneath the counter. 'Dogs eat first.'

3

'Is that it?'

Sid looked at the largely empty storage unit. The mental image he'd had moments before Colin had rattled the sliding door upwards – of a unit cluttered with antique furniture and exotic dusty curios – had come crashing down around him. He was presently staring at three stacks of blue plastic storage crates in the middle of the floor and a lot of absolutely nothing else.

'Oh God, I'm so sorry, mate,' said Colin.

'Two hundred quid,' muttered Sid.

Colin's face coloured at Sid's disappointment. The old man had really needed a win, even a small one. 'I honestly thought it was going to be a juicy one. I'm so sorry,' Colin said again. 'You can pick the unit we bid on next time. I just had a stupid feeling about this one.'

Sid sighed. 'Can't help it, I s'pose, mate. Luck of the draw.'

Colin stepped into the unit and pulled the door halfway down. The last thing either of them wanted right now was for one of the other panners peering in and guffawing at their bad luck.

'Well, let's see what's in them, then,' said Sid. 'Maybe it's some DVDs... I could try flogging them this Sunday.'

'DVDs,' repeated Colin. 'I bloody hope not.' He suspected the world's landfills these days were a mix of DVDs, CDs and Covid-testing kits. Gone were the days when folks collected boxed-up movies, neatly stacked on MDF shelves in their home libraries. Every movie ever made was streamable from somewhere now, and, he reflected, pretty much nobody actually watched them any more... They were just background noise while people endlessly doom-scrolled on their phones.

He approached the stacked crates and pulled out a Stanley knife as he spotted the packing tape wrapped generously around the plastic lids.

'Could be comics, maybe?' said Sid hopefully. Now *those* definitely did have a collectors' market.

There was still hope.

Colin reached up to grab one of the topmost crates. 'Christ, it's heavy. Can you give me a hand?' And Sid helped him ease it down onto the dusty floor.

'Heavy is promising,' grunted Sid. 'Books, d'you think?'

Sid's warehouse had a corner devoted to worthy collectibles: sets of the *Encyclopaedia Britannica* and leather-bound *Collected Works of Shakespeare* that looked nice all lined up with their spines facing out.

Colin gently slid the blade along the tightly taped edges of the lid. The packing tape had clearly been applied carefully, creating a proper seal. He grinned at Sid. 'Maybe it's a stack of signed Harry Potter first editions, hey?'

Sid lifted one side of his bushy grey, walrus-like moustache with a wry smile. 'Now that would be a bloody good find, wouldn't it?'

Colin finished slicing through the tape. He could feel the lid, loose in his hands, waiting for the big '*Ta-da!*' lift-and-reveal.

He puffed his lips. 'Okay.' And he pulled the lid off.

Although it took their eyes a moment to work out what they were staring at, the fetid odour was unmistakable.

4

'You look like shit this morning, babycakes.'

Okeke looked up from the kitchen table at Jay. 'I had that frigging dream again,' she said.

'The ninja sword one?'

She nodded. She'd begun to hope that she'd got away with the incident in Karl's mothballed brewery. The events of that particular night in Brighton had been months ago, and, perhaps naively, she'd started to believe that her recollection of them was becoming manageable, successfully boxed up and sealed away in her mind, like toxic waste. But instead the memory – and one moment in particular – had begun to leak into her dreams. It was the *sensory* memory that haunted her: the impact of the sword slicing into the man's torso, the sickening sound as it caught his ribs, followed by his gurgling groan as he'd slid to the floor. And the last image she'd had of him: eyeballs rolling upwards in their sockets, mouth silently opening and closing like a dying fish in a wet market.

'Yup. The ninja sword,' she said finally. Jay had been there but he hadn't witnessed it.

Meanwhile, he shrugged on his jacket and wrapped an arm around her neck, kissing the top of her head. 'You should see someone at work about that,' he advised.

'Can't,' she replied, looking up at him, 'can I?'

Their desperate fight in that building was something that had 'never officially happened'. It was their secret. Forever. Boyd's, Warren's, hers and Jay's.

The old brewery had burned to the ground, the three bodies of the Russian mobsters inside had never been identified. The four of them had their pact. They would never speak of it again and they were never there. So confessing her flashbacks to a police shrink wasn't really on the cards.

'Then try not to think about it,' he offered helpfully, kissing her again. 'It's done. We won. We got away with it.'

Okeke shook her head. 'It really is *that* simple for you, isn't it?'

He shrugged. 'Well, they weren't very nice men, were they?'

To Okeke, Jay seemed to exist in a simple world of black and white. Good guys and bad guys. The bad guys had killed his friend Karl... and had been intent on killing him too, which meant they were fair game and had deserved what they got.

'It's over,' he said, stepping back from her and adjusting his tie. 'We gotta move on, babes.'

She nodded. 'I'll be all right,' she said, sipping her coffee. 'You'd better get off to work or you'll be late.'

Today was his Big Day. His first shift at McGuire and Hampton. The Eastbourne-based private investigation firm had somehow managed to see past his lumbering Jason Statham-like exterior and spotted some potential. Jay had given up on his hare-brained notion of joining the police –

to Okeke's relief – and had scraped together enough NVQ credits to qualify as a PI gopher.

He leant over her shoulder and kissed her lips, which she puckered sideways to meet his. 'Maybe you should pull a sickie?' he said.

'I'll be fine,' she replied. 'Go on, bugger off. You don't want to be late on your first day.'

'Right.' He kissed her again, grabbed his work bag and left the kitchen. A moment later the front door *thunked* heavily behind him.

She gazed out of the kitchen window at their messy backyard, still cluttered with Jay's unfinished furniture projects.

Move on, Sam. They were Bad Men. And now the world has three less sadistic bastards living in it.

5

Boyd reached the top of the stairs to the CID floor, sweating already. Today was looking like another scorcher. He took the last step, *oofﬁng* like an old man as the persistent stitch in his side stabbed painfully at him once again.

He pushed open the double doors and stepped into the familiar muted hubbub of the main CID floor. It was stuffy. None of the big windows opened properly. Instead, they magnified the sunlight spilling in, making the space feel like one big sodding greenhouse.

Boyd stepped into Sutherland's glass-walled office, which was even stuffier, if that was possible. He had only just dumped his jacket, loosened his tie and sat down when DSI Sutherland's perfectly round head and Penfold-like thick-framed glasses appeared in the open doorway.

'Morning, Boyd,' he chirped with syrupy cheerfulness.

'Morning,' Boyd grunted.

Sutherland stepped in. 'Is this a bad time for you?' he asked.

'Well, umm... I only just...' Boyd began.

Sutherland ignored him and settled down in the visitor's seat of what had been, up until a few months ago, *his* office. 'Boyd, I have a couple of things to mention,' he said.

'Not departmental cost spreadsheets, please,' Boyd cut in.

Sutherland wafted his hand. 'Oh, no, no, no – nothing like that.'

'Thank Christ,' Boyd muttered.

'Did you know,' Sutherland began, 'that DI Fox has requested a transfer to Brighton?'

Boyd shook his head. That was the first he'd heard of it. 'Really? Why?'

'He said he feels he's got more chance for a promotion over there than he has here,' replied Sutherland. 'Said he's felt overlooked. A bit of a spare wheel.'

Boyd pursed his lips. That was fair enough, he thought. Fox had been ditched from Flack's team – Flack had given no reason that Boyd knew of – and had been a 'floater' on the CIDs main floor ever since. Boyd could have, and probably should have, made more use of him, but... instead he'd got into the habit of using the same small team: Minter, Okeke, Warren and O'Neal. The dynamic between them worked well and tossing into the mix a DI who he didn't really know that well, who was also a rank above the perfectly capable Minter, would have meant shuffling the pecking order and probably also result in a few out-of-joint noses.

'Well anyway, Fox has put in for his transfer,' continued Sutherland. 'It's a done deal. Which means –'

'Which means,' cut in Boyd, 'there's room for internal promotion?'

Sutherland nodded. 'And I'm guessing you've got a suggestion for me?'

'DS Minter,' replied Boyd, without hesitation. 'He SIO'ed the Argyle House case and he did a fine job with it.'

'In between prancing around in budgie smugglers,' said Sutherland with a chortle.

Boyd grinned. 'He assures me his modelling gigs are mostly knitwear now.'

'Are you sure?' Sutherland asked. 'He's not planning a repeat performance ... or worse? I can't have my DIs running around in leather thongs now, can I?'

Boyd pulled a face. 'I suspect that pier gig has given him PTSD. He told me he's being a little more circumspect about the bookings he accepts going forward.'

'Well, I should ruddy well think so,' Sutherland said. 'Sussex Police has a serious reputation to protect.'

'Exactly,' Boyd said. 'Now can we talk about Okeke?'

'What about her?' Sutherland asked.

'I'd like to recommend her to rank up and take Minter's place,' Boyd said.

'To detective sergeant?'

Boyd nodded. 'She's long overdue.'

Sutherland made a gurgling sound. It was the kind of uncomfortable noise that Boyd would have made paying for a meal out in London. 'She can be arsey,' said Sutherland.

'She can be *difficult*,' Boyd agreed, 'but I think that's a good thing. She's definitely no pushover. You'll be glad to have her as a DCI one day. Trust me.'

'God help me,' Sutherland muttered.

'To be honest, she should have been ranked up to sergeant when she transferred from Kent. She's more than capable of the role,' Boyd pressed. 'It's not going to add to your budget. She'd be filling a vacant slot.'

'I suppose you want to promote Warren. And O'Neal too?' Sutherland grumbled.

'Relax. It's just Minter and Okeke,' Boyd said. 'The other two need a few more years under their belts.' He shrugged. 'Although Warren's showing promise.'

'He's got his court appearance today, hasn't he?' Sutherland said.

Boyd nodded. 'I'm going in with him in a bit.'

Sutherland took a deep breath. 'All right, then,' he said. 'Send me your forms for them both and I'll get them booked into the NPPF exam in August.' He stood up.

'You said there were a couple of things you wanted to talk about?' Boyd reminded him.

Sutherland paused. 'Oh yes, the other thing...' He puffed out a breath of air and his round head seemed to shrink slightly, like a punctured balloon. 'Hatcher's coming back.'

BOYD WAITED until Sutherland had left what was soon to be *his* office again, then wandered out onto the main floor to find Warren. He wasn't at his desk. Boyd nudged O'Neal, who was sitting at the next desk along, and the young man removed his headphones.

'Where's the Boy Wonder?' Boyd asked.

'In the bog.' O'Neal looked up at him. 'He's shitting himself about the court appearance. Literally.'

Boyd entered the gents to what sounded like someone emptying a bag of potatoes into a well.

'Is that you in there, Warren?' he called out.

'Uh, yessir,' came the muffled reply from one of the cubicles.

'Is this nerves? Or have you eaten a dodgy kebab?' Boyd asked.

'Just a bit of anxiety... I think,' Warren replied.

'You'll be fine. They may not even call you up to the stand today,' Boyd reassured him.

'Hopefully,' Warren said, sounding doubtful.

'Look, we've got an hour before we need to head over to the court. Do you want to practice giving your evidence?' Boyd asked.

'What... now?' Warren asked.

A short squeak from the cubicle punctuated the silence.

'What! No, Warren, not *right* now.' Boyd grimaced. 'My office... when you've finished!'

He stepped back outside, flapping a hand in front of his nose to chase away the fumes that had followed him and was almost bulldozed by Minter and Okeke hurrying towards the double doors.

'What the –?'

'Got us a shout, boss,' said Minter, pausing. 'Bodies in a storage unit.'

'Bodies? Plural?' Boyd asked.

'Plural.' Then Minter wrinkled his nose.

'That's Warren, by the way,' Boyd said. 'Not me.'

6

Okeke pulled up outside the yellow-painted cinderblock wall of the imaginatively named Best Price Storage, which was in fact a large warehouse backing onto the barns and outhouses of a neighbouring farm in Little Fritton.

The sun was out in force this morning and made the yellow wall look insanely cheerful, like a soft-play centre for kids. The vehicles parked on the gravel outside were mostly Sussex Police ones. There were two squad cars, a CSI van, a civilian car that Okeke recognised as the SOC manager Leslie Poole's, and a white transit van marked 'Holmes Removals'.

'Okay, division of labour... Who's doing what?' she asked, pulling up the handbrake and switching off the engine.

'I'll interview our finders,' replied Minter. 'You go and check out the bodies and trade theories with Sully.'

She turned to look at him. 'Christ. Please don't tell me you're going all Boyd on me.'

'What?' he asked, confused.

'The first sight of blood and you...'

'Oh, behave,' Minter replied. 'You're the one with the medical knowledge.' He opened the passenger-side door. 'And you're the only one who has even half a chance of understanding Sully's rambling monologues,' he added before stepping out and shutting the door.

'Well, maybe some of it,' she muttered to the empty front seat, then climbed out and looked around at the rustling green farmland. There were heads of broccoli as far as the eye could see. Little Fritton really was in the middle of nowhere.

Minter glanced at her, reading her mind. 'No danger of a cuppa round here, I'm guessing.'

She smacked her dry lips. The day was getting unpleasantly warm and muggy already. 'I could murder an ice cream.'

They waved their lanyards at the officer waiting outside the warehouse and stepped inside the front door and into a small office. An agitated civilian was sitting on a chair behind a messy desk, nursing a steaming mug of coffee in both hands.

Minter nudged Okeke. *Or maybe there is*, he hoped.

They approached the desk and introduced themselves.

'Are you the one who called this in?' Minter asked.

'Yes,' the man replied. 'I'm the owner.'

Minter pulled out his notebook. 'And your name, sir?'

'Gareth Jones.'

Minter nodded approvingly. 'Gareth Jones,' he repeated, emphasising his Welsh accent. 'Good solid name, my friend. And are you the owner of the farm too?'

Jones nodded. To Minter, he looked to be in his fifties. His curly greying hair formed a misty horseshoe round a wide tanned bald spot. He had the ruddy and weather-worn complexion of a farmer used to 4 a.m. starts and late finishes.

'One of the bidders found the bodies in Unit Thirty-Seven,' Jones explained. 'And I'm the one who called the police.'

'Bidders?' Okeke asked.

'Yes. I was auctioning off some of the units this morning,' Jones explained. 'Their leases lapsed and we haven't been able to get hold of the renters.'

'Did you get their names?' asked Okeke. 'The bidders who got the Unit Thirty-Seven.'

'No, but they're outside in the car park,' Jones replied.

Minter turned to look at her. 'Haven't you got somewhere to be?'

She raised her brows at him, then turned to address Jones again. 'Where's the unit?' she asked.

Jones nodded at the only other door in the small office. 'Through there.'

Okeke stepped over to it and pulled it open. 'I'll have a coffee, Minter, if there's any danger of one.' She disappeared into the warehouse beyond.

Minter pulled up a spare seat and sat down. 'Right then,' he said to Jones. 'Talk me through this auction, will you?'

Okeke spotted Unit 37 immediately. Halfway down the dimly lit passageway she could see Leslie Poole armed with her clipboard, and next to her a uniformed officer standing in the glare of a brilliant light, which was spilling out through a pulled-up shutter door. She headed over to them.

'Morning, Leslie,' she said.

Leslie greeted her with a smile. 'Morning, Sam.' She held out her clipboard for Okeke to sign. 'It looks like an archaeology dig in there.'

Okeke peered into the unit and saw a figure in white

overalls squatting over a blue storage crate. A plastic sheet had been spread out on the floor and on it were what looked like several brittle parts of a desiccated body: a number of limb portions that looked like dried branches, and three heads that could have been props from an old Hammer Horror movie.

Okeke pulled on a pair of gloves and stepped inside.

Karen Magnusson looked up cheerily at her. 'Ah, hello there, Samantha. It looks like we have three bodies... All in kit form.'

Okeke joined her and squatted down beside the open storage crate. It was filled with granules of gritting salt. Poking out where Magnusson had been carefully digging, she could see the leathery nub of what looked like the top end of a humerus bone.

'There are twelve crates in total,' declared Magnusson. 'I've dug into four of them so far.'

'Where's Sully?' Okeke asked, peering around.

'He's on leave this week,' Magnusson said behind her mask. Her eyes wrinkled with a smile. 'He'd have jolly well loved mucking about with this one.'

'I'm sure.' Okeke examined the limb that was gradually being exposed as Magnusson scooped out grit. It looked like a joint of serrano ham; the flesh clinging to the bone was a rich, dark burgundy.

'By the flaying and splintering of the bone, I'd say these bodies were dismembered using an axe or machete. A lot of elbow grease went into breaking them down enough to fit into these crates.' Magnusson gently eased the humerus out of the grit. It came with the lower arm still firmly attached by the dried flesh, and was followed by a wrist and a complete hand. The fingers were curled like claws, halfway towards forming an accusatory fist.

'I love the dismembered ones,' said Magnusson glee-fully. 'Especially multiples. You get a satisfying puzzle to piece together.'

Okeke glanced over at the heads on the sheet of plastic.

'Those were all in the top crate,' said Magnusson, following her gaze. 'But, looking at that one, it's far more recent than the other two.'

The withered flesh on the one she'd pointed out looked significantly paler than the others and sported a full head of short blonde hair.

'Do you know if they are male or female?' Okeke asked.

'They're all males,' Magnusson replied confidently.

'Are there any obvious indicators of cause of death yet?' Okeke asked.

'Apart from being chopped up into human kindling, you mean?' Magnusson snorted, then she pointed to the paler head. At its crown was a very clear canyon where the skull had caved in. 'That looks like blunt-force trauma to the head with a blade. Probably from the same tool that was used to dismember them. Same for the other two.' She lifted one of the older, darker heads and, with the side of her gloved hand, she made a slow karate chopping motion. 'One big mighty blow, probably from behind.' She turned the head round to show Okeke the shrivelled face. 'And this is interesting.'

'What?' Okeke asked, studying it.

Magnusson reached in between the two rows of teeth, which were set in an unpleasant long-toothed snarl caused by the receding gums, and pulled out a small handful of dried twigs and leaves. 'Apparently he was munching on forest floor at the time of his death.'

~

'So, was there any particular reason for the auction of these storage units?' asked Minter.

Gareth Jones shrugged. 'Once every quarter... if there are clients who have lapsed on their payments, we send them a notice that we intend to sell their contents. They either pay their arrears or let the unit go. Most often it's the latter.'

'Really?' Minter asked, surprised.

'Yeah. Most of our notice letters go out to dead clients and it's usually a relative or executor who's tidying up their affairs who replies.' Jones shrugged. 'They're dealing with a will, bickering beneficiaries, funeral arrangements, maybe a house sale... The last thing they want is to pick through some unwanted old junk in a storage unit.'

'Right,' Minter said.

'The panners who turn up...' Jones continued.

'*Panners?*'

'As in gold panning?' Jones said. 'You know, like the Westerns... Some old prospector panning river pebbles for gold nuggets?'

Minter nodded. 'Ah, okay.'

'Well,' continued Jones, 'most times they can turn a decent profit selling on the stuff that's in there. Or at least I assume so, since there's always a dozen or so who turn up for the auction days. There's always a few old faces too.'

'Speaking of old faces... The two who found the bodies, are they regulars?' Minter asked.

Jones gave it some thought. 'They're not ones I've noticed before, no. There's a lot who come and go. And it's usually a cash transaction. They have to sign a form if they win the unit, so we do have a name. Can't vouch whether the name's legit, though. Second-hand junk's always been a cash-in-hand business, you know?'

'I presume you keep up-to-date records of who owns and who pays for your storage units, though?' Minter said.

Jones looked irritated. 'Of course. But that's confidential.'

'Not, I'm afraid, to the police. We will need to know who previously owned Unit Thirty-Seven,' said Minter, closing his notebook and looking up. He had one last question. 'Cheeky, I know...' He glanced at the mug in Jones's hands and gave him a winning smile. 'Any chance of a brew?'

'Sorry, detective,' Jones said, looking anything but. 'I've only got one mug out here. It may be chipped and dirty, but it's mine. The rest are back at the house. This is a storage warehouse, not a Starbucks.'

'Fair enough.' Minter sighed, then dug out a business card from his jacket pocket and handed it over. 'If there's anything else that comes to mind, my number's on there.'

Jones briefly examined the card and dropped it on his cluttered desk.

'Since this is a murder investigation,' Minter added, 'at some point we will need you to come in to give a formal statement.'

Jones blew out a sigh of irritation. 'As I keep telling you, I run a farm as well, mate. It's busy this time of year.'

'And, as I have told *you*, this is a murder case,' Minter reiterated. 'I'm sure we can work out a convenient time.' He turned to leave the office.

'Are you going to need to look through all the other units?' asked Jones.

Minter paused in the doorway. 'Possibly. Actually probably. At some point.'

'Great,' Jones said with a sigh. 'Just great.'

Minter stepped out into the sunshine and shaded his eyes. He spotted two civilians sitting on a stack of pallets. A uniformed officer was standing next to them. He wandered over.

'I'm DI Minter,' he said, waggling the lanyard around his neck. 'And you're the lucky devils who found the bodies, I take it?'

7

'Now, Mr Warren, you claimed in your statement that you turned up at Mr Knight's house with absolutely no intention of arresting him; that in fact he was not even a person of interest in the case. It was simply an errand. A bit of procedural box-ticking, if you will. Is that correct?'

Warren sat forward in his seat on the witness stand and nodded. 'Yes, sir.'

'In fact, these are your words, DC Warren,' said Knight's barrister. He turned to look at the jury and cleared his throat. '*I was sent to Mr Knight's home to hand over a release form that would allow Mr Knight to resume restoration work on the Martello tower, as it was no longer required as a source for forensic evidence.*'

Warren nodded.

'So,' continued the barrister, 'in the short space of time that you were at Mr Knight's house, he went from being a completely innocent man, to – in your mind – becoming the number-one suspect. Is that correct?'

'Yes. That's correct.'

'Based simply on the fact that he possessed a Swiss Army penknife?'

Warren nodded.

'For the court records,' cut in the judge, 'we do need a verbal response, Mr Warren.'

'Yes,' said Warren. 'He had a Swiss Army knife with a serrated blade that exactly matched the wounds on –'

'*Exactly matched?*' The barrister tutted. 'That's a forensic grey area, isn't it? I mean –' he turned to the jury – 'I'm sure most of you have seen true-crime documentaries on television, such as, for example, *The Staircase*?'

Some of the jury members stirred at his mention of the reality-inspired series.

'For those of you who are unaware of the show, it features a murder victim who displayed wounds on her scalp that various experts claimed could have been anything from the claw marks of a barn owl to the impact wounds of a fireplace poker.'

Boyd noticed some of the jury members nodding along to that.

'The forensic match with the victims wasn't with the *soft tissue*. It was matched against markings on bone,' replied Warren. 'Knight used the same penknife to gouge out the victim's eyes, making score marks on the orbital sockets.'

A muted gasp came from the jury box.

Knight's barrister stood up. 'Excuse me? We have a matter of legal protocol to discuss.'

The judge raised a hand and nodded. 'Yes, quite.' He turned to address Warren. 'Mr Warren, it is proper form to use the word "allegedly" with regard to someone who has not been proven guilty yet.'

Warren's face pinked a little. 'Sorry, Your Honour.' He looked at Stephen Knight, tidily groomed and sitting in a smart suit beside his barrister. 'Allegedly,' he added, then glanced at the gallery and caught a glimpse of Boyd in the back row.

Boyd winked and smiled. Warren had successfully managed to plant the ghastly image in the jury's mind. *Good job, lad.*

MINTER HELD the dashboard tightly as Okeke sped her Datsun along the winding country lanes back towards Hastings. 'Their names are Colin Holmes and Sid Beckett,' he told her.

Okeke chuckled. 'Holmes and Beckett. Sounds like a pair of Victorian grave robbers.'

'I suppose they kind of are the modern-day version,' he replied. 'Picking through the belongings of the dead.'

'What were your impressions?' she asked him.

'They're a bit like Del Boy and Rodney,' Minter mused. 'Actually, that's not quite right. They're more like Tyson Fury and Steptoe. Colin Holmes is Tyson Fury. He's got a face that looks like a melted welly. And Sid's like Steptoe.'

'Who's Steptoe?' Okeke asked.

'Never mind. It's an Old Fart reference. The boss would probably get that one. Colin and Sid were hoping to score big with a unit full of antique furniture to upcycle and sell on, and they were very disappointed with their haul, as you can imagine.'

She looked at him. 'They weren't in shock?'

'Well, that too, yes. Both of them were chugging on their cigarettes like they were lollipops.'

'Speaking of which...' Okeke took one hand off the steering wheel and fumbled in her bag.

'Here, let me,' Minter said, in a bid to keep *both* her hands on the steering wheel, especially at the speed she was going. He unzipped her bag, stuck his hand in and felt around gingerly, mindful that a woman's handbag was a potential Aladdin's cave of awkward surprises. He felt her box of Berkeleys and her lighter, and pulled them out. 'Windows open, though, please,' he told her. 'I don't want my lungs caked with your soot.'

Okeke wound down the window on her side, then fumbled out a cigarette and sparked up.

'I also got the name of the person who'd originally rented the unit,' Minter said. 'Alan Smithee.'

'Right.' Okeke nodded. 'Thanks. I'll look him up when we get back. Then we can chat to the guv and work out what the action points will be.'

Minter resisted the urge to shake his head. *I'm the SIO here.* The woman was virtually impossible to line-manage. '*I'll* chat to the boss when we get back and *I'll* sort out what the action points are,' he said pointedly.

'Get my phone out,' she said, nodding towards her bag. 'I took some photos of the bodies if you want to review them.'

He wasn't particularly keen on that, but, still, he delved into her bag again and this time his fingers brushed against the rounded end of something. He pulled it out.

'Okeke... what's –' he asked.

She glanced over at it. 'Pepper spray,' she replied.

Minter looked at her. 'Actual *illegal* pepper spray?'

She nodded. 'I know, I know. I bought it online. And not through Amazon. Obviously.'

Pepper spray was banned from public use under the Firearms Act. If that canister spilled out of her bag at work in front of Sutherland, she'd be in big trouble.

'Something going on I should know about?' he asked.

She shook her head. 'I've just been on too many unsupported forced entries with Boyd to wander around completely empty-handed.'

Minter could understand that. On Boyd's first case after arriving in Hastings, he'd dragged her into a house where he'd almost had his ear sliced off by a Russian hitman.

'I'll pretend I didn't find it,' he said, dropping it back into her bag. His fingers finally found her phone in a side pocket and he pulled it out.

'Zero-two-two-one-six-five,' she said.

He tapped in the code and unlocked the phone. The picture of Jay's grinning face was immediately replaced with another face. This one looked as though it was grinning too, the desiccated flesh of its lips pulled back to reveal a tidy row of yellowing teeth.

'Oh, bloody hell!' Minter yelped. 'Can I have a bit of warning next time, Okeke?'

'Magnusson found three heads in the first box and it looks as if there'll be enough body parts in the unit to put together three complete bodies,' she said.

He swiped through her pictures. 'Jesus.'

'So the question is –' She blew a cloud of smoke out of her open window – 'have we found ourselves the dumping spot of a serial killer?'

'Another one?' he replied. 'Christ. We seem to be tripping over the buggers.' He swiped through a few more images. There was one of Magnusson smiling, squatting beside a plastic sheet of leathery body parts like a child ready to assemble a giant Lego set. 'They're very old bodies,' he noted.

'Two very old ones. One more recent. They were buried in gritting salt. The old ones might not be that old. The salt in there would have drawn out the moisture pretty quickly, making them look worse,' she explained.

'Three bodies,' mused Minter. 'Two older than the other one. Any idea what sort of a timescale we're looking at?'

'None at all.' She shrugged. 'To be determined. Maggs said they're all male, though.'

Minter nodded. 'If two of them were killed at the same time, that suggests to me something gang-related and not some lone killer.' He clicked her phone off; he'd seen enough. 'Christ, who'd have thought sunny old Sussex could end up looking like a Colombian cartel warzone?'

'Assuming it is about drugs,' she said. 'Could be human traffickers.'

'True.' He nodded. 'There's lots of that going on these days.'

To Minter's relief, Okeke pulled up at a junction and turned onto a nice straight A-road with no more blind bends.

'There's a small service station with a KFC not so far off,' she said. 'Fancy?'

His mind's eye replayed the images on her phone of crinkled, dark flesh clinging to splintered shards of bone.

'I think I'll pass thanks,' he said.

JAY RAPPED his knuckles gently on the door to Mr Adrian McGuire's office.

'Yes?'

He eased the door open and cautiously poked his head in. 'Would you like a brew, boss?'

The old man hadn't been the one who'd interviewed him a fortnight ago – that had been the office manager,

Janice: a stern-faced matriarch with lips so stiff she could have given Maggie Smith's Dowager Countess of Grantham a run for her money.

'Ah, you must be our brand-new hire. Mr Jason Turner, isn't it?'

'Jay,' he replied, 'if you like, sir.'

Mr McGuire waved him in. 'Let's get rid of all that "boss" and "sir" nonsense, shall we? We're not a wretched cavalry regiment here. "McGuire" will do.'

'Ah, right.' Jay grinned, and he set the cup and saucer down in the middle of McGuire's desk.

'Not on the leather, not on the leather... Here...' McGuire moved a pad of lined paper and placed his cup and saucer on top of that. 'That's Saffiano calfskin leather,' he explained. 'Jolly expensive stuff.' He picked up the notes from Jay's interview and quickly scanned them. 'You've got all the necessary NVQs, which is helpful.' He looked up from the notes. 'But, honestly... I think they're a big waste of time, a box-ticking exercise – necessary for our insurance and PI licence. Fieldwork is ninety per cent common sense and ten percent initiative.'

Jay grinned at the mention of *fieldwork*. 'I was worried you were going to use me as a tea boy,' he said.

'You'll be on fieldwork almost straight away,' continued McGuire. 'Burning some shoe leather. Your work will mostly be watching someone or following them. *Very* discreetly. With a little bit of bin-rummaging every now and then. I believe your wife is a detective in the Sussex Police?'

'My partner. Yeah,' Jay said.

'Good. Then you'll be used to the idea that work isn't discussed in bed. If she asks you how your working day has been, "all right", "fine", "ghastly" would all be acceptable answers, but no more.'

'Gotcha,' Jay said.

McGuire paused, then he looked up from the notes again and studied Jay for a moment. 'You're quite a well-built chap, by the look of it. I'm presuming you can handle yourself?'

'You mean, like...?' Jay raised a hand and formed it into a fist.

'Well... our work rarely comes to anything like that, but there will be times when a stern word and a little squaring up may be required. We can't have someone who's going to burst into tears if a little harsh language is thrown their way.'

'I've been a doorman for several years,' Jay reminded him. 'I can handle a bit of attitude, McGuire.'

The PI nodded thoughtfully. 'I imagine you probably can.' He set his notes down and raised one bushy eyebrow just a fraction.

Jay took this as his version of a 'welcome aboard' smile.

'Good chat,' McGuire said, and nodded at the door.

8

Boyd left Warren having a celebratory smoke outside the entrance to the station. He'd treated the lad to a pub lunch at the Pump House for his sterling performance in court. The penknife evidence was almost certainly going to be the thing that would put Knight away for good, and the mental image of striation marks around the orbital sockets of those poor girls' skulls was going to stick with those jurors for life.

Warren had ordered expensively and eaten heartily. Boyd, who'd picked up the bill, had made sure to ask for the receipt afterwards.

He climbed the stairs to the first floor in a good mood, but at the top that persistent twinge near his hip made him wince. *Need to see a physio about that*, he reminded himself.

Boyd entered the CID main floor to see that Minter and Okeke had just returned from their call-out and were dropping their jackets over the backs of their seats.

'What have you got?' he asked as he approached them.

'Three desiccated and dismembered bodies,' answered Minter.

'Jesus.'

'All male, all adult,' added Okeke.

Boyd put a hand on his hip, subtly massaging the pain away. 'A gang hit?' he wondered.

'That's what we were thinking, boss. OCG activity,' Minter said. 'Wouldn't be the first time. Or they could be traffickers?'

Okeke side-eyed him for stealing her suggestion. 'That was *my* view. The bodies could be trafficked migrants,' she said. 'This doesn't seem like county-lines style to me.'

Boyd nodded. Turf wars between the groups of London-based gangs had expanded their franchises out to the south coast, which had led to drive-by shootings or scuffles outside night clubs. Either way, they left their victims bleeding behind them in their haste to scarper before any flashing blue lights turned up.

'Right,' said Boyd, 'Minter, you're with me. We'll have a chat upstairs with Sutherland, update him and set up the team.' He turned and headed back to the double doors.

More bloody stairs. Great.

Minter took the steps effortlessly, chatting all the way. 'I'll open an action log, boss. Okeke can be my second-in-command...'

'Ah.' Boyd paused on the second-floor landing.

Minter looked wary. 'I *am* SIO... right?

SUTHERLAND STEEPLED his fingers thoughtfully beneath his chin while Boyd and Minter waited patiently. Finally he spoke. 'If it's a drug hit, this goes straight over to DCI Flack, okay?'

Boyd nodded. 'But we're not sure it is.'

He explained his thinking. It was too tidy and, because of that, probably pre-meditated and not the result of a chance encounter and subsequent skirmish between rival gangs of dealers and their foot soldiers.

'You think it's something more structured?' Sutherland said. 'You're thinking organised criminal gang stuff?'

Boyd and Minter both nodded.

Sutherland lowered his hands to the desk. His miraculously round head defied gravity and remained perched on his narrow shoulders. 'So not a serial killer?' he asked.

'Another one?' said Boyd.

Sutherland shrugged.

'We've stumbled upon two in as many years,' replied Boyd. He was going to volunteer some pithy remark about Sussex not being some trailer swampland populated by Edmund Kempers and Ted Bundys but settled for something less flippant. 'Statistically speaking, a third one feels unlikely.'

'Plus,' cut in Minter, 'two of the victims look like they were boxed up in road grit at around the same time, sir. With most serial killers being loners... Well, their victims tend to be killed one at a time, out of necessity.'

'And they're all adult and male,' added Boyd.

'Another Dennis Nilsen?' Sutherland suggested. 'And of course there's our very own Kristy Clarke...'

'Kristy targeted young and vulnerable teenage boys,' said Boyd. 'According to Magnusson, these are mature adult males.'

'Hmmm...' Sutherland looked a little disappointed. 'All right, then.' He eyed Minter. 'You've explained to Minter about –'

'Hatcher coming back?' Boyd shook his head. 'Not yet.'

'Hatcher's coming back?' parroted Minter.

'Yup,' said Boyd. 'Everyone's back to their old seats.'

Boyd was the only one in the room to be pleased about the news: escaping the role of stand-in-Sutherland and budget wrangling was almost the best news he'd had today.

The best, of course, had been Knight's prosecutor telling him – *sotto voce* – that Warren's testimony was the back-of-the-net winner.

'All right, then,' Sutherland said again, managing a wan smile in Boyd's direction. 'Your purgatory in my office appears to be over. You're SIO on this, Boyd.' And he pushed his chair back to signal that the meeting was over.

Boyd looked at his assembled team, sitting round the conference table in the Incident Room once more. He was experiencing mixed emotions: a complex trifle of layers. He was relieved to be off paperwork and a little bit excited to be running a case again, but felt a large dollop of guilt that he'd displaced Minter as SIO. The Welshman had a face on him like smacked bearded arse.

Boyd's eyes wandered around the table at Okeke, Warren and O'Neal – his usual go-to team – then onto Magnusson, who was taller than anyone, even when she was seated.

'Where the hell's Sully?' he asked.

'He's on annual leave, if you want to know,' was Magnusson's curt response. 'I'm minding the shop in his absence.'

'Ah... right,' said Boyd. 'Thanks. Well, let me just start by telling you all that Her Madge is returning to work on Monday, which is why I'm here with you and Sutherland's in his glass box. So everything's back to how it was.' He looked at Minter. 'Sorry about that, mate.'

'It's good to have you back, guv,' said Okeke.

Boyd acknowledged her with a brief nod; anything more would have felt like rubbing Minter's nose in it. 'Minter... do you want to get us all up to speed?' he asked.

'Sure, boss.' He had his notebook out on the table in front of him. 'Three bodies have been discovered in a storage unit out near Little Fritton,' he began. 'The storage warehouse owner was holding an auction on a batch of units for which people had defaulted on their rent.'

'Like *Storage Wars*?' asked Warren. 'Is that even a thing over here?'

'Yes, evidently it is,' Minter replied. 'The bidders who won, Sid Beckett and Colin Holmes are the ones who discovered the bodies in the unit. The three bodies had been dismembered and sealed in some crates that had been filled to the top with road grit. The grit, essentially unrefined salt, has basically preserved the bodies.'

'The victims are all male,' added Magnusson, 'and all mature adults. I'd guess in their thirties or forties.'

'Any identifying marks? Any tattoos?' asked Boyd.

Okeke and Magnusson both shook their heads. 'Nothing that we could see as we pulled the pieces out,' said Okeke. 'Mind you, the skin on them is so dark it was hard to tell.'

'Well, I presume Ellessey Forensics will spot anything if there is anything useful there,' he replied.

'They were dark-skinned?' asked O'Neal. 'All of them?'

Okeke nodded.

'It's gotta be migrants then,' said O'Neal. 'Sounds like people smugglers had some bodies to dispose of.' He looked around the table. 'Could have been some truck driver? Maybe he took money to smuggle them through in his container? They died in the back... and he had to find some way to deal with the bodies...'

Boyd raised a hand to shut him up. He got up from the table, grabbed a whiteboard marker and scribbled '*storage unit*' and '*truck driver/smuggler?*' on the board. He also scrawled '*people traffickers?*' and '*drug gang?*' below.

'What about the previous renter of the unit?' Boyd asked.

Okeke flipped a page in her notebook. 'Alan Smithee. I looked the name up on LEDS. There's nothing.'

'There wouldn't be.' Boyd smiled. 'It's an obvious alias. It's a pseudonym, actually. A tradition in the film business, Hollywood specifically,' he continued. 'If a director wanted their name removed from the credits of a crappy film, the pseudonym Alan Smithee was always used to fill in the blank credit.'

'How do you even know that?' asked Warren, impressed.

'He's watched too many crappy films apparently,' said Minter.

Okeke stirred. 'Well, maybe our unit renter is, or was, a bit of a film buff?'

'Not your average trucker, then,' added Magnusson.

Boyd scrawled the alias on the whiteboard. 'It *might* be helpful. I mean if you're hiring a unit and giving a false name, you'd go with something random – John Smith or something equally neutral. Unless you're wanting to make a point.'

'About crappy movies?' queried Magnusson.

Boyd turned to Minter. 'The manager has records, right?'

'Owner,' Minter corrected. 'He's the local farmer – one Gareth Jones, great name. Yeah, he has basic records in a knackered old filing cabinet.'

'Nothing digital?' said Boyd.

'He has a laptop in his office,' replied Minter. 'So there might be some digital records too. I'm not holding my breath, though. The storage business seems to be something of a sideline for him.'

'The name again?' asked Boyd.

'Gareth Jones.'

Boyd scribbled it on the board. 'And the auction winners? Who were they?'

Minter gave him the names and Boyd wrote those down too.

He stood back. 'All right, then – we've got some ink on the board. That's a start.' He returned to his seat and sat down. 'Jones, Beckett and Holmes will all need to come in and give a statement. Meanwhile, we're waiting on Ellessey to look over the bodies.'

He twisted in his seat to look at the board for inspiration. 'It might make sense for someone to go back to the unit with Magnusson and give it another once-over. Fingerprints on the crates, possible DNA traces. We'll need Jones, Holmes and Beckett to give us elimination prints and swabs in case they touched them.'

'Beckett and Holmes certainly did,' said Okeke.

'Right. Okay then. Jobs. Minter, you're my second. Action log, please.'

'Righto,' Minter replied.

'Okeke, you'll be going over to Ellessey tomorrow. Actually, I may come with you. O'Neal, go back to the unit and give it another look-over with Magnusson. Are you okay with that?' he asked, looking at Magnusson.

'I'll have to make sure he doesn't smear his own DNA all over the place. Might it be better if I do it alone?' she said.

'It's just dusting for fingerprints and UV-light blood tracing. It'll be a useful refresher course for him.' Boyd looked at O'Neal. 'Won't it?'

'Uh, sure. Yeah,' O'Neal said, nodding.

Magnusson sighed. 'Fine.'

Boyd turned back to Minter. 'You and Warren can do the interviews. We'll want prints and swabs from all three men.'

'On it, boss.'

Boyd planted his hands on the table. 'Well, that's it for now. Sorry, Minter,' he added, 'but it's good to be back.'

9

Friday was another scorcher. The sky was an unbroken blue and the nettles that covered the verge on either side of the winding country road were beginning to lose their perky green lustre.

'How's Jay's new job going?' asked Boyd.

'It's only his second day,' Okeke replied. 'He started yesterday.'

'Sorry, that's what I meant. How was his *first* day?' Boyd tried again. He could see another hairpin bend approaching up ahead and realised he was distracting her. 'Maybe slow down a bit, Okeke?'

She eased her foot off the pedal. 'Sorry, guv... It's cos it's my car, not a pool car.'

The vehicle manager back at the station had messed up his rolling maintenance schedule and, rather than taking just a couple of CID pool cars out for servicing, he'd had to take out the whole lot. So they were using their own this week.

She slowed down to a more sensible 30 miles per hour

as they rounded the blind bend, still managing to kick up a tail of dust in her wake.

'He's loving it,' she replied to his question. 'They've already got him out snooping after people.'

Boyd shook his head and laughed. 'I still can't believe he's actually a... PI.'

She shot him an accusatory glance. 'Why?'

'Sorry, it's not that I don't think he's up to it... It's just...'

'Just... what?' she asked.

He realised he'd dug himself into an awkward hole. 'It's just that, well...'

'You *don't* think he's up to it?' she suggested.

'No, not at all. It's only that a few months ago he was a bouncer and a carpenter. And now...'

'Well, you're entirely to blame for it,' she replied.

'What? How is it my fault?' he asked.

'He's so flipping... enamoured with you, guv. He bloody hero-worships you. After all that Russian mafia shit, it was hard enough talking him down from trying to join the police.'

'Why'd you do that? He'd probably make a good beat officer,' Boyd said, hoping he'd made up for his earlier slip.

'No, he wouldn't,' she replied. 'He's too hot-headed. He'd fail his probation in a heartbeat.' She glanced his way. 'He thought he was Jason Statham even before he decided to take on the Russian mafia. Now he thinks he's Jason Bourne.'

'Ah.'

'Yeah, ahhh,' she replied. 'You're a bad influence.'

'You sound like his mum,' Boyd said, laughing again.

Okeke huffed. 'Sometimes it feels like I am.' She sighed. 'At least he's working as a private dick,' she continued. 'It's only surveillance and eyeballing rather than, you know, actual hands-on stuff. He's loving it so far.' She couldn't help a small smile as she recalled how excited he'd been when he'd come home yesterday. 'Hey... change of subject. You caught sight of Her Madge yet?' she asked, glancing across at Boyd.

He gripped the dashboard as her speed began to creep up again. 'Not yet. She's been in, though. I spotted her car in the reserved spot.'

'*All change!*' she cawed in a fair imitation of DSI Hatcher's voice. 'Musical seats.'

Boyd grinned. *Well, now's as good a time as any,* he thought. 'Oh, by the way, DI Fox has put in for a transfer.'

'I'm not surprised,' Okeke said. 'He's been in a constant sulk since Flack dropped him. Where's he off to?'

'Brighton.'

'That figures. There's usually plenty of action over there.'

Boyd nodded. 'Which means we'll have a slot to fill. I've recommended Minter to Sutherland for promotion to DI.'

She puffed air out. 'It's probably well overdue. You worried he's going to quit and become a catalogue model full-time?'

He shrugged. 'Not after that swimwear gig. He's still traumatised.'

'So are we.' She laughed. 'You really should've been there, guv. It was hil–'

'And,' he cut in, 'I've also recommended you for promotion to DS.'

Her mouth clapped shut mid-sentence. Then: 'Seriously? You're not shitting me?'

He nodded. She was silent again. For longer this time. He turned to look at her and thought he caught the rare glint of a tear in her eye.

'That's also overdue,' he said. 'Long overdue.'

'Not... Warren? O'Neal?'

He shook his head. 'They're both a little green, still.'

Warren had done some great detective work over the last eighteen months, O'Neal too, but both, as far as he was concerned, needed a couple more years of experience. Okeke, on the other hand, was the complete package – oven-ready, to quote an idiot ex-PM, who was now making a fortune doing after-dinner speeches around the world.

'It's time you took a step up, Okeke.'

She met his gaze. 'I... I... don't know what to say. Thanks, guv. I –'

'Eyes on the road, please, Okeke,' Boyd cut in, 'or Sutherland will have two more slots to fill.'

Dr Palmer's eyes rounded behind her glasses as she watched Boyd and Okeke enter Studio Three. 'DCI Boyd! What an unexpected and pleasant surprise. I didn't think I'd see you here this morning!'

'My shackles have finally been released and cast aside,' he replied, smiling.

'No longer chained to a desk, then?' Palmer asked him.

'Well, less so than I was yesterday,' he replied. He looked past her at the examination tables. There were three of them, spread out beneath the glare of the ceiling spotlights. 'I see you've made a start.'

'Yes. It's a bit of a mix-and-match puzzle... I've been having fun linking all the parts together.' She led them over to the tables. 'These are three *very* complete bodies; there's nothing missing.'

Boyd let Okeke go first and therefore stand closest to the table. He could see well enough from where he was. He was operating on a belly full of eggy bread" another of Emma's weird pregnancy-induced culinary compulsions.

'So what have we got?' he asked.

'I'd say all three were in their mid thirties,' replied Dr Palmer. 'If I recall, we covered the subject of the fusing of the diaphysis with the epiphysis what, last year, wasn't it?'

Boyd nodded. 'Thereabouts. The flared end of the tibia bone?'

'Well remembered.' She smiled approvingly. 'So that's our marker for adulthood. Beyond that we can look at the fusion of other bones to place an approximate age. Specifically, the ossification fusion of the manubrium and sternal body, which starts to happen to all of us in our thirties...'

She pointed to the withered torso on the table, which was turned over onto its front to reveal a pair of dented and misshapen buttocks. They looked, to Boyd, like two oversized dates. She pointed at an incision she'd made beneath the shoulder blades. The leathery skin had been pulled back and clipped in place to reveal the vertebrae.

'So, as I said, this chap was in his mid thirties.'

Magnusson's on-site best guess was spot on. Boyd made a note to tell her that.

'I'm going to open up the rest the same way to get a better idea of their ages. While we're here, I want to point something else out to you.'

With her gloved hands, she attempted to spread the buttocks. 'They're stiff,' she said, 'but they give a little... There...' She pointed to the rectum. 'There is some tearing, some abrasions.' She reached for something in a metal tray on the table and held it out towards them.

'What's that?' asked Okeke. 'It looks like a pine cone.'

'That's exactly what it is. Quite a thick and gnarly one. I found it inserted into the rectum.' She turned and gestured at the other two bodies. 'I found a pine cone inserted in each of them.'

'Ouch,' muttered Boyd, involuntarily clenching his buttocks.

'What are we looking at?' asked Okeke. 'Some sort of torture?'

Palmer shook her head. 'There are no signs of inflammation or blood around the torn flesh. So I'd suggest that this occurred to them all post-mortem. If I was to don a profiler's hat, I'd say it was a message.'

'Be careful where you sit?' asked Boyd, wincing.

The two women turned to look at him. He cleared his throat apologetically and Dr Palmer resumed. 'Also, I found leaves and twigs had been stuffed inside their mouths. That, I think, was done while they were all still alive.'

'Based on what?' prompted Okeke.

'One of them – this one, actually – had managed to swallow some of it.'

'So, our CSI reckoned the two darker skinned men were killed around the same time and the paler one much later,' said Boyd.

Dr Palmer nodded. 'That's fair. This was done over a spread of a few years. The desiccation is noticeably less advanced on that one,' she said, pointing at the paler torso on the other table. 'A number of factors affect the rate. Temperature, humidity, method... The amount of moisture and fat in a body varies; gender and age can have an effect. If we assume that all three bodies were processed in the same way and kept in the same location... A storage unit, I read in the report?'

'Correct.'

'Then any minor variation is down to the bodies themselves.'

'Ethnicity?' said Boyd. 'Would that have an effect?'

She shook her head. 'Don't be fooled by the variation in skin colour. We'd all turn mahogany if we sat in a bed of salt for long enough.' She turned to look at the paler cadaver once again. 'That one was definitely processed a number of years after the other two.'

'How long ago?' asked Okeke. 'Roughly.'

Palmer made an unconscious clucking sound as she evaluated the body before her. 'It's a wild guess until I consult one of our comparison charts, but I'd estimate between ten and fifteen years for the darker two. The pale one, less than five.' She looked at Boyd. 'And to address the ethnicity issue... they were all white.'

10

Sid Beckett and Colin Holmes came into the station together. They'd arrived in the same beaten-up old transit van Minter had spotted outside the warehouse. Minter watched Colin park it, badly, exhaust fumes pluming out of the back.

He went down to reception to escort them up to CID, while Warren got them a coffee each from the kitchenette, then all four of them grabbed a seat around the table in the interview room.

'Thank you both for coming in so quickly,' Minter began

Sid and Colin nodded in unison.

Minter pointed at the recording equipment. 'Do you mind if I record this?' he asked.

'Are we suspects?' asked Colin.

Minter shook his head. 'You've probably seen these things on crime dramas. It doesn't mean you're under suspicion. It's just easier to transcribe the interview later. Are you okay if I switch it on?'

They both nodded again, and Minter signalled to Warren to hit the record button.

'Statement interview with Sid Beckett and Colin Holmes,' he began. He added the date and time and then turned to look at them. 'Right, talk me through yesterday morning, please. What exactly happened?'

'We turned up for the auction,' said Colin. 'There were quite a few units up for grabs.'

'Lapsed payments?' Minter asked.

Colin shrugged. 'I don't know. I heard the owner's looking to close it down, though.'

'Close it down?' queried Minter.

'So I heard from one of the other regulars,' replied Colin. 'He's got plans to empty it all out, knock the old warehouse down and sell the land to some developers.'

Minter noted that down. Jones hadn't mentioned anything about closing his business when he'd spoken to him. 'All right... Go on.'

'We bid on Unit Thirty-Seven and won,' continued Colin. 'We signed for it, got the key, opened it up and found the crates. Sid and I opened the top crate and saw the top of a head. That's when we came out and told the owner. He made the call.'

Minter smiled. 'Can you expand on that a little?'

'We scrambled out of there, all but screaming,' said Sid. He grinned, revealing

a mouthful of wonky tobacco-stained teeth. Truly, all he needed to do was don a pair of fingerless mittens and he could be Steptoe in the flesh.

'Let's wind things back,' said Minter. 'Why did you bid on that particular unit?'

'It was my mistake,' Colin admitted. 'I told Sid it looked promising. The manager said that it had had a ten-year lease on it and the rent had expired; the older ones tend to have more stuff in them.'

'All right. And do the pair of you do this kind of thing often?' Minter asked.

'It was my first one,' said Sid. 'Colin convinced me to pool some petty cash.' He sighed. 'That was two 'undred bob wasted.'

Colin looked at him. 'I'll make it up to you.'

'Don't worry.' Sid waved it away. 'Shit luck.'

'What about you, Colin? You mentioned regulars earlier – are you a regular?'

'No, but I've gone to a couple of auctions like that to see how it all works. It was the first time I actually won a bid, though.' He paused. 'I'm a man with a van,' he continued. 'I do removals, clear-outs, that kind of thing. And if I spot any junk that's worth flogging, then its car-boot sales or Facebook Marketplace.'

'Is this kind of thing your main occupation?' Minter asked.

Colin nodded.

'And I've got a warehouse on George Street,' said Sid. 'Second-hand furniture mainly. Some nice antique pieces. But recently there's not been a lot coming through. So Colin suggested I come along to the auction.'

'Okay,' said Minter. 'So... you win the unit... and then what happens?'

'Like we told you...' Colin shrugged again. 'We signed the paperwork and got the padlock key. We opened it up.'

'Was there anyone else around?'

Sid grinned toothily. 'You mean... anyone *suspicious*?'

Minter shrugged. 'Were there any other people there showing a particular amount of interest in that unit?'

'Everyone gets nosy when the shutter goes up,' Colin replied. 'They want to see what they missed out on.'

'There was that lady,' said Sid. 'With the ginger 'air?'

Colin nodded. 'Yeah.'

'You got a name?' asked Minter hopefully.

Colin shook his head. 'I don't know any of the other panners. Like I said, I'm not a regular.'

'Did she say anything?' Minter asked.

'I told her to bugger off,' said Colin. 'She was a nosy cow.'

'And?'

'She did...'

Minter decided the woman was probably a distraction. 'So you went in,' he prompted.

'Right. We went in. I was kind of embarrassed,' said Colin.

''E promised me a pirate's fortune, 'e did.' Sid cackled good-naturedly. 'You big ugly mug.'

'I'll square up with you, Sid,' Colin promised.

'You'll buy me lunch at the Lord Nelson after this. And pay for me beer.'

Minter couldn't help smiling. Steptoe and Tyson Fury – they made an endearing double act. He pressed on. 'So, you opened just the top crate?'

Colin nodded. 'We lifted it down onto the floor. There was tape around the lid. I thought it was to make it airtight. It was heavy, so we were both sort of hoping it might be first editions.'

'First editions?'

'Every now and then you'll find a first edition of a book that can make quite a few quid,' Sid chipped in.

Minter nodded. 'Right. Like a first edition of *Harry Potter* or something?'

Colin smiled. 'Chance would be a fine thing. You can get thirty thou' off a mint one with J. K. Rowling's signature inside.'

Minter whistled.

'We was hopin' for something' good,' said Sid. 'You never know.' He cackled again. 'Someone's gotta hit the jackpot, right?'

'And that top crate was the only one you touched?' asked Warren.

Both men shrugged.

'I might have shoved a couple aside,' said Colin. 'Then I got my Stanley knife out. Cut through the tape –' he mimed – 'and lifted the lid.'

'And your blimmin' face,' said Sid. He looked at Minter and chuckled. 'His face. Bloody hell. He nearly crapped 'imself.'

'Yeah, it was a shock. And you were just as bad,' Colin replied defensively.

'Well, we'll need to take your fingerprints,' said Minter. 'Just for elimination purposes.'

'I presume, when you opened up the first of those boxes, you weren't wearing gloves?' asked Warren.

Both men shook their heads.

'Wish I had done,' said Sid. He shuddered. 'I keep feeling the need to wash me 'ands.'

'So we're probably going to find your fingerprints on some of those crates and that's why

we're going to need to take your prints and get a DNA swab from both of you,' Minter explained.

The men both looked perturbed.

'Will we end up in some police database?' Colin asked.

'Would that be a problem?' Warren looked at him.

Colin shrugged like that was no concern of his.

Sid, though, appeared confused. 'I'm going to be on one of your registers?' he asked.

'As a rule, if we go to the trouble to take prints and a

swab, they go on a national database, but it's only for three to five years,' said Minter. 'It's just routine. It doesn't mean we suspect either of you of anything.' He tried a friendly, reassuring, smile. 'If we're going to get ink all over your fingers, we might as well log the details, eh?'

Sid grinned. 'We're doing the whole ink-pad thing?'

Minter nodded.

'Just like they do it on *The Silent Witness*?'

Minter nodded again. 'Exactly like that.'

11

'Mid thirties?' Magnusson whistled. 'I was spot on.'

Boyd scribbled Palmer's guestimates on the Incident Room's whiteboard. 'As for how long ago, she reckons between ten and fifteen years for the darker two. For the most recent one, she said less than five years.' He paused. 'So a significant gap between the first two and the last one.' He turned to face his team. 'Taking all this at face value, it's looking even less like a gang hit. The murders were probably done one at a time.'

'A serial killer, then,' said Magnusson. 'How exciting.'

Boyd shook his head, still not entirely happy to jump to that conclusion. 'We also made a bit of a dumb assumption based on the darkness of their skins. They were all white.'

'That doesn't mean they *weren't* migrants,' said Minter. 'Ten, twenty years ago it was all about Turks, Bosnians and Albanians, wasn't it?'

'Right,' said Boyd. 'True. So, yes, it's *possible* that we've discovered a dumping ground for three unwanted, trafficked men.'

'Maybe they were ones who were proving too difficult to manage?' offered O'Neal. 'Maybe they were threatening to go to the authorities?'

Okeke made a kissing sound with her lips. Loud enough that Boyd couldn't ignore it. 'You're not convinced by that?' he said.

'Guv... it's just...'

'Go on.'

'The pine cones Palmer found? You know, rammed up their...'

Boyd explained what Palmer had found. As he did, Warren, O'Neal and Minter all pulled the same face that he'd undoubtedly pulled in the examination room. 'That occurred post-mortem for all of them,' he added, 'which, yes, I suppose, is more of a serial-killery thing to do.'

'That's the technical term for it, is it?' asked Magnusson.

O'Neal laughed.

'Anything done to a body post-mortem that doesn't have any practical purpose,' cut in Okeke, 'has to be considered a part of the killer's pathology, surely?'

'A message of some sort,' clarified Minter.

Boyd sighed.

'You seem a little reluctant to go with that, guv?' Okeke noted.

Boyd shook his head. 'That would make it our third serial killer. They just aren't that common.' The truth was that statistically serial killers were a rarefied breed. The vast majority of detectives were unlikely to encounter one such case in an entire career.

'All right,' he said finally. 'For argument's sake, let's keep that option on the board. What narrative are we looking at?'

'The anally inserted cones,' said Magnusson. 'That

strikes me as a very clear message. Perhaps our killer was raped that way?'

'You're thinking a woman did this?' asked O'Neal.

'Not necessarily,' she replied, rolling her eyes. 'The killer could have been a male prisoner and raped while in prison? That does happen, particularly to sex offenders... if the cops can get their hands on them.'

'And what?' O'Neal shrugged. 'This is some sort of revenge thing?'

Magnusson hunched her shoulders and spread her hands. 'That might explain the distribution across ten years. Waiting for them to come out on licence and then jumping them one by one.'

Boyd got up and scrawled '*rape/revenge*' on the board.

'We also have to look at why the killer would have let the lease lapse on his storage unit,' said Minter.

'Maybe he's dead?' said Okeke. 'Revenge mission done. He takes his life?'

'Or he died of natural causes or an accident?' offered Warren.

'Or he's back in prison,' added Minter.

'Or sick in a hospital, or maybe even broke?' said Warren. 'There's a lot of that going on these days.'

'Whatever the case is,' Boyd said, interrupting them, 'we're probably going to make more headway if we start by ID'ing our John Does. Dr Palmer said she's going to have one of her techies photograph the body parts with a UV-light filter to see if there are any distinctive markers such as tattoos that jump out. And she's also going to hopefully come back with a more precise timeline for each of the bodies. In the meantime, we can surmise they were all in their mid thirties, they were all white males, and we have a rough timescale. Warren...?'

'Mispers?' Warren said with a sigh.

'Correct,' Boyd said. 'Minter, you're interviewing...'

'Beckett and Holmes. Done them already, boss. I'll type it up this afternoon. Holmes said that they handled more than one of the crates, so...'

'Did you get their prints?' Okeke asked.

Minter rolled his eyes.

'Right,' Boyd said. 'Magnusson, you been back to the storage place yet to check for latent forensics?'

'Not yet, *Boyd*... I had some suspected narcotics to test for DCI Flack yesterday.'

'Jesus. This is a bloody murder –' Boyd stopped himself and tempered his voice. *Probably not her fault.* Flack must have badgered her into dropping what she was doing. 'Flack's lot can wait. Could you take O'Neal with you and go over this afternoon?'

'Be a pleasure,' she replied.

'Okeke, you're on LEDS. Have a look to see what you can find there. He – or she – may have struck elsewhere. He might have used another storage business.'

'On it, guv.'

'Right then...' He glanced at his watch. 'It's lunchtime.'

12

Charlotte sat down with her bag of chips, while Mia settled down on the decking by her feet.

'Well now, I've just booked a practising witch into our summer schedule at the theatre,' she said.

Boyd remained standing, one hand cradling his own portion of chips – he was damned if he was going to trust the circling gulls not to dive-bomb as soon as he placed them down on the table. For some reason, it appeared, the birds had clearly come to an agreement with Charlotte not to pester her.

In his other hand was Ozzie's lead; the spaniel was on high alert for any chance of anything remotely food-like dropping onto the decking. With gaps between the planks, he seemed well aware that if anything did drop, he was going to need to intercept it or risk losing it to the sea.

'A witch?'

She nodded. 'Uh-huh.'

'What's her act going to be?' he asked. 'Summoning Beelzebub for a Q&A?'

She laughed. 'She's giving a talk about the history of witchcraft. She's written a book about it.'

'And the Lord of the Underworld's happy to sign a few copies afterwards, is he?'

She sighed. 'Witches aren't necessarily in cahoots with the devil, Bill. Most are white ones, and they're pagans. Anyway, the devil is a Christian bogyman.'

'Oh, right. That's me told.' Boyd eased himself down onto the bench seat, wincing as he did so.

'Is that ache still there?' she asked, concerned.

He nodded, rubbing at his side. 'I thought it was a pulled muscle but it's been lingering.'

'For a while now, I think,' she said. 'You really should go and see a doctor about that.'

'Ha. Chance would be a fine thing. You hang on the phone for hours, only to be told that there aren't any appointments for days.'

'Well, I'll have a go for you this afternoon. I can work and be on hold at the same time,' Charlotte said firmly.

Boyd wasn't particularly keen to make an appointment; from his experience, GPs had a tendency to find some lifestyle choice that needed correcting. Usually the fun stuff.

'I can see you're not thrilled,' she said. 'But it could be something like kidney stones. Those can get awfully painful, Bill.'

'Right. Okay...' He sighed. 'Can I have an early-morning appointment if you can bag one?'

They worked their way through the rest of the chips, half a dozen finding their way out of the wrapping, through the slats of the picnic table and into Ozzie's poised and waiting jaws, and then they headed back across the road to the White Rock Theatre.

He let Charlotte have Ozzie's lead on the steps. 'Still up for a pub dinner, tonight?'

She nodded. 'Let's bring Emma. She seems a bit fed up.'

He shrugged. 'If she feels up to it.'

'I'll text her.'

Boyd gave Charlotte a kiss, then headed uphill towards the station. Bohemia Road felt like a bloody mountainside this afternoon.

She was right... If it was kidney stones, which would only get worse, better to get seen sooner rather than later.

RETURNING TO HIS DESK, Boyd spotted Minter and waved him over.

'What was your take on – dammit, I keep forgetting their names – Hinge and Bracket?' he asked.

'Steptoe and Tyson Fury?'

Boyd laughed. He'd got a glimpse of Minter walking them in. They really did look like an unlikely pair.

'Holmes and Beckett,' said Minter. 'They seem like a couple of wheeler-dealers, hoping to strike gold.'

'And you got their prints and swabs.'

Minter nodded. 'Sid, the older one, seemed a bit twitchy, though. Might be worth running his prints and DNA through the system once it's on the NDNAD.'

'You think he's suss?' Boyd asked.

'Maybe. I mean, I hate to prejudge the whole second-hand business, but...'

'His prints might turn up from a burglary?' Boyd filled in and nodded. 'Okay. It's always a pleasant win, catching a little bonus crime while you're trawling.'

'Like finding a tenner, eh?' Minter turned to go, then

paused. 'Oh yeah, I forgot to mention. Holmes said the guy who owns the storage business is actually in the process of closing it down.'

'So?'

'He didn't tell me that when I spoke to him,' Minter explained. 'He said he was just auctioning units that had lapsed rents on them.'

Boyd nodded. 'Okay, that's something to press him on, then.'

'Will do.' Minter went to head back to his desk.

'Oh, one more thing...' Boyd said.

'Boss?' Minter said, turning back.

'You coming down to the pier after work for Friday beers?'

'Maybe,' Minter replied. 'Why?'

'Great.' Boyd winked. 'I've got a bit of good news for you.'

13

O'Neal watched Magnusson inching around the edges of the storage unit in a squat, aiming her UV light up and down the corrugated iron walls. Even huddled over, she looked large in this small space. Not overweight large, but large as in a wrongly scaled figurine placed in a diorama: a PlayMobile character roped in to join a Lego playset. She was scanning for droplets of blood on the lower walls and floor, or other bodily fluids... 'Who knows what a psycho gets off on when no one's looking,' she'd explained.

The single bulb in the low ceiling was off and the only illumination – her UV torch – was casting wild looming shadows around the small space.

'Hmmm,' she muttered. 'It certainly doesn't seem like any chopping was done in here. Which makes sense.'

'So it was done elsewhere and then the crates brought in?' asked O'Neal.

'Indeed. The chopping would have been very noisy and very messy. Dr Palmer guessed that the older bodies might have been in these crates for ten to fifteen years. But you know, O'Neal... it's quite likely that the bodies would have been sealed in the crates before they were brought here. They could have been sitting in someone's spare bedroom or garden shed a few years before they ended up here.'

'Nice,' said O'Neal.

Magnusson completed her shuffling inspection, stood up, then switched on the overhead bulb. 'Well, that's the UV pass done. Now then, let's take a closer look at these 'ere crates.'

She dropped down to a squat again, delved into her equipment bag and produced a dusting kit. She looked up at him. 'When was the last time you dusted for prints, O'Neal?'

It was ages ago. He'd been on a taster course just after he'd joined the force. 'About four years ago, I reckon.'

'Not since?' she asked.

'That's what we've got you lot for,' he replied.

Magnusson tutted. 'It's always good to keep your skills up to date.' She surveyed the

plastic storage crates. There were twelve of them, four to store each body. They'd started out as three tidy stacks of four; now they were spread out across the floor, most still half-filled with salt.

'They're too large to fit in a fuming chamber,' she said, 'so we'll have to dust. What's the first rule of dusting, O'Neal?'

The detective constable cast his mind back and came up with a blank.

'Identify the most useful contact points,' she answered for him. 'Which would be...?'

O'Neal looked at the nearest crate. 'The red lifting handles?'

She smiled. 'A sensible guess. But wrong. Our killer would most likely have been wearing gloves.'

He looked again. The lid was off and leaning against the crate that it had been removed from. 'The lid?'

'Same answer,' she replied. 'Try again.'

The crates had all been sealed with a strip of masking tape running around the edge of the lid to create an air-tight seal, presumably to prevent any foul odours from escaping.

'The masking tape?'

'Good boy,' she said, grinning. 'Have you ever tried working with a roll of tape with a pair of gloves on?' She pulled a roll of Sellotape out of her kitbag and tossed it to him. 'It's a nightmare constantly trying to find and re-find the start of the tape, correct? You've got to feel for the wretched thing with the tips of your fingers, or your nails if you're not a chewer.'

He ran his thumbnail around the tape until it finally caught and found the leading edge of the tape. 'So, the killer's gloves might have come off to do the taping?'

She nodded. 'That's where I'd make a start.' She pulled out her dusting kit: charcoal dust, fingerprint-lifting tape and a large brush with a coral pink handle. She noticed him staring at it. 'It's a make-up brush, far better than the ones that come with the standard-issue kit. Let's get started, shall we?'

O'Neal was keen. It was gone four in the afternoon and it would probably be gone six before they'd returned to the station and logged any lifted prints. The siren call of 'Thank fuck it's Friday' was summoning him.

'Let's move the crates beneath this light,' she said, nodding up at the bulb.

He bent down to pick up the first crate, grabbing the red handles in his gloved hands. It was heavy, still being half full with grit. He grunted with the effort as he lifted it from the floor and shuffled over with it and set it down.

Magnusson got busy with her kit as he turned to pick up the next crate. It was then that he noticed it... lying within the dust and grit-free footprint marking where the crate had been standing in darkness for the last eleven years.

'Did you bring a takeaway coffee in here with you yesterday?' he asked.

'Hmm?' she replied, distracted with setting her kit out.

'A takeaway coffee?'

She looked up at him and then followed his gaze. A paper cap, crushed like Wile E. Coyote beneath an Acme anvil, lay perfectly flat on the floor where the crate had been.

BOYD BROUGHT the tray of drinks up to the Bier Garden's rooftop area. It was busy this evening; every wooden table was occupied by after-work drinkers – a good proportion of them from Hastings police station. He offered a polite nod to DCI Flack at another table, surrounded by his Operation Rosper team. It looked as though they were celebrating something, a birthday, a drugs bust... or simply that it was the end of the working week.

'Here you go, kids,' he said, setting the tray down. Okeke, Minter and Warren helped themselves.

'No Jay?' he asked Okeke.

She shook her head. 'He's working late. He might join us later.'

Boyd smiled. 'On some covert op, is he?'

She shrugged. 'I presume so. He says he can't tell me anything. Client confidentiality,' she added, laughing.

Boyd eased his leg over the bench, wincing with the effort and sat down. 'He's taking it very seriously, then.'

'Very. I reckon he thinks he's been recruited by MI5.' Okeke pulled open a bag of crisps. 'No Charlotte, guv?'

'Not tonight. We're taking Emma out to the Pump House later.' He checked his watch. 'One pint and I'm going to have to love you and leave you.'

Minter took a sip of his beer. 'So, boss... what's this bit of good news you've got?'

Bugger. He'd been hoping to catch Minter alone to share it. 'Fox has put in for a transfer to Brighton. Which means there's a slot to fill,' he said.

Minter froze, pint in hand, mouth open, brows raised with hopeful anticipation.

Boyd hesitated for a moment, enjoying the look on his face. 'I discussed it with Sutherland and I've put you forward to go up to DI.'

'You are shitting me, boss!' Minter replied.

'And Okeke to DS,' Boyd added, glancing at Warren, who looked both surprised and a tad disappointed.

Minter turned to Okeke to clink his pint glass with hers. 'Congratulations, Detective Sergeant Okeke.'

Okeke clinked his glass and smiled. 'And up yours, Detective Inspector Minter.'

Warren lifted his glass to them. 'Congratulations, both of you.'

Boyd nudged Warren's arm. 'Your time will come soon enough.'

Warren nodded mutely. Boyd realised the lad had been hopeful for a minute there and now – dammit – Boyd felt like a shopping-centre Santa Claus having handed out the last present in his sack.

14

Boyd woke to the delightful sound of Emma puking in the bathroom down the hallway. He could hear her heaving and spitting, heaving and spitting, followed by a long, frustrated groan.

He had a flashback to her as a child: the tips of her long mousy brown hair spotted with regurgitated cake as she dangled her head over the toilet bowl in a play-barn cubicle. It had been her sixth birthday party. There had been cake and a kids' buffet at a soft-adventure centre and the excitement of that, combined with all her school friends arriving with gifts, had resulted in an embarrassing tsunami at one end of the birthday table and a frantic rush to the toilets with Emma under one arm.

He decided to go and sit with her, as he had back then (while Julia had the unenviable task of wrapping the party up and apologising to the other mothers). He winced as he sat up and swung his legs over the side of the bed.

'Poor girl,' muttered Charlotte, still half asleep. 'It's not a lot of fun... baking a bun.'

He padded barefoot across the floorboards into the

hallway and tapped his knuckles gently on the bathroom door.

'Is it okay to come in?' he asked.

Emma grunted.

He entered to find her sitting on the floor beside the bowl, arms cradling her three-month bump, legs drawn up and head resting pitifully on the seat.

'You look a sight,' he said as he sat on the rim of the bath beside her. 'Morning sickness?'

She raised her head to look at him. 'You think?'

He ran his hand over her damp forehead as he had done years ago. 'It should be easing off now, though, right?' he asked.

She shrugged. 'I googled it... It can last into the second trimester...' She spat into the toilet bowl. 'For the lucky few.'

He stroked her back as she dipped her head down to rest on the seat again. 'I saw Dan last night,' she muttered.

'Really?' Boyd thought that Dan had given up his job in the Pump House. His band was making enough money with various downloads and streams, and the bar work was no longer a necessity.

'He was there as a patron, not pulling pints,' she added, guessing his thoughts.

'I didn't see him. Did you speak to him?' he asked.

'Briefly.' She lifted her head and ran a hand through her hair to tame it out of the way. 'He was there with some of his bandmates –' she managed a bitter smile – 'and a gaggle of dewy-eyed groupies.'

Boyd juggled his feelings about the lad: on the one hand, he was pleased for him. Having tried to become a rock star himself once upon a time, Boyd was well aware of the hard work, the relentless gigging, the constant humping of guitar amps out of and back into a transit van, and the endless, exhausting hope that one day it would all pay off. On the other hand, the scrawny little bugger had got his daughter pregnant and had scarpered like a frightened rabbit on hearing she'd decided to have the baby.

'He said...' she began, then waggled her hand in the air. 'Water. Please.'

He turned to see she'd set a glass down on the sink. He passed it to her and she took a hearty slug. 'He said,' she resumed, 'that he's done some soul-searching. He wants to help.'

'To help?' Boyd asked.

Emma shrugged. 'We're going to meet for a coffee,' she replied. 'And try to decide exactly what that looks like.'

Boyd sighed. 'He could come over here, you know? I'm not going to eat him. Though he more than deserves it.'

She looked at him. 'He's frightened of you.'

'What?!' he exclaimed.

Emma laughed wearily. 'You know. You're an angry, over-protective patriarch. That old cliché.'

Boyd could imagine that Dan had visions of him as a surly Don Corleone, demanding Dan did the decent thing and make an honest girl of his daughter... and if he didn't, he'd wake up with a horse's head in bed with him. Boyd grinned. He quite liked that. 'I'm not going to have a go at him,' he replied. 'Well, maybe just a little.'

She reached over and patted his knee. 'Leave that to me, Dad.'

~

JAY FOLLOWED his surveillance target from a discreet distance. Michael Tebbutt was thirty-seven and married with kids. His thinning hair was tied back in a lank ponytail, and he sported a goatee to hide a generous chin. And this morning he was wearing a baggy *Red Dwarf* T-shirt and three-quarter-length khaki shorts as he led his kids through the arcade machines, all blinking lights and noisy jingles, penny falls and crane grabbers that promised to grasp and deliver tempting prizes but in reality merely caressed them in their limp claws.

Tebbutt was in the process of making an insurance claim against Conquest Hospital. Specifically, that the paramedics who'd collected him from his home several months ago had not exercised due care in transporting him and had caused irreversible damage to his lower back in the process. His claim had been supported by pictures taken by his wife of some bruising on his back and a video clip of him shuffling around his house using a Zimmer frame, wincing and groaning as he did so.

There was none of that going on this morning, though.

Jay raised his phone and took a couple of snaps of Tebbutt lifting his boy up to slot some coins into one of the machines in Pelham Arcade.

'Oh dear, mate,' he muttered as he swiped the screen to review the image. He had a nice little collection on his phone now. One with Tebbutt in a dodgem car – a nice action shot as his car rear-ended someone else's. One with him and his boy clambering aboard the busy Ferris wheel. Several with Tebbutt and family playing crazy golf: one shot with him bending down to collect a golf ball. And in none of the pictures was he clutching a Zimmer frame, or balancing on crutches or even holding his supposedly ruined lower back.

Jay supressed a smile of satisfaction. McGuire was going to be pleased with the photos he'd managed to take so far. He'd just get a few more, then he was going to melt away into the bustling crowd like a stealthy ninja. He raised his iPhone once again, zoomed in on Mr Tebbutt so as to get a clear shot of his face as he held an arcade gun and readied himself to mow down a horde of zombies on the screen in front of him.

Except, as the focus settled, the face of Mr Tebbutt was looking directly at him and wearing an expression of both alarm and anger. Jay looked up from his screen to see the man was striding over, remembering halfway to add a theatrical limp to his movement. He drew up in front of Jay and reached out to grab his phone.

Jay lifted it up out of his reach. He was an easy foot taller than Mr Tebbutt. 'Oh no, you don't,' he told him.

'What the hell are you up to?' Tebbutt demanded.

'Nothing that concerns you,' replied Jay coolly.

Tebbutt's eyes narrowed. 'What are you? A pervert? Why else would you be taking pictures of all these kids?'

There were a lot of children milling around, to be fair.

Jay tucked his phone into his back pocket. 'As I said, mate, it's none of your concern.'

'Gimme that phone!' Tebbutt barked. 'Let me see what you've been snapping, then.'

Jay smiled as he shook his head. 'Nope.'

'Right, I'll...' Tebbutt looked around and spotted what he was after. He pointed towards a security guard who was sitting on a stool in the corner of the arcade and looking bored to death. 'I'll get him to make an arrest.'

'He doesn't have that authority,' said Jay calmly. 'He's just a civilian wearing a T-shirt with "Security" on it.' There was something very satisfying about saying that with a hundred per cent certainty. He'd done his homework; he'd read the IPI's guidelines... and of course, from his experience as a doorman working at CuffLinks nightclub, he knew that wearing a uniform and a plastic name tag conveyed no legal authority whatsoever.

Tebbutt looked as though he wanted to punch him but was unsure as to whether Jay's muscular bulk was just for show – a prancing gym bunny, or a warning sign that he might end up biting off more than he could chew.

Instead, Tebbutt, moving with surprising agility and speed, reached around Jay and pulled his phone out of his pocket. Jay managed to grab Tebbutt's forearm before he could run off with it.

'I'll have that back, thanks,' he said.

Tebbutt opened his hand. And the phone began to drop to the floor.

Jay let go of his arm, ducked quickly and managed to catch his phone just as it was about to hit the ground. 'Nice try, Mike. Nice try,' he said.

Tebbutt's eyes widened as he rubbed his arm. 'How do you...?'

Jay had realised his mistake as soon as the words had left his mouth. *Hardly the stealthy ninja*, he scolded himself. Michael Tebbutt was going to figure out what was going on, maybe not right now, but later as he replayed today's events in his mind. The only way forward, Jay decided, was to double down.

'Mr Tebbutt,' he began, adopting his best attempt at an official-sounding voice, 'you might want to reconsider your insurance claim against the NHS. That or face charges for attempted insurance fraud.'

God, he mused. *He sounded good.*

15

What Boyd really *should* have been doing right then was herding his team into the Incident Room and getting an update on where everyone was with the investigation. Hatcher was back at work this morning and would be wanting to make sure she was seen. Given that there was a homicide case on the go, she'd almost certainly want to pop into the morning briefing to appraise the situation.

But no, here he was, sitting in a rammed surgery waiting room, watching for his name to pop up on the screen above the reception desk. It was now ten minutes past his appointment time. He was about to get up and check with the harried receptionist when, miraculously, 'William Boyd – Room 4' appeared on the screen.

He made his way into the room and took a seat. The GP, Dr Ho – a man who looked younger than Warren – glanced up from his notes and greeted him with a cheery professional smile that Boyd very much doubted would last the day.

'Good morning, what can I do for you?' he asked.

Boyd explained.

Dr Ho listened thoughtfully. 'Like a jogger's stitch, you say?'

Boyd nodded.

'And how long's that been going on?'

Boyd pursed his lips. He'd first become aware of it back in May. In fact, not long after Emma had announced she was pregnant.

'A month or so.'

Dr Ho nodded. 'I see. Which side is it on?'

Boyd indicated his left.

'And have you noticed any changes to your stool?'

'You mean my poo?' Boyd asked.

'Yes. Its consistency, colour?'

'I can't say I've taken a look. But, now you mention it, yes, it's been... uh... looser than normal.'

'Have you had any unexplained nausea?'

'No.'

'Any sign of blood in your urine?'

'Not that I've noticed.'

'Inexplicable fatigue?'

Boyd gave that a moment's thought. To be fair, he had been walking to work less often recently, despite the weather warming up and the blue skies. But he'd put that down to weary resignation at the prospect of spending the day dealing with Sutherland's paperwork.

'Yes, actually,' he replied.

'Have you had any bloating? Feeling uncomfortable after meals?'

That was another 'yes' and he didn't like the serious look on Dr Ho's face.

'Can I have a feel?' asked the doctor.

Boyd nodded as Ho snapped on some nitrile gloves.

'If you could remove your jacket and just lift your shirt, please?'

He pulled his shirt up and Dr Ho wheeled his chair forward and began gently prodding and probing the left side of his abdomen. Boyd couldn't help wincing as his fingers worked around the side.

Dr Ho's eyes flicked up, catching his grimace. 'Painful?'

'A little uncomfortable, yup.'

Dr Ho stopped and wheeled his chair back to his desk. 'Right, Mr Boyd… I think it would be prudent to get a stool sample from you.' He handed him the tube. 'You can return the tube to the sample box at reception.'

'Is this anything I should be worried about?' Boyd asked.

The young doctor pressed his lips together for a moment, considering how to present his thoughts. 'Statistically speaking, Mr Boyd, you're relatively young for this to present itself. Your age is…?'

'Forty-eight,' said Boyd.

'Right.' Dr Ho nodded, checking the notes on his screen. 'You are approaching the statistical bell curve.'

'For what?' Boyd had a horrible suspicion he was going to regret asking that.

BOYD ARRIVED AT THE STATION, just after ten. He parked his Captur in the space next to Okeke's beaten-up Datsun, locked up and entered the building. He waved his lanyard robotically at the desk sergeant and climbed the stairs to the first floor, more aware of that stitch in his side than ever before. He entered CID's main floor and walked over to his desk, playing and replaying Dr Ho's tentative, carefully phrased explanation.

His phone had buzzed several times in his jacket pocket as he'd driven to work. It was Charlotte wanting to know how the appointment had gone. At some point, very soon, he was going to have to reply. And that reply was going to have to include those three scary words.

Possible colorectal cancer. Although, to be fair, Dr Ho had said 'worst case'.

'Are you all right there, guv?' asked Okeke. She seemed to be in a surprisingly perky mood this morning. She glanced at her watch. 'Are we having a morning briefing?'

'Yeah... I need a few minutes first,' Boyd replied. 'Give the others a coffee warning,' he added. 'Be in the Incident Room in, say, fifteen minutes?'

The faintest trace of concern spread across her face. 'Is everything okay?'

'I'm fine.' He nodded, then forced a smile. 'Just rally the troops for me, would you?'

She nodded and turned away. His phone started buzzing repeatedly in his pocket and he pulled it out. It was Charlotte calling.

Not now. He wasn't ready for the conversation. And, in any case, it wasn't a done deal. Only a *possible* one. He let it go to voicemail, then tapped out a texted reply.

Have to drop a sample in later. Doctor wanted to tick ALL the boxes.

He inserted an eye-roll emoji.

Got a meeting right now. Will call you when I can x.

16

He'd been right about Hatcher. She turned up just as his team meeting started, with Sutherland in tow. She nodded politely at Boyd and waved him on, a signal to not mind her and continue as though she wasn't there.

'Right then,' he began, 'let's start with you, O'Neal. Any joy at the storage unit?'

O'Neal seemed pleased with himself this morning. 'I've got good news and bad news, chief,' he stated.

'Let's get the bad news out of the way first, shall we?' said Boyd.

'Well, we dusted the crates for fingerprints... and all we got were Beckett's and Holmes's prints. No others. Our killer is clearly very careful and forensic aware.'

'Or was,' added Okeke. 'We can't assume he's alive, given that he allowed the lease to expire on the unit.'

'We also can't assume the killer's male,' cautioned Magnusson. Okeke looked irritated with herself for making that particular slip.

'All right, so now let's have the good news,' said Boyd.

'We found an old paper coffee cup crushed beneath one of the crates.'

'An old coffee cup? Are you sure it was old?' Boyd asked.

O'Neal nodded and pulled out a printed photo from a folder. He slid it across the conference table towards Boyd. 'It was within the imprint of the bottom crate.'

Boyd picked it up and examined the image. O'Neal's photograph included an evidence measure stick and he had made sure to include the rectangular outline of dust that indicated where the crate had been standing for years.

'The logo on the cup is Nesso. I looked that up. It's a small chain of coffee shops that went bust at the end of 2021. So, obviously, it's been stuck under there for at least two years,' O'Neal added.

Boyd nodded and slid the photo back across the table. 'Please tell me it had something on it...'

Magnusson piped up. 'There was a thumbprint on the plastic lid. I've swabbed the rim of the cup for traces of DNA and I'm just waiting on the result.'

'I ran the thumbprint through our database,' added O'Neal. 'Unfortunately there wasn't a hit.'

'Well, if our killer was careful enough not to leave prints on the crates, then that's no surprise.' Boyd wandered over to the whiteboard and scrawled '*coffee cup*' on it and drew a line linking it to '*storage unit*'.

'I also ran the prints for Beckett and Holmes on Friday night,' continued O'Neal.

Boyd almost smiled. The mention of Friday night was obviously for Her Madge's and Sutherland's benefit. Evidently O'Neal had caught wind that there'd been talk about promotions and wanted it known that he was putting in long hours.

'And?' Boyd asked.

'Sid Beckett's got some form for burglary. It's going back a bit, mind.'

That explained his discomfort during the interview around letting them ink him. Boyd made a note on the board. 'Okay. Good work. Okeke?'

'Guv?'

'Any luck on LEDS with similar MOs? Specifically, the pine cones?'

She shook her head. 'No.'

'Pine cones?' queried Hatcher.

'Pine cones,' said Magnusson. 'Inserted up the bottom. They had one each.'

'Good God!' breathed Hatcher.

'Post-mortem,' Magnusson added.

'We're working on the theory it's an emotive message, ma'am.' Boyd turned back to Okeke. 'Has anything come back from Ellessey yet on any identifying marks on the bodies?'

'Not yet,' Okeke replied.

'Then chase that, will you? We need an ID on at least one of those men if we're going to get anywhere at all with this.'

She nodded.

'Minter? The bloke who owns the business...'

'Gareth Jones, boss. I'm going up this morning to talk to him again; see if we can get any records he has on the unit's owner. I'm not holding my breath, mind you, judging by the state of his office.'

Boyd scribbled a question mark on the board beside Gareth Jones's name. 'You might want to quiz him on why he's wrapping things up there and why he forgot to mention it to us.'

'I'm planning to, boss,' Minter replied.

'Do you think *he* might have done it?' asked Okeke.

'Owning your own storage warehouse would be handy if you've got bodies to hide,' said Boyd. 'We'll certainly look into any link or motive between Jones and those three. But if he had hidden bodies in one of his units, I doubt very much he'd have invited a bunch of people to bid on it. Anyway...' He capped the marker pen. 'Warren? Any luck on mispers?'

'Nothing useful so far, sir.'

'Any hits on Alan Smithee?'

'No, sir.'

'*Nothing?*'

Warren shrugged. 'Sure, some Alan Smiths, but no Smithees.'

'It's an odd surname,' said Hatcher. 'Sounds too obvious as an alias.'

'It's meant to be, ma'am.' Boyd explained the use of it in Hollywood. 'It's meant to *clearly* be a fake name. As in "I'm *clearly* too embarrassed to be associated with this movie".'

'I see.'

Boyd turned to look back at the whiteboard. 'Our focus at the moment is on ID'ing those bodies. And I want all eyes on that. Any questions?'

Hatcher stirred. 'I notice you have "drug gang" on the board? Why's that?'

'We initially thought two of them were killed at the same time, ma'am. Which could have meant something other than a lone killer. However, the timing's inconclusive. Dr Palmer said that two of the victims were likely murdered ten to fifteen years ago, but it's hard to tell any more than that. Could be a few years or just months between them. But, definitely, given both bodies were stored in the same way, in the same kind and amount of road grit, there's enough variance in their condition to indicate they weren't done at the same time.'

'Good God, not another serial killer in Surrey?' She sighed. 'We're going to get a reputation.'

Boyd shook his head. 'I'm not sure it's one in the classic sense, ma'am. It *feels...*' He hated using that word; it sounded unprofessional and was the kind of word that belonged in the mouth of some improbably on-the-nose TV drama inspector. 'It feels emotive. The insertion of those cones suggests that perhaps there was some sort of personal connection. My hunch is that our killer could have known these men.'

'Well, we're going to have to present this to the press in the next couple of days,' said Hatcher. 'But I really don't want them going down the serial-killer route if I can help it.'

'Then it's important we mention that we *believe* the killer may have known his victims,' replied Boyd.

She nodded. 'Fine. But it's probably not a good idea to mention the pine cones.'

'Agreed,' Boyd said, looking around at everyone. 'That's a detail we're keeping to this room.'

17

'Hello. It's me again, I'm afraid, Mr Jones,' said Minter, brandishing his CID lanyard in the doorway.

Gareth Jones appeared to be in the process of tidying his scruffy little office. He sighed. 'What now. Can't you lot see I'm busy?'

'Clearing the place out?' Minter asked.

'Cleaning up,' Jones corrected.

Minter stepped inside, uninvited. Gathering a stack of box files, Jones looked even more harried and irritable than he had last time.

'Mr Jones, a little birdie told me that you're wrapping the business up and closing down? And I said to myself, *No, that can't be right. Surely Mr Jones would have mentioned it to me when we had our chat the other day.* So, I thought I'd come back over and ask you, man to man. Is it true? Are you closing down?'

Jones dumped the box files on his desk. 'Who told you that?' he asked.

Minter didn't answer.

Jones hesitated for a moment longer, then finally nodded.

'And can I ask why that is, and why you forgot to mention it?' Minter asked.

'It's no big secret,' Jones replied tersely. 'It's just not making enough money to be worth my frigging time.' He sighed again. 'I need to focus on the farm or...' He paused.

'Or?' Minter prompted.

'Or I'll risk losing the bloody lot.'

'Are you in financial difficulty?' Minter asked him.

Jones looked at the detective sergeant with incredulity.

'Have you ever tried running a farm, detective? Particularly in times like these, the supermarket buyers are squeezing the bloody life out of us. We can't find British fieldworkers any more and we sent all the Poles home. There are no subsidies these days. And don't get me started on the cheap unregulated produce that's coming in from outside the EU. Add that to the price of fuel, and do I really need to go on?'

Minter shook his head this time. 'Right. But, again, you didn't mention this last week.'

'Because it's none of your bloody business!' Jones snapped.

Minter raised his brows.

'Look,' Jones said. 'I'm closing the units down because I'm selling off the land that the warehouse is sitting on. Because I need the money to keep the farm going. Or, like I said, it won't be long before I don't have a bloody farm to worry about.'

His answer stacked up. Minter had noticed the farm machinery sitting idle and little sign of any activity given it was June.

'Okay,' Minter said. 'So let's move on to the reason for

my visit today, shall we? I've come to collect everything you have on the person who was renting Unit Thirty-Seven. Alan Smithee, isn't it?'

'Right.' Jones let out yet another deep sigh; this time accompanied with an eye-roll. 'You could have bloody well asked me for that last time you were here.' He nodded at the stack of box files.

'It's all paper records?' Minter asked.

'I'm not that good with computers,' Jones replied, opening up one of the box files. 'Unit Thirty-Seven, then... It'll all be in here somewhere.'

OKEKE'S DESK PHONE RANG. She picked it up. 'Hastings CID, Detective Constable Okeke speaking.'

'Ah, just the person I'm after. Dr Palmer here,' came the reply. 'I've got something for you. We've been over the bodies in fine detail and finally picked up an identifying mark on one of them, you'll be pleased to hear.'

'What have you got?' Okeke asked.

'There's a tattoo on the upper left arm of one of the bodies. This one, by the way, I've refined my post-mortem estimate to ten years. I've just emailed you a picture. It was incredibly faint and we had to play with various filters to sharpen the image.'

Okeke tucked the phone between her shoulder and ear and opened her inbox. 'Ah, okay, got it. Let me just open it now,' she said.

She double-clicked and the image expanded on her screen. She was looking at what appeared to be a heraldic shield with a lion holding a ball.

'Looks like a rugby club logo,' she mused.

'That's exactly what it is,' said Dr Palmer.

Beneath the lion were several smudged letters: N. R. F. C.

'I'll save you the googling,' Dr Palmer said. 'It's the logo for Norton Heath Rugby Club.'

Okeke grinned. 'Oh God, really? You're a lifesaver.'

'Not a problem. I'm still waiting on the DNA chromographs, but as soon as those come back I'll forward them to you,' said Dr Palmer.

'Great, thank you.' Okeke hung up and immediately googled the club. She navigated to the club's modest one-page website where she found contact details for a Mr. Julian Hollander. She dialled the phone; it rang several times before finally tipping over to voicemail. She decided to leave a message.

'AH, HERE WE GO,' said Gareth Jones. He pulled a few tattered sheets of paper out of the box file. 'This one is the registration form for the client. Alan Smithee.' He handed one of the sheets to Minter.

Minter stared at the obviously self-made form with its misaligned entry boxes, typos and cut-and-paste terms and conditions. It was the original, though, and not some blurry photocopy, which was something. He immediately placed the dog-eared sheet on Jones' desk and pulled a pair of nitrile gloves and an evidence bag out of his jacket pocket.

'I need to bag that,' he explained, carefully easing the paperwork into the plastic bag, sealing it and writing his initials and date on the bag. He peered through the plastic to read the various entries.

. . .

NAME: Alan Smithee

D.O.B.: 12/06/77

Date: 27/04/2012

Payment details: cash, annually

ID: driving licence

Contact: 07439 123 657

THERE WAS A SCRAWLED illegible signature just underneath the terms and conditions.

'Christ,' said Jones. 'Is that piece of paper important?'

Minter nodded. 'We might be able to get some useful forensics from it.'

'I tried that phone number when he didn't renew,' said Jones. 'I got a "this number isn't recognised" message.' Jones carefully handed him another piece of paper. 'I took a photocopy of his driving licence too.'

Minter stared at it. The quality of the scan was bloody awful. It was littered with the obligatory print smudges and flecks of a badly maintained photocopier. The driving licence details were legible, luckily. The tiny image of the face on the licence, however, was next to useless; all he could get from it was that the person was male and white with short hair.

So, that's our killer's face, then.

'Thank you,' said Minter as he slid the scan into the same evidence bag. 'Would you be able to recognise Alan Smithee if he walked in right now?' he asked.

Jones shrugged. 'I doubt it. He only came here that one time eleven years ago, when he filled out that form.'

'But it says here that he paid in cash annually,' Minter queried.

'By post, he did. Yes,' Jones said.

'That's a lot of cash to send in an envelope,' Minter said.

'£450, to be precise,' said Jones. 'But it came on time every year... Otherwise I would have chased him for payment earlier.'

'And when did you last try chasing him?'

'About three months ago,' Jones said. 'Like I said, the phone number was no longer recognised. Or maybe it was never even a proper number.' He shrugged. 'Who knows?'

Minter tucked the evidence bag into his jacket pocket. 'All right, well, thank you very much for your help. This has been very useful.'

'So you think you'll be able to find this sick bastard?' Jones asked.

'That's the plan, Mr Jones,' Minter replied. 'That's most definitely the plan.'

OKEKE DECIDED to stick to her desk over lunchtime in case she got a call back from the rugby club; stupidly, she'd given the desk extension and not her mobile. She had just made it back to her desk with a sandwich from the canteen when she got the call she'd been waiting for.

'Detective O...Okay-key?'

'Samantha Okeke,' she helped him. 'Is that Julian Hollander?'

'Yes, it is. You left a message for me to call you?'

'Yes, I did. I presume you run the Norton Heath Rugby Club?' she asked him.

'I'm the club secretary,' Hollander told her. 'I handle the boring side of things, the paperwork.' He had the kind of comedy nasal voice that Okeke associated with trainspotters and stamp collectors.

'We're chasing up on an old misper case –' she began.

'Misper?' he interrupted.

'Sorry, a missing person's case,' she explained. 'We're looking for a man who would have been in his mid thirties when he went missing. We believe he might have had something to do with your rugby club.'

'How so?' Hollander asked.

'He had your club's logo tattooed on his arm,' Okeke said.

'Ah... yes, some of our more enthusiastic members have been known to do that,' Hollander said. 'What's the name?'

'We don't know,' Okeke said.

'You don't know,' he repeated. 'Then I'm confused. How...?'

'A body was recovered,' Okeke explained. 'Male, white, mid thirties. And that's all we know about him so far – other than the tattoo, that is. He would have been a member of your club, maybe ten years ago, give or take. Do you keep a register of past members?'

'Oh, crikey,' Hollander said. 'That's dreadful. Well, we do have a subs register. Our members have to pay a small subscription every quarter to keep things ticking over. If your missing person was once a member of our club, I imagine his name should be in our paying-in book somewhere.'

'You'll need to look back a few years,' Okeke reminded him. 'I'm after someone who would have suddenly stopped making his payments. If he was an enthusiastic club member, then he might have been one of your regular players? Stopped turning up to practice sessions, perhaps?'

'Members do come and go, Ms Okeke,' Hollander told her.

'But I presume they contact you to say they're dropping their membership, right?' she said.

'Well, yes, usually,' he agreed.

'If a member stopped paying his subs...' pressed Okeke, 'I presume you would chase them down in the first instance? And make a note?'

'I don't *chase them down*... as you say, but, yes, I do make a note to tactfully press them the next time they turn up for a practice session. I can dig out our past yearbooks for you.'

'Could you start with 2011, 2012. Maybe earlier... 2010?' she asked.

'Crikey. That's before my time as club secretary, I'm afraid,' he replied.

'If you could take a look for me, though? Even if it's just a list of lapsed members from those years. I appreciate that's a bit of work for you.'

'No, that's all right. Anything I can do to help you find your man.'

'That's incredibly helpful. Thank you.'

'I'll crack on with that now,' he said, and hung up.

18

'Don't make me drag it out of you, Bill...' said Charlotte. 'I want to know everything.'

Boyd ambled along the shingle in silence, wondering how to tell her. The beach was populated with enough people taking in the sun with their packed lunches that both Ozzie and Mia were confined to a lead walk.

'Bill? I checked the terms and conditions of being a couple... You're supposed to be honest with me,' she told him.

He sighed. 'The doctor insisted I drop in a sample to get a better idea of what we're dealing with.' He looked at Charlotte; her brows were locked together with concern. 'The doctor mentioned the C-word,' he admitted.

Charlotte's eyes clamped shut for a moment.

'Yeah, it's a bit of a bummer. No pun intended. But... it's only *possible*. It could still all be fine. It's not a certainty, by any stretch,' he said, attempting a smile.

'Oh no,' she whispered.

'He also said that, given my age, if it is bowel cancer... it would probably be very treatable.' He smiled. 'The doc said, "If you're going to get cancer, this is a good one to get."'

Dr Ho had actually said nothing of the sort.

'Worst case, it's just a quick bit of colon editing,' he added, 'and the job's a good 'un.'

Charlotte took a deep breath. 'When will you know, one way or the other?'

'He said the turnaround for the test result would be pretty quick. A day, maybe two. They don't mess about with this kind of thing.'

He could see she was wrestling with tears. She noticed him studying her and flashed a stoic smile back at him.

'I mean, it could just be irritable bowel syndrome. Or an infection, you know? Probably is,' he said hopefully.

Charlotte stopped walking and planted her feet in the shingle with a resolute clatter of stones. 'Bill, we're not going to do that. You're not going to sugarcoat things for me, okay? It's all right to be worried. And if it's the worst case, then –' she paused to steady her voice – 'we'll jolly well beat this fucker together.'

Boyd smiled and cupped her chin in one hand. 'God, I love it when you go all potty-mouthed on me.'

She leant forward and kissed him. 'It's been a long wait finding a man like you, Bill. I'm damned if I'm going to let anything happen to you. Are we sharing this with Emma?'

'Not yet,' he replied. 'I want to find out what we're dealing with first. It could be something or nothing,' he reminded her. 'A twisted bowel, constipation. A long overdue fart that's been waiting to express itself...'

'God help me.' She punched him gently. 'You can be so uncouth, Bill Boyd.'

~

Boyd returned to his desk to find Okeke hovering around it like a wasp over a dustbin.

'You look remarkably pleased with yourself,' he noted.

'I am,' she replied. 'We just got a possible ID for one of the John Does.'

'Really?' Boyd dropped his jacket over the back of his seat. 'Do tell.'

'Mark Meadows. Aged thirty-six when he went missing in 2011.' She relayed to him the tattoo that Dr Palmer had found – the club crest for Norton Heath Rugby Club – and club secretary Julian Hollander's swift help in coming back with a very short list of lapsed members.

'Meadows is an unresolved misper. His wife raised the alert –' she checked the notes in her hand – 'in October 2011. There was no reason she could think of for him to disappear. There were none of the usual triggers: gambling debt, depression, stress. He just didn't return home from work one day.'

'Sounds promising,' Boyd said.

'More than promising. She confirmed he had the club tattoo and there's more...' She looked around the CID floor. 'Where's Minter gone, for God's sake?' she muttered.

'Did he turn something up too?'

She nodded.

'Well, don't keep me in suspense,' said Boyd. 'What is it?'

'I should really let him tell you. It's *his* find,' Okeke said, glancing around again.

Boyd rolled his eyes. 'I promise he'll still win a sticky bun. What's he found?'

'He's got photo ID of the guy who rented the unit. A driving licence.'

'Well, that'll be faked, I assume,' Boyd said.

'Obviously. But the photo on it would have had to have

been genuine, because he'd have needed to show it to Gareth Jones when he first went in to rent the unit.' She held out a photocopy of the scanned licence.

Boyd squinted at the tiny ID photo.

'I know,' she said. 'The quality of the image is shit.'

He nodded. It was little more than a dark blob of smeared printer ink. 'So, that's our killer, eh?' he mused aloud.

She nodded eagerly. 'It probably isn't going to be good enough for facial recognition software, though.'

'Not even close,' said Boyd. If real life was like fiction, some technical whiz would have whipped it away and managed to sharpen up the image with some hi-tech gizmo to produce something cleaner. But a smudged array of printer ink dots was all they had and it was unlikely to yield anything more.

'Minter also picked up a registration form. Not a copy. The original,' she told him.

'Well, that's better news, I suppose.'

Okeke nodded. 'It's with Magnusson right now. She's going to dust it for prints and swab it. She offered to run the swab over to Ellessey herself so they can run it for DNA. We might get lucky, you never know.'

Boyd nodded. 'Right. Good.'

Okeke looked exasperated. Obviously, she'd been hoping for a more animated response from him. 'You okay, guv?' she asked.

'Yup. I'm fine. Just flagging a bit today. That's all,' he replied.

'Okay, well, we reached out to Mark Meadows' wife...' Okeke began just as Minter arrived with a fresh cup of coffee in hand.

He took one look at the photocopy in Boyd's hand and groaned with disappointment.

'It's my fault,' Boyd said. 'I pressed her. Go on, Okeke, you were saying... Mark Meadows' wife?'

'Okeke gave her a call, boss,' Minter answered. 'Hope you don't mind?'

He shook his head. That was why he'd nodded them through for promotion. Having two detectives with initiative was a godsend, especially at the moment.

'So...' Minter continued. 'Me and Okeke are popping up to interview her tomorrow morning. Do you think we should take a FLO with us?'

They were going to have to tell the poor woman that there was a body that could be her husband. Twelve years might have passed since he'd gone missing, but being an unresolved misper – rather than a resolved bereavement – tended to place grief in a state of suspended animation. It was probably going to be an emotional one.

'Might be a good idea,' he replied.

19

McGuire reviewed the pictures that Jay had printed out and brought into his office.

'Good work, Jay,' he said, running a finger along his top lip. 'Love the one of him hefting his sprog out of the bumper car. Marvellous action shot. Nice composition.'

Jay smiled. 'Thanks, sir.'

McGuire lifted a brow. 'Sir? I remind you, we're not a cavalry regiment.' He settled back into his seat. It let out a soft creak. 'Incidentally, I got a call from the trust to say that Tebbutt's solicitor had been in touch first thing this morning. Mr Tebbutt's decided to drop the claim.'

'Nice one,' grunted Jay. 'Result, eh?' he said, grinning.

'Indeed. A result. The *right* result for our client, but...'

Jay felt the smile freeze on his lips. He hadn't been expecting a 'but'.

'Mr Tebbutt, I presume, must have suddenly realised his fraudulent claim was in danger of getting him into trouble. I do have to ask myself why he made a very timely and abrupt U-turn on the matter.'

Jay had decided not to mention the altercation in the arcade. It had seemed like an unnecessary detail. He'd got the job done, got the pictures, and they were damned good ones.

'According to Mr Tebbutt, you physically threatened him?' McGuire said.

'What? No!' Jay replied.

'Apparently there was some sort of an exchange between the two of you?'

Jay nodded reluctantly. 'He... uh... he caught sight of me taking a picture. He stormed over and accused me of being a perv taking photographs of kids at the arcade.'

'I see.' McGuire resumed stroking his lip. 'To which you responded?'

'I told him he was rumbled. I told him I had pictures of him driving bumper cars, lifting his kid up, playing Crazy Golf and stuff.'

McGuire's brows bounced impatiently, waiting for more.

'I... uh... I said his claim was clearly fraudulent and he needed to bloody well pack it in.'

'Ahh...' said McGuire. He leant forward in his seat. 'There are a couple of small learning moments here, Jay, and they're worth pointing out... if I may?'

'Sure.'

'It's covert surveillance you were doing, not *overt*. In other words, the trick is not to be spotted,' McGuire explained.

'Yeah, I know... but... he –'

McGuire raised a finger to show he was not finished. 'And if a target does spot you and, in this instance, thought you were a pervert taking photos of kids... then that is exactly what you should have pretended to be.'

'Oh, I see.'

McGuire's mouth lifted slightly, a ghost of a smile to take the sting out of his words. 'We're in the business of observing, *discreetly*... not publicly rebuking, Jay.'

'Right.'

'That said... the trust will be happy he's dropped his claim. So, all's well that ends well.'

Jay nodded, grateful that McGuire was taking that approach. 'Thanks, McGuire.'

He turned to leave the man's office.

'Jay?'

He turned back to face him. 'Yeah?'

McGuire was thoughtfully stroking his top lip again. 'How would you feel about going on a training course?'

'Uh... yeah. That would be, yeah, great.' Jay realised he should probably ask – in what? 'What kind of –'

'Spy craft,' said McGuire, his crooked lips spreading into a broad smile.

20

'You really should put an air freshener back here,' said Minter from the rear seat. 'It reeks of stale fag smoke.'

'No one sits back there... normally,' Okeke replied as her beaten-up brown Datsun sped along the eastbound M25 as they headed for Dartford. 'Except when I have to give my brother's kids a lift somewhere.'

'You make actual children sit back here? In this toxic mess?' Minter asked, horrified.

'They get used to it, or they walk,' Okeke replied. 'Now stop fidgeting and kicking my seat. Don't make me pull over and smack the back of your legs.'

The family liaison officer, PS Gayle Brown, who was in the front passenger seat, chuckled.

'I didn't know you were an auntie,' said Minter.

'Auntie Sammy,' she said with a sigh. 'Yeah. Best contraceptive ever, that, you know... Someone else's kids.'

'I hear you,' said Brown. She adjusted the tight, fraying seat belt across her front. 'I've made a solemn vow never to spawn any rug rats. Too messy, too noisy and too expensive.'

Okeke had made a similar pledge at the start of her career. Having a baby on a PC's wage would have been foolish. Especially if things hadn't worked out and she'd ended up being a single mum. Of course, though, she had Jay and two steady wages coming in now. There was also the exciting prospect of a promotion to detective sergeant... It had started her thinking. With her internal body clock ticking away, maybe the question was worth revisiting... She knew Jay was keen to have a family at some point.

'So what's the situation with this Mrs Meadows?' asked Brown. 'Do we know how she is? How she's likely to take the news?'

'Her husband's been missing for over a decade,' answered Minter. 'We don't know if she's with someone new or keeping a candle-lit vigil.'

'How much info are you planning to share with her?' asked Brown.

'Only that a body's been found,' said Okeke. 'That could *possibly* be her husband's.'

'No mention of his murder and dismemberment,' added Minter. 'We'll keep it light on details.'

Brown turned in her seat to look back at him. 'Okay. Sounds good.'

THE ANSWER as to whether Marjorie Meadows was going to need a bit of hand-holding and back-rubbing became quickly apparent. She'd moved on. The man who opened the door to them and introduced himself as Jim told them that he was her partner.

'She's in the front room. Can I make you guys some tea?' he asked.

Minter smiled. 'I'll have a coffee, if it's going?'

'No problem.' Jim led them through into the living room.

Marjorie Meadows was waiting for them. She got up off the sofa and shook hands with the three of them as they gave her their names.

'You're the lady I spoke to yesterday?' she said to Okeke.

'That's right.'

'Please, take a seat,' she said, gesturing at the armchairs. 'Jim'll be through with the tea and biscuits in a minute.'

Minter nodded at Okeke.

'Mrs Meadows...' Okeke began.

'Just Marjorie,' she cut in. 'And I use my maiden name now. Barlow.'

'Right.' Okeke made a note of that. 'So, as I mentioned yesterday afternoon, a body was recovered that we think may well be your missing husband, Mark.'

Marjorie nodded.

'We've compared the body with the details you gave the police twelve years ago,' said Okeke. 'And I'm afraid it's looking likely that it could be Mark. It was his rugby club tattoo that helped us make the link.'

Marjorie nodded. 'He was a keen player.'

'What position did he play?' asked Minter.

'Prop forward,' she replied. 'He had the build. You know... chunky.' She turned back to Okeke. 'So how did Mark die? Where did you find him?'

'We do need to wait for confirmation that it's him,' Okeke said gently. 'Can you tell us a bit more about him? About the day he disappeared and what reason might he have had, if any, for taking off?'

'None... *really*,' Marjorie replied. 'I mean, he went to work as usual that day and just never returned.'

'What did he do, job-wise?' Minter asked.

'He was an estate agent,' said Marjorie.

'And there were no problems to speak of? Debts maybe?' Okeke paused. 'Marital issues?'

Marjorie stiffened slightly. 'To be honest, we weren't getting on that well at the time,' she admitted.

'How do you mean?' Okeke asked.

'You know. Arguments and the like.'

'And what were they about, if you don't mind me asking?' Okeke said.

Jim entered the room with a tray of mugs and a plate of chocolate digestives. Marjorie remained silent until he'd handed them out and left them to it.

'Mark had a temper on him,' she said eventually. 'He could be a little too handy with his fists, especially after he'd had a drink or two.'

'He was violent with you?' said Minter.

She shrugged. 'Once or twice. That's what we argued about. I'd decided I wasn't having any more of it. I'd had enough.'

'You said he could get "a little too handy with his fists" after a couple of drinks. Did he drink often?' said Okeke.

Marjorie shrugged again. 'He liked a few beers with the lads at the club after a session. Once a year he used to go on a complete bender with some old friends of his. He called it their "annual review". But the reunion was basically just a massive piss-up.'

'Do you know who they were?' Minter asked.

She shook her head. 'There were four of them – at first, anyway. Over the years the others dropped out, I think, and it was just Mark and the other one.' She looked at Okeke. 'Those were the times when he got particularly drunk... and violent.'

'Okay, and what about this remaining friend? Do you have a name for him?' She paused. 'Or her?'

'It was Andy... something.' Marjorie frowned as she tried to remember his surname. 'When he came back from those drinking sessions, Mark always seemed... different.'

'How do you mean, *different*?' asked Minter.

'He was distant. Closed down. Angry. I met Andy once. I think it was the year before Mark went missing. Mark brought him back after one of their sessions because he was worried about him making his own way home.' She sipped her tea. 'Andy was blind drunk that night, kept rambling on about something or other.'

'What something?' asked Okeke.

Marjorie shook her head. 'I don't know. Some secret or other that Mark didn't want me to know. He kept trying to shut Andy up. Told me to leave them be and go up to bed.'

Okeke jotted that down. 'Did you get a sense of what this secret could be? Was it about money?'

Marjorie shrugged. 'Could have been. I know that Andy was always asking Mark for money. Now *he* was a bit of an alcoholic, I'd say. But, anyway, by the way Mark kept telling him to shut up that night, I think there was definitely something going on.'

'Right. And you say they were *old* friends?' Minter asked.

'Going way back, I think.'

'Do you know what school Mark went to?'

'Some grammar school near Harsham, his home town,' Marjorie said.

Okeke scribbled that down. Harsham was an hour or so from Hastings. The school would be easy enough to find.

'Andy didn't manage to make it to their last reunion,' added Marjorie. 'He went missing apparently.'

'He was missing too?' Okeke said sharply, looking up from her notebook.

Marjorie nodded. 'And that was only a few months before Mark went missing as well.'

Okeke glanced at Minter.

'Oh...' Marjorie raised her hand. 'I remember now.'

'What?' Minter and Okeke asked in unison.

'His surname. It was Westford. No, that's not right.' She frowned. 'Andy West... *field*. That's it. Andy Westfield.'

21

Boyd herded his team into the Incident Room. Okeke, Warren, O'Neal and Minter reeked of cigarette smoke as they filed past him.

Boyd sniffed in Minter's direction. 'Surely not you too?' he asked. 'It's a filthy habit, Minter.'

Minter paused. 'Very funny,' he huffed. 'I'm going to have to dry-clean my suit to get the reek of Okeke's bloody car out of it.'

They took their seats round the conference table and Boyd was just about to start the meeting when Sutherland poked his head round the door. 'Mind if I sit in, Boyd? I'd like to catch up on things.'

Sutherland looked hot and bothered; his white shirt was sporting damp patches under the armpits. Clearly he'd already had enough of being slowly baked alive in his glass vivarium.

'Feel free, sir,' Boyd said, and waved him in.

Boyd went over to the one window in the room that could be cracked open just a couple of inches and opened it.

The novelty of seeing blue skies over Hastings and feeling the sun on his face was beginning to wear thin.

'When the hell is the air conditioning going to be switched on?' he asked, shrugging off his jacket. The others shed theirs too.

'July,' replied Sutherland. He spread his hands apologetically. 'It's a budget thing. July for air-con, November for heating, Boyd. Sorry.'

Boyd loosened his tie as he sat back down. 'Okay then – updates, ladies and gents, please.' He turned to Minter. 'Let's hear about Mrs Meadows first, shall we?'

'Righto.' Minter checked the notes in front of him. 'Mark Meadows' wife is Marjorie Barlow; she's going by her maiden name now,' he explained. 'It was a very interesting interview, boss...' He relayed a potted version of their conversation with her and took a swig from his water bottle when he was done.

'So,' Boyd summarised, 'we have Mark Meadows and Andy Westfield, two friends from childhood, both going missing within months of each other back in 2011.' He got up slowly and approached the whiteboard. He scribbled their names on the board.

'I already checked LEDS,' added Minter. 'Westfield's in the misper database too. He was the same age as Meadows.'

'Who reported him missing?' Boyd asked.

'His mother. I skimmed the interview notes. She hadn't heard from him for months. Normally he kept in regular touch, usually tapping her for money.'

'He was an alcoholic, according to Meadows' wife,' Okeke added.

Boyd scribbled '*alcoholic*' and '*money*' beside Westfield's name. 'So then, you say, according to the wife, Meadows and

Westfield were in the habit of going for a reunion pint or several every year?'

Both Minter and Okeke nodded.

'And she mentioned something about a secret?' Boyd said.

'Yes,' Okeke replied. 'She said there was definitely something going on between them.'

Boyd went back to his seat and eased himself down. The stitch in his side was particularly irksome this afternoon. He tried not to think it might be some gnarly tumour slowly eating away at him. Other explanations, he reminded himself, were still in the running.

'You all right there, Boyd?' asked Sutherland.

He nodded. 'Pulled a bloody muscle.'

'Aha!' said Sutherland, puffing up his chest. 'Finally joined us on the old exercise front, have you? Well, see me afterwards and I'll give you some tips on how to avoid the pitfalls. It's very easy for a novice to overdo it, Boyd.'

Minter choked on a mouthful of water and Okeke snorted.

Boyd glared at them. He handed Okeke his whiteboard marker. 'Note the secret on the board, will you?'

Boyd scratched his beard as Okeke added '*secret*' to the board. 'So that's two out of the three, then. And both disappeared in 2011, before that storage unit was taken on in 2012.'

'So our serial killer may have stored them somewhere else for a while,' suggested Magnusson.

Boyd nodded, then added, 'But can we stop using the term "serial killer"?'

'Well, technically –'

'Guv, we haven't a hundred per cent *confirmed* the identities of the bodies yet,' cut in Okeke. 'Just saying.'

Boyd nodded. 'But it's looking somewhat more likely now.'

'The third one could be another school friend?' suggested Warren. 'In on this secret?'

'The Ellessey write-up indicated all three men were about the same age,' Magnusson confirmed. 'Mid thirties.'

'Okay. Well, let's run with that. School mates. Potentially,' muttered Boyd. 'Interesting.'

'So that really could rule out a serial killer, then,' said Okeke.

'The definition of a serial killer is more than three victims across a time span greater than thirty days,' said Magnusson. 'So, by that definition, our killer *is* a serial killer.'

'They're most often random profiled victims,' Okeke corrected. 'As in, not known to the killer but strangers of a certain type.'

'Okeke's right,' said Boyd. 'If all three of them were known to him, then it's not a serial killer in the classic sense.' He absently tapped a pen against his chin. 'Since Meadows and Westfield knew each other... the chances of both being randomly selected victims of a type seems highly unlikely.'

'But still possible,' said Magnusson. 'If they had similar traits? A similar lifestyle?'

Boyd tilted his head from one side to the other, to indicate he was at least giving her suggestion consideration. 'This *secret*, though... If we're going to give that some weight, it's another factor that links the pair of them.'

Magnusson settled back in her seat noisily. '*If* we're giving this notion of a *secret* serious consideration. Although, personally, I much prefer to deal in facts.'

'That was Mrs Meadows' word, right?' asked Boyd.

Minter and Okeke nodded.

'And did Mrs Meadows say if this secret went back all the way to childhood?'

'She didn't say that,' said Minter. 'But she did say that four of them got together every year for a while before they started dropping out.'

'So then...' Boyd mused, absent-mindedly tapping his chin with the biro again. '*Four* men, possibly linked by a shared secret that possibly goes all the way back to their childhood. And three of them are now dead.'

'That's a lot of speculative "inking in",' said Magnusson. 'Just saying.'

'That's what we do on our side of the floor,' cut in Sutherland. 'CSI do facts; CID do theories.'

'Let's just indulge it for the moment,' said Boyd coolly. 'A secret that four men know about. Three of them are dead. Either the fourth one killed the other three... or...'

'Or?' prompted Sutherland.

'There's a fifth person who wants all four of them dead,' Okeke said.

Sutherland turned her way. 'Now that *is* inking in, detective.'

'It could have been a playground pact,' Warren suggested.

Sutherland cut in again. 'Good God, let's never use that phrase again. If the press catch wind of that, it'll be all over the place. They love a bit of ruddy alliteration.'

Boyd twisted carefully in his seat and looked back at the board.

'All right,' he said. 'Let's find out what schools Meadows and Westfield attended. If it's the same school, then maybe we're looking at something that happened when they were school age. If they *didn't* go to the same school, then they might have met each other through some club or other. Maybe they were just friends because they knocked around the same neighbourhood?'

'Maybe they became friends later in life?' added Warren. 'Like university or something?'

'You're right,' said Boyd. 'Perhaps I'm leaning too hard on the childhood angle?'

'Meadows' wife was quite specific... that their friendship seemed to go back a long way,' said Okeke.

'Right.' Boyd nodded. 'Well, let's give the school a try and we'll go from there.'

'I'll take that,' volunteered Okeke.

'No,' replied Boyd. That was going to be relatively easy work and Okeke was good at the more important face-to-face stuff. 'O'Neal. You check the schools.'

'Right, chief,' O'Neal replied.

'Minter, Okeke... you go and interview Westfield's mum. Let's find out some more about him. Did he have money troubles? Was he actually an alcoholic? And, yes, dive into his childhood. Did he have any particularly close friends. Get names if she can remember them.'

'Righto,' Minter said.

'Warren?'

'Yes, sir?'

'We really need to know who body number three is. Keep trawling the misper database and liaise with O'Neal. Remind me – how old was Mark Meadows when he went missing?' he asked Minter.

'Thirty-six, boss.'

'Right. So John Doe number three looks as if he was boxed up about five years ago. So carry on with the search – white, male and mid thirties – and look at records from four to six years ago.'

'And Okeke... can you get a DNA swab from Westfield's mother while you're there? We need to confirm that the body is definitely her son.'

'On it, guv,' Okeke replied.

'You still don't have a one hundred per cent DNA certainty that Mark Meadows is one of those bodies,' cut in Magnusson sharply. 'You're working on an assumption, Boyd.'

Boyd did his best not to grind his teeth too obviously. 'Yes, Magnusson. Admittedly, it's an *assumption*. But it's a promising enough one to run with at the moment.'

Magnusson raised her brows sceptically and tucked her chin into her neck in a way that irritated him.

'We're still waiting on some bits and pieces from Ellessey, aren't we?' he asked her.

'Only the DNA swab from the coffee cup. And potential forensics on that storage unit registration form,' she replied.

'Chase them up, will you?'

Her chin disappeared deeper into her thick neck. 'Of course... *sir*.'

22

Boyd's personal phone buzzed on his desk with an unknown caller ID. He let it roll over to voicemail. Being an unknown, it was more than likely he was going to be informed by some AI spam-bot that he'd recently been involved in a traffic accident.

It started buzzing again.

He picked it up, intending to remain silent so that the bot would figure out his number was a waste of time and move on.

'William Boyd?' It was a female voice. A human one.

'Yes?'

'My name's Kath Middleton. I'm ringing on behalf of Dr Chudasama from the oncology department.'

It took him a moment to assemble that in his head. 'Oncology. The cancer people?'

'Yes, at Conquest Hospital.' Her voice sounded vaguely apologetic. 'I'm calling about your stool sample. I just need to check a couple of details before we can talk...'

Boyd got up and wandered over to the window that overlooked the car park at the front of the station, away from the other desks. 'Go on,' he said.

'Can you confirm your date of birth, please?' she asked. 'And the first line of your address.'

Boyd did so.

'Thank you, William,' she replied. 'Your sample was sent to us by Dr Ho from Ore Surgery and it's just been tested –'

'Blimey, that was quick. I only made the...uh... *deposit* yesterday.' He put a smile into his voice. 'And there was me thinking the NHS was backed up for months.'

'I'm afraid,' she continued, 'that a couple of positive markers turned up in the sample.'

'Positive markers... meaning?' he asked.

'It means we'd like to take a closer look at you, William.'

'Are we talking –' he looked around to make sure no one was nearby – 'cancer?'

'Not necessarily,' she replied. 'The positive markers can mean a number of things.'

'But they *include* cancer?' he pressed.

She hesitated for a moment. 'Yes. Among other things. Dr Chudasama has requested that you come in for a colonoscopy as soon as is convenient.'

Convenient seemed a vaguely reassuring word to hear. So not *that* urgent, then. 'Well, I'm quite busy with work at the moment,' he tried. Refraining from mentioning that in fact it was three dismembered, desiccated bodies he had, figuratively, in his in-tray.

'It's quite *important*,' she responded.

Okay, so *possibly* urgent.

'Colonoscopy,' he said cautiously. 'Is that the camera up the...' He paused. 'Back passage?'

She laughed politely. 'Yes. It's not as uncomfortable as it

sounds, though. It can be done with a local anaesthetic if you're... uh...'

'Not used to that sort of thing?' he helped her.

'Indeed. We're ideally looking at some time in the next couple of days. It's best to investigate these things as quickly as possible to rule out anything serious. How does Thursday morning sound?'

The day after tomorrow. They really weren't hanging around.

'All right. Yes. Okay,' he heard himself say.

'Great. I'll book you in for nine. We'll prescribe you CitraFleet to be taken on Wednesday evening and on Thursday morning. Full instructions will be with the pack.'

He heard the photocopier firing up behind him and looked over his shoulder to see O'Neal waiting patiently beside the machine. He took a couple of steps further away and turned his back on him.

'What's that for?'

'It's just to flush you out so your bowels are nice and clean. No breakfast Thursday morning, all right?'

'All right.'

'You just need to mix it into a glass of water. Tastes a bit yucky, I'm afraid,' she continued. 'Shall I have the prescription sent to the pharmacy at Ore Surgery?'

'Great,' muttered Boyd. 'I mean, yes.'

He heard the tapping of a keyboard down the line. 'Right, that's all booked in. You'll receive a letter telling you how to find the colonoscopy theatre, as well as information about the procedure, and –'

'Kath? It's Kath, isn't it?' he interrupted her.

'Uh... yes.'

'Can you be blunt with me...? So I need to worry about this?' He hated how that had come out sounding. A little desperate. 'Is this a box-ticking exercise or is this colonoscopy more of a confirmation-of-diagnosis thing?'

There was another hesitation. A long one. 'We find it's best to retain a positive frame of mind, William. We'll see you on Thursday morning, all right?'

'Yes, okay,' he replied.

'Take care.' She ended the call.

Positive frame of mind? Okaaay. So, no. Not good news, then.

The rest of the afternoon spun out with little to distract him. Minter updated him to say that he'd managed to contact Westfield's mother and set a time for himself and Okeke to visit her in the morning and O'Neal proudly announced that he'd found Meadows' grammar school and spoken to the headmaster's secretary. They were going to email him the registration list for the first-year students for a few years from 1986 onwards.

Other than those welcome interruptions, Boyd spent the afternoon wondering how he was going to break the news to Charlotte. He wasn't sure he'd get away with wry humour and macho stoicism.

He'd managed to resist the urge to google 'bowel cancer' so far. He almost felt as if having the term in his search history would increase his chances of having it from 'possible' to 'definite'.

Another thought occurred to him. At some point, and pretty soon too, he was going to have to let Emma know.

23

Emma met Dan outside the Nelson pub, and then on a whim they decided to grab a takeaway coffee and wander among the tall net huts and beached, bleached hulls of Hastings' small fishing fleet. For once there were no dogs in tow; it was just the two of them.

'There was another way you could have handled all this,' Emma said after the small talk had whittled away to nothing. 'You know, better than throwing your toys out of the pram and running for the hills?'

'I know,' Dan replied. 'I'm so sorry.'

'I wasn't expecting you to give everything up, get an office job and rot away at a desk so you could keep me in nappies and formula milk,' she continued.

He pushed a floppy tress of dark hair out of his eyes. It had grown much longer over the last few months and, she wasn't sure, but it looked as though he was possibly having a stab at a goatee. All part of the band's grungy image, no doubt.

'But that's how it goes, though, isn't it?' Dan replied. 'You have a kid... you've got responsibilities, so you get a job.' He shrugged. 'And that's your life over and done with.'

'It doesn't have to be,' she replied.

They paused by the old stone jetty that stretched out from the shingle beach and bordered Rock-a-Nore. She recalled her dad telling her about the yacht that had been tethered there on his very first day of work here in Hastings, complete with bloody mess in the cockpit. His first case with Sussex Police.

'Thing is –' Dan sipped his coffee – 'you can't be a just little bit parent-y... Like you can't be just a little bit pregnant. It's all in or all out.'

Emma stroked her bump subconsciously as she shook her head. It was showing enough now that an oversized hoody wasn't going to hide it for long. 'It's all in for me, but it doesn't mean you have to be all in too. There's room for the band as well as a baby.' She came to a halt and leant on the wall. 'I mean, Kurt Cobain had a baby, right?'

Dan huffed dryly. 'Didn't end so well for him, did it?'

'I'm pretty sure it wasn't his baby that did it for him. More like the drugs. The fame.'

He smiled and rested his cup on the wall. 'Can't say I object to the comparison, though.'

She laughed gently. 'How's it all going, anyway?'

'Good.' He nodded. 'Unsettlingly good. We hit fifty thousand downloads last month; we're getting some decent bookings. There was an article on us on LADBible last week.'

'Wow,' she replied, even though she didn't know the website. 'You got a manager yet?'

He shook his head. 'We want to go as far as we can before we get some guy bossing us around.' He sighed. 'I keep wondering how long it's going to last.'

'It'll last as long as you keep writing good songs, I suppose,' Emma said.

'Nah... it lasts until some other shiny new band comes along and takes the fans with them.'

'Nothing lasts forever,' she said quietly.

He nodded. 'I was thinking about that while I was waiting for you to turn up. You see these sad crinkly pop stars on reality shows, trying to rekindle the old magic. It must be, like, a lifelong nightmare... being famous, briefly, for you know, eighteen months, then fading into obscurity and spending the rest of your life trying to get it back.'

'Looking at your old videos on YouTube? Listening to your old songs?' she added.

'Right. Seems to me you get two choices with success in this business: die young and become a tragic legend, or, you know, have your brief window of fame and then spend the rest of your life pining away for it.'

Emma let out a deep breath. 'You're not really selling me on the idea of rock-star fame.' She sipped her coffee. 'You're supposed to be making a strong case for running off to London or LA, or wherever it is that rock gods live, and leaving Hastings far behind you.'

'And winding up twenty years from now,' he continued, 'on *The Mask* wearing a stupid feathery disguise and singing – badly – someone else's song. Being that guy from that band that most of the audience won't really remember anyway.'

She nodded. 'Or playing a walk-on part in *EastEnders*.'

'If you can act.'

'Oh, is that what they're doing?'

They both laughed.

'But...' Dan sighed. '... there's a chance, right? A chance that we'll amount to something, at least for a while...?'

Emma looked at him. 'Which is why you should go for it, Dan. See how far this thing will take you.' She reached out for his hand and placed it gently on her belly. 'And you can still be a part of this. I'm not going anywhere, nor is the bump. I've got Dad and Charlotte as my support network anyway.'

'I can help with money?' he offered. 'There's enough coming in that I can buy stuff you need.'

'No need for subs, Dan. Just... I don't know... drop by sometimes –'

'What about your dad?' he asked nervously.

Emma laughed. 'He *isn't* going to arrest you and read your rights,' she said. 'For some bizarre reason, he seems to quite like you.'

'Even though I cut and ran?'

She nodded, then let his hand go. It lingered on her bump. 'You can, in fact, do *both* things, you know? The band *and* be a part of my family.'

Danny nodded. Grateful. 'I miss you, Emma.'

She put her hand on his. If this was a cheesy nineties rom-com with Jude Law and Renée Zellweger, there'd be a conveniently and timely kick that would melt his heart and deliver a hopeful denouement. But the bump remained still.

'I miss you too... you doofus,' she said.

24

Okeke resisted the urge to wrinkle her nose at the overpowering odour in Bridgette Westfield's tiny flat. She shared it with four fat tan-coloured bulldogs, none of which looked as if they'd had a walk for some time. In the corner of the front room was a litter tray that was garnished with several recent turds and surrounded by over a dozen Febreze air fresheners, presumably run dry long ago.

Minter was pulling a face behind the woman's back and both Okeke and PS Gayle Brown shot him daggers in a bid to lock it down before Bridgette turned and glimpsed the look on his face.

'I can make you all a cuppa and some sandwiches if you like?' Bridgette wheezed as she sat down.

All three officers politely declined her offer. 'We've just eaten, thank you,' replied Minter quickly.

Okeke settled down on the sofa opposite her. PS Brown took a seat beside her and Minter remained standing – the only other chair was occupied by two of her bullies, both daring him to even think about trying to shoo them off.

'Now, Mrs Westfield,' began Okeke, 'if you recall, my colleague DS Minter mentioned yesterday afternoon that we found a body that we believe may be that of your son.'

Bridgette nodded. Her thinning white hair was rucked up on one side and her eyes were puffy and red from crying. On the coffee table beside her, Okeke could see that she had pulled out a dozen photos of her boy. Okeke suspected she'd spent the night on the sofa, leaking tears onto the faded cushions, going through old photo albums and pondering the many different – better – paths her son's life might have taken.

'I'm so sorry,' Okeke added.

Bridgette nodded. She'd had the night to start to come to terms with the news. 'How did he die?'

'We suspect he was murdered, Bridgette. Again, I'm so sorry,' Okeke said.

'No need to keep apologising, love.' Bridgette sighed. 'It's actually a bit of a relief, truth be told. To know, I mean. I always thought he'd come to an unfortunate end. That he'd die of a drugs overdose or drink. He was an alkie-holic, you know?'

'Yes. We have heard that,' Okeke replied.

'Did he get in a fight with someone? Is that what happened?' Bridgette asked.

'We're still trying to work out exactly what happened,' Okeke told her. 'Whatever it was, we think it took place about twelve years ago.'

Bridgette laughed humourlessly. 'And there's me waiting all this time like an idiot. Waiting for him to knock on my door and ask for another tenner.' Her face crumpled.

Okeke picked up one of the photos on the coffee table – a school portrait of Andrew Westfield, kept in a dog-eared cardboard frame with the school's logo embossed at the top.

'That's from his school, that is,' Bridgette said, wiping her eyes. 'When he was at Harsham Grammar. He was a clever boy, Andrew. He passed the exam that got him in, instead of going to the local comprehensive.'

Okeke smiled. 'You must have been very proud of him.'

'I was. He was a good boy...' Bridgette shook her head. 'I was convinced that school would set him up for life, you know? Get him some decent grades... Give him a chance to do well.'

'How did he get on there?'

Her smile was tight-lipped and spare. 'Good, for the first year. Then he started hanging around with a gang of boys.'

'What gang?' asked Minter.

'There were four of them, I think. Thick as thieves, they were.' Bridgette shook her head and scowled. 'They went everywhere together. I didn't like them. I made supper for them all once... I could hear them sniggering and whispering behind my back.'

'Can you remember their names?' pressed Minter.

'There was...' She frowned with concentration. 'There was Mark. Another boy – can't remember what his name was. And then the fourth... I really didn't like him at all.' Her eyes glazed over and she bit her lip. 'I think his name was Richard. He bossed them around. He was the ringleader, all right. A right little shit, but Andrew thought the sun shone out of his behind. "*Richard says this, Richard does that.*" On and on.'

'Can you remember this Richard's surname?' Minter asked her.

Bridgette shook her head again. 'They spent most of their time around his place.' She looked up at Minter. 'It was because he was rich. They had a proper snooker table.

Andrew was always saying how big and fancy his house was. They had a hot tub, don't you know?'

'And the boys were friends for some time, were they?' prompted Okeke. 'Sometimes friendship groups change or break up completely during the school years.'

'No. They stuck together all the way through school,' Bridgette replied. 'I think Andrew only stayed on for A levels because he wanted to keep hanging around with them.' She sighed. 'He struggled with those exams, though. He should have gone for an apprenticeship instead. He could have made something of himself if he had.'

'What about after school?' asked Minter. 'Did they remain close as adults?'

'Not really,' Bridgette replied. 'I don't think so. I mean, Andrew stayed friends with Mark for a while, I think. The other two... Richard... Oh...' The distant look on her face cleared. '*Robin.* That was the other one's name. Richard and Robin, that's it. Those two went on to better things. Well, that's what Andrew always said.'

'Better things?' Okeke echoed.

'You know, she replied, 'where the smart ones go. University. Nice jobs...'

Okeke made a few notes and looked up. 'And you say Andrew and Mark remained in touch?' she said.

Bridgette nodded. 'I think so. I'm pretty sure I remember Andrew telling me once that that they met up every now and then for a pint of beer... That was after Andrew moved out.' She dabbed at her puffy eyes. 'He couldn't wait to get away from me,' she mumbled.

'What makes you think that?' asked Okeke.

Bridgette looked up at her. 'I think he was embarrassed by me.' She sighed. 'I think he thought he could do better. Having seen how rich people lived.'

'But he visited, didn't he?' Okeke asked.

She huffed. 'When he needed a bit of money, yes. To buy his drink.'

Minter caught PS Gale Brown's eye. She nodded – they probably weren't going to get much more from Bridgette this morning.

'Right,' he said. 'Thank you, Mrs Westfield. You've been extremely helpful.'

'Oh, I doubt that.' She reached for a crinkled tissue from the box next to her. 'I'm a bit of a mess at the moment.'

'Actually, I do have one more question,' said Okeke. 'Was there ever an incident between the boys? Or an incident involving them?'

'What do you mean?' Bridgette asked.

'Trouble with the police maybe? Trouble at school? Were any of them disciplined?'

'Andrew got a few detentions, but nothing more serious.'

'Did he mention any disagreements between them? Any arguments? Fights?'

Bridgette shook her head. 'Like I said, they were a tight-knit bunch.' She looked at Okeke. 'Too tight, I sometimes thought.'

'In what way?' Okeke said.

'Richard, the rich one, was very controlling. Manipulative. He had those other three wrapped around his little finger.' She narrowed her eyes. 'He had a sly look about him. I can imagine he could have done it.'

'Done what?' Okeke asked.

'Murdered him. Some children are born evil. Born rotten. They grow up, but they don't change; they just get smarter at hiding it.' She began to sob. 'And they always end up getting away with everything.'

'We're going to try to find these friends of Andrew's. And

talk to them,' Okeke assured her. *Particularly this Richard, if he wasn't one of the three bodies.*

Minter caught her eye. *We're probably done here.*

Okeke rested over and placed a hand gently on Bridgette's arm, then she reached into her bag. 'One more thing. Do you mind if we take a DNA swab?'

She pulled out a small glass pot with a cotton bud inside.

'Like a Covid test?'

Okeke nodded. 'But not so it'll make you gag. I just need to swipe your gums. It's so that we can ID the body. To be sure whether we really have found Andrew.'

The old woman nodded and Okeke made quick work of it.

'Thank you,' said Okeke as she dropped the bud in and screwed the cap onto the pot. 'You've been really helpful, Bridgette.'

'You make sure you find that boy, Richard.' Bridgette narrowed her eyes. 'He was a nasty one.'

25

O'Neal had Harsham Grammar's first-year registration list from 1986 printed out in front of him. It spread across four sheets of paper.

'How many students are there?' asked Minter.

'The year's intake was two hundred and fifty-four. The school secretary said it was a larger year group than normal.'

'Of course it was,' Minter muttered dryly.

'So what names are we looking for?' O'Neal asked.

'Mark Meadows and Andrew Westfield are on there. So, we're looking for a Richard and a Robin.' Minter pointed to a page. 'Richard Edward Daley.' He clapped O'Neal on the back. 'There you go – I've got you off to a grand start.'

'You're not helping me?'

'It's an easy one, O'Neal. A five-minute job,' Minter replied. 'I'm off to update the boss.'

~

Boyd was relieved to have Minter and Okeke for company up in the canteen. He'd spent way too much time this morning googling 'bowel cancer' and the fun and games to be had with colostomy bags.

Okeke brought a tray of coffees over. 'Are you sure you don't want a pastry, guv?' she asked him as she handed out the cups.

'I'm not hungry,' he replied.

She sat down. 'That's not like you.' She checked her watch. 'It's three. You're normally on a carb binge round about now.'

Boyd picked up his coffee. 'Not today. Right then... what did you get from Andrew Westfield's mother?'

'Well, we didn't eat or drink anything – so luckily not food poisoning,' said Minter. 'It was bloody rank there.'

Okeke tutted. 'Poor old woman.'

'Did you manage to get a swab from her?' Boyd asked.

Minter nodded. 'Evidenced and with Magnusson as we speak. She's going to get it over to Ellessey.'

'Good,' Boyd said. 'So then... tell me about the interview.'

Okeke gave him a summary of the interview from her notes.

'O'Neal's going through the school's registration list for Andrew's year now,' added Minter. 'We'll have a few names to chase up by the time we get back downstairs.'

Boyd ran a finger over the bristles around his mouth. 'Four schoolboys, thick as thieves and potentially with something to hide... '

'She seemed to think Richard was the bad apple, leading the other three astray,' said Minter.

'If we're giving this secret pact idea any credence,' Boyd

said, shrugging, 'we're looking for something bad enough for those boys to keep a vow of silence over all these years.'

'Sexual assault?' offered Okeke.

'Murder?' added Minter.

Boyd shrugged again. 'Could be.'

'You think they could have killed another kid?' Minter asked.

Boyd nodded. The horrific James Bulger case had briefly occurred to him as Okeke had been relaying her notes. His mind raked back over it: the press coverage, the shock, grief and outrage that children could kill children. He remembered the heated exchanges on shows like *Kilroy* and *This Morning*.

A talking point had been 'Who had been the main instigator?' with both boys pointing the finger at each other, claiming they'd been forced by the other one into taking part. If Mrs Westfield's cautionary words about Richard being the ringleader were to be taken at face value, then, presumably, if whatever they'd done came out while they were all alive, *he'd* be the one with most to lose. All the more reason then for this Richard to decide many years later that some remedial action needed to be taken.

'If it was something like that,' said Boyd finally, 'then there surely must be something we can dredge up from the time. A newspaper article or a case file. But I'm not convinced. Something that horrific would have made national news.'

'It could be a lingering misper?' Okeke said. 'I could take a look?'

Boyd shrugged. 'Let's not get sucked too deeply into anything yet. Magnusson raised a valid point... We're just throwing theories around here. It might not even be murder.

It could be something as simple as a grudge. Some kid was bullied at school and getting his revenge years later maybe?'

'Murder's a bit extreme, though?' said Minter.

'I don't know,' said Boyd. 'Lives can be ruined by what happens in the corner of a playground.'

'And we're also assuming whatever happened involving them took place during their school years,' added Okeke.

'Right, there's that too,' said Boyd. He was beginning to wonder whether the secret that Mark Meadows' wife had mentioned was getting a little too much attention. However, for the lack of any other driving narrative, it wasn't something they could ignore either.

'We need to confirm ID on Andrew Westfield and find the other two... Robin and Richard,' he said eventually. 'If they're on that school registration list, then we may be able to positively ID the third body in the box. And then... we can go down the path of looking into what those boys may have done together with a little more certainty.'

'It could be something one of them had done and then told the others about,' offered Minter. 'Maybe he felt it left him vulnerable?'

'It's got to be worth trawling around in the past a bit,' said Okeke.

Boyd nodded. 'If they were at the same school, then you're looking at, what, five years.'

'Seven,' said Minter. 'If you count the A-level years.'

'We could also concentrate on the area where they lived,' added Okeke. 'They'd be too young to drive anywhere. So whatever happened would probably have been local to Harsham.'

'Well, now there's a thing,' said Minter. 'What if they'd nicked a car?'

'A theft from thirty years ago? That's a bit of a reach for murder, isn't it?' Okeke replied.

Minter frowned. 'Well, not if they'd run someone over. Or caused a fatal RTA and fled the scene.'

Boyd shook his head. 'Okay, enough. Fine. Dig back a bit. Pull up any mispers, murders, assaults, manslaughters, RTAs... from 1986 to, say, '96? And in the Harsham area. But, let's not get tunnel vision here. We're sitting on a big fat assumption that at least two out of four schoolboys took a secret to their graves. The priority here is to figure out who the bodies in the boxes are.'

26

'Here you go, boss,' said Minter, handing the list to Boyd. 'O'Neal managed to find five Richards and two Robins.'

'And just checking... Andy Westfield and Mark Meadows are on the list too?'

Minter nodded. 'I can't believe how many Marcs with a "c" there are in this list, though. Was there a super-famous Marc around when they were all born?'

'Marc Bolan maybe?' Boyd suggested.

Minter looked at him blankly and shrugged.

'Never mind,' Boyd said. 'Run the names O'Neal has highlighted through LEDS. Also, you might want to get back in touch with the school to see if they have copies of any of their old school reports.'

'Righto,' Minter said. 'On it, boss.'

Boyd looked at the accumulated notes on his desk, his mind running through the theories that had been voiced up in the canteen. They had two very probable IDs now – Mark Meadows and Andrew Westfield – provided the DNA was matched with Westfield's mother. The third body would hopefully belong to either the Richard or Robin on the list. If it was... then all well and good. But if not, then what? Could it be sheer coincidence that two boys from the same school gang happened to be murdered within a few months of each other twelve years later?

Coincidences happened, of course, and when they did, they had a habit of blindsiding an investigation. If the last John Doe turned out to be someone else, then it would be back to the drawing board. They were going to have to consider other investigative tangents: commonalities between Meadows and Westfield that had nothing to do with childhood friendships and more to do with adult life choices that would have put them in the wrong place at the wrong time. Serial killer territory? God, he hoped not. As Her Madge had said... Sussex Police were going to pick up something of a reputation.

OKEKE STARTED with the *Sun*'s news archive. The tabloid had an insatiable appetite for grisly news stories, particularly ones with some kind of shock value attached. She tapped in a string of keywords that she thought might yield something useful: '1980 .. 1989', 'Harsham Grammar', 'Harsham Town, 'murder', 'missing', 'body found', 'feral youths', 'hit and run'.

While the searches returned a slew of articles that ticked a couple of boxes, she found herself sidetracked by the headlines. There had been a wave of outrage going in 1988 directed at Acid House and a pandemic of pill-popping.

'Acid Party Army of Baseball Bat Brutes!' stood out. There were various others.

She shook her head at the shouty capitals. It seemed that every decade had its own enemy for the red tops to jab their fingers at. Apparently outrage sold as many newspapers back then as it did mouse clicks now.

The detour into the past – before her time, before she was born even – led her to consider another possibility. Could drugs have played a role in whatever had happened? Could they have been on some crazy hallucinogenic trip? She jotted the thought down. She was still lost in one hyperbolic horror news story after another when Minter tapped her on the shoulder.

'Shit,' she said with a start. 'What time it is?'

'It's nearly home time,' Minter said, waving several pages of printed text in her direction.

'What's that?' she asked.

'They're various school reports on our Richards and Robins.' He waved them at her again. 'Harsham Grammar were very keen to assist.'

'Is there anything helpful in there?' she asked.

'I should say so, potentially.' Minter held up one of the sheets. 'This is a school report for one Richard Philip Leeder,' he told her. He had underscored several lines with a highlighter. 'Let me read it out to you,' he said.

'No need – I can read it myself,' she said, swiping it out of his hand.

'Snatchy, snatchy,' he tutted. 'That's not a good look, Okeke, and not at all becoming for a potential detective sergeant.' He grabbed it back and cleared his throat. 'Ahem...'

'Oh, for fuck's –' she muttered.

'*Richard is a natural leader and appears to be one of the more influential pupils in his year, with a firm hold over a number of boys in his class. While Richard is clearly intelligent and we predict he will effortlessly do well in his exams at the end of the year, we are concerned about him leading others astray...*'

Okeke held her hand out for the sheet of paper.

Minter ignored her and grinned. 'Wait – this is the best one.'

'On several occasions this term, we've had cause to discipline him over reported incidents of bullying boys in a lower year group. While the incidents were of a relatively trivial nature, I'm concerned that his behaviour has the potential to escalate...'

Minter finally handed Okeke the page.

'I think we may have found our Richard,' he said.

27

Boyd was quite happy for Her Madge to take the press conference instead of him. He wasn't in the mood, or right headspace to stand behind the small lectern and deliver the press briefing, and Hatcher had decided to step in and do it. Boyd wondered if Sutherland had shared his supposedly confidential Bad News with her and she was doing her bit to take some of the weight off his shoulders, or whether she was keen to demonstrate to the force and her superiors based over in Brighton that she was back, match fit and on everything – Sussex East-wise – like a rash.

Nonetheless, she'd insisted Boyd be close by in the room and ready to consult, or more likely, pass the ball to, if a question popped up that she couldn't answer.

Boyd handed her the crib sheet before they entered the press room – changed at the last moment, as a result of a call from Dr Palmer, to show the familial DNA swabs were a match and the wording on the crib sheet had been changed from 'likely identities' to 'identities confirmed'.

Hatcher had looked pleased when Boyd had pointed out the last-minute change.

Now, standing behind the nest of microphones, she raised her hands to quieten the room and draw cameras and attention to where they should be – on her.

'Thank you all for attending at such short notice. I'm going to start by giving you a brief update on the three male bodies found in...'

'THANKS.' Boyd took the mug of coffee from Charlotte and budged up to make room for her on the couch.

'Don't forget: no more eating and no breakfast tomorrow,' she said softly as she kicked her slippers off, pulled up her feet and snuggled up beside him.

They could hear Emma in the kitchen pouring herself a late-night bowl of Weetos, giving them a brief window of opportunity to talk about... *it*.

'I put that sachet of CitraFleet on your bedside table so you don't forget it in the morning,' Charlotte told him.

'Thanks,' he replied.

'Are you nervous?' she asked.

'Nah.'

She nudged him.

'Okay, well, maybe a little,' he conceded.

'I'm coming with you tomorrow,' she said firmly. They'd already discussed this and Boyd had been adamant that he'd be okay going to the hospital by himself. He had the letter telling him where to park and where to go.

'I can manage,' he told her again. 'I'll pull my Big Boy trousers on and I'll be fine.'

She shook her head. 'I'm coming.'

'You know what it's like,' he told her. 'Endless waiting around and I won't get any news tomorrow anyway. It'll be a bit of lube and "*Up we go, Mr Boyd*"...' He did a *Carry On* comedy whistle as he raised his index finger. 'Then: "*Off you trot, Mr Boyd.*"'

Charlotte didn't laugh. 'I'm coming, Bill,' she repeated in a voice that suggested the matter was settled.

They heard Emma rounding up the dogs and making her way back to the lounge.

'They might tell you if they see something,' Charlotte said in an undertone. 'I want to be with you if that happens, Bill.'

Emma entered the room, bowl in one hand, phone in the other, the dogs in her wake.

'You chatting to Dan?' Boyd asked, changing the subject sharply.

Emma sat down in the armchair opposite. 'We're texting,' she said.

'And how is Danny Boy?' he asked her.

Emma placed the bowl down on the side table and resumed tapping something out on her phone screen. Ozzie and Mia were sitting stock-still beside the table, their eyes glued to the bowl of Weetos.

'Looks like you've lost her,' Charlotte said to Boyd softly.

Boyd bounced his brows in a way that said, *Kids, eh?* He picked up the TV remote and flipped over to BBC One. The local news was on and he was treated to an image of Her Madge in the station's press room behind a bank of microphones. He'd forgotten that today was the day.

'Ah, here we go,' he said, raising the volume slightly.

'... found in a storage unit located near Little Fritton. At this stage we are treating this as a murder enquiry. The identities of two out of three bodies have now been confirmed, and their families and loved ones have been informed.'

Hatcher looked up from her script. 'Thank you. I'll take a couple of questions.'

She pointed at someone off-screen.

'You say three bodies... Are we looking at another serial killer in Sussex?'

She shook her head. 'At the moment we are keeping open-minded about the investigation. All three victims were male, white and potentially in their thirties... and we strongly suspect they were known to the killer.'

She moved onto another reporter. 'Yes?'

The question was inaudible on TV.

Hatcher shook her head. 'No, at this stage we don't have a suspect, but we are pursuing several promising lines of enquiry.'

Charlotte nodded at the TV. 'Is this one of yours?' she asked.

Boyd nodded.

'Three bodies in a storage unit?' She looked at him. 'Like in one of those storage warehouses?'

'Yup. And we have IDs confirmed, by the sounds of it.'

'Oh my God,' she whispered.

He could see she was reliving the traumatic memories of what had happened to her last year. Her ex-husband was dead and buried, literally. Her decades-long ordeal of abuse and the fear of being found by him was all in the past. But it was a very recent past and she was, quite understandably, still seeing the ghost of Ewan Jones in every shadow. She was last to bed every night, checking the downstairs doors and windows sometimes several times – a habit she'd got into at her own place and brought with her to Boyd's house.

Boyd squeezed her hand.

'It's nothing like that,' he said softly. 'We're not looking for a random predator roaming East Sussex. We're looking for someone with a grudge.' He nodded at the screen. 'Those murders happened a while back. We're not expecting any more.'

28

'This won't hurt, but it may feel a little weird.'

'No kidding,' muttered Boyd. He felt gloved hands on his behind. 'Sorry, I should've waxed or something. It's probably a bit of a jungle down there.'

The consultant was too busy lubricating his camera and setting up the screen to respond. The anaesthetist smiled on his behalf. 'Relax, we've seen worse.'

'Here's some gas and air,' said the anaesthetist, handing Boyd a tube to suck on. 'To use if it starts to get uncomfortable.'

Boyd took a hit straight away. He wasn't going to wait until he needed it. He was lying on his right side, the one that didn't hurt, but it meant he was staring at the wall, not the screen. And he wanted, out of morbid curiosity, to see what the inside of his bowel looked like.

He glanced over his shoulder into the eyes of the consultant.

'Keep perfectly still please, Mr Boyle.'

'Boyd,' he corrected him. He held his position. Over the doctor's shoulder, he could see a small LCD screen mounted on a wheeled stand. The image was unpleasantly clear.

'I *did* take the powdered drink,' he assured the doctor.

'Relax, I can see that. It's a nice clear run... Okay, bend in the road coming up. This might get a little uncomfortable.'

Boyd sucked again on the tube in anticipation. Then he felt it: a small stab of pain followed by a wave of a nausea.

'Think I'm going to be sick,' he mumbled.

'That'll be the gas,' said the anaesthetist, patting his shoulder. 'Little sips. Not gulps.'

Boyd fought the urge to throw up. Not that he had anything to give. He'd had nothing to eat since seven o'clock last night, even though Emma had pestered him to help her finish off the apple pie that was in the fridge. She was still wholly in the dark about all this and Charlotte had covered for him, insisting she was starving and that she'd help her out with the last slice.

'Hmmm.'

Boyd twisted his head to look back over his shoulder.

'And there we have it...' The consultant twisted the camera and took several close-up shots of what looked like a dark purple Twiglet.

RELIEVED TO BE out of the arseless surgical gown and back in his work clothes, Boyd and Charlotte looked at the printed page of pictures on the consultant's desk.

'It's a tumour, protruding about three centimetres into the colorectal channel. I'm presuming the aches and pains you've been having were generally after mealtimes?' Dr Chudasama said.

Boyd nodded.

'Well,' the doctor continued, 'the good news is, from what I can see, it isn't that big. Your surgeon Mr Mumford will probably excise a section of colon, maybe twenty centimetres long to be sure he's got it all out with good margins. But...'

Charlotte clutched Boyd's hand tightly beneath the desk.

'But...?' prompted Boyd.

The consultant pressed out a worryingly thin smile. 'It looks as though it could have burrowed through the bowel wall. There may be – in fact, there probably will be – more of it outside. The question is how much.'

'Is there a scan you can do to find out?' asked Charlotte.

He nodded. 'We'll book you in, William, for an abdominal CT scan as soon as we can next week. Probably Monday morning.'

'Right.' Boyd sighed. That meant bumping another team update briefing. He'd bumped this morning's, which he was hoping to get away with without having to explain himself. But another one? Okeke was undoubtedly going to notice and ask him what was going on.

29

Boyd's drive to work, first stopping to drop Charlotte off at the White Rock Theatre, before continuing five minutes up Bohemia Road to the station, felt like the backdrop to a movie: a projection of someone else's humdrum daily routine.

He parked, entirely on autopilot, flashed his ID at the front desk, climbed the stairs and entered CID. His mind was swimming. The consultant's debriefing had been steeped in positivity and sugarcoated with upbeat phrasing; it looked entirely fixable, and for it to be caught at this stage was... *lucky*.

But, of course, everything that had been said to him after the word 'tumour' had fallen on deaf ears. It had been Charlotte who'd been listening closely, asking all the questions for him.

And now here he stood at his desk, with his jacket dumped on the back of his chair and the computer booting up. Everything was entirely normal. Except it wasn't. Still coasting on autopilot, Boyd went to the kitchenette and slapped the kettle on.

'It looks to be nicely contained to one area, William ... I know it all sounds ominous but it should be a straightforward operation to remove it. We'll discuss chemotherapy afterwards.'

'Guv?'

Okeke's voice broke through his brain fog.

'You all right?'

It was a welcome relief. Boyd turned away from the kettle to look at her, a cheerful smile thrown onto his face. 'Morning!'

'You looked like you were away with the fairies there,' she replied.

'I'm just a bit knackered.' He pulled a mug out from the cupboard. 'Another sleepless night.'

'Tell me about it.' She joined him and pulled a mug out for herself. 'I keep getting flashbacks in my sleep.'

'Hmmm?'

'Brighton. The Russians?' She spooned coffee granules into her cup and his. 'And what I, you know, *did*.'

A distraction. Perfect.

'Georgians,' he corrected. 'And you did what you had to,' he replied solemnly, quietly. 'We *all* did.'

'I know. But...'

'What?'

'It's the sensations that I'm struggling with. The sound he made... when I –' She looked down at the floor.

'You need to put a lid on that, Sam,' he told her. 'It's done with. It's history.'

She nodded.

'And if you'd hesitated,' he went on, 'even for a second, we wouldn't be talking now.'

'I know.' They both stared at the rumbling kettle. 'I can live with it. But I could do without the playbacks in my sleep.'

He patted her awkwardly on the back. 'I get those too, mate. They linger... They don't ever fade, but they do become less frequent.' At a guess, it had been a month since he'd last pictured Julia and Noah in their crumpled car. A fleeting replay at best, which he'd quickly pushed back into its box at the back of his mind and snapped the lid on tight.

The kettle clicked off.

'So... what's the latest?' he said, changing the subject as he poured the water into their mugs.

'We've ID'd our Richard,' she told him.

'And?'

'His full name is Richard Philip Leeder. I've gophered up some intel on him... and we've got some more stuff back from Ellessey.'

'Good. Incident Room? Five minutes?'

She nodded. 'I'll go round up the rabble.'

'So, let's have the forensics stuff first,' said Boyd. 'Magnusson?'

She flipped open the folder in front of her. 'The DNA chromograph for the coffee cup –' she sighed – '*finally* came back. I ran it through the NDNAD.'

'And?'

'There's nothing on record, I'm afraid. Our coffee drinker isn't a habitual crim. Under Good News, however, Ellessey came through very quickly on Mrs Westfield's sample. It's a familial match for lucky victim two. He's confirmed as Andrew Westfield. Dental records have given us a match for Mark Meadows too.'

'I know already,' said Boyd. 'Dr Palmer came through with that yesterday.'

'Yesterday?' Magnusson looked irked. 'I only just got the email this morning!'

'She rang,' Boyd replied, then got up from his seat, approached the whiteboard and wiped away the question marks beside the names on the whiteboard. 'So, that's two out of three.' He returned to his seat. 'Now then, what have we got on this Richard Leeder?'

'Right,' began Minter, 'he's the only child of Dereck and Alison Leeder. Dereck was a property developer and builder. Like Bridgette Westfield said, Dereck was very wealthy indeed.'

'*Was?*' Boyd asked.

'He passed away during the pandemic, boss.'

'Of Covid?'

Minter shook his head. 'No, he was involved in a building site accident. The report says he was checking on a stalled project when he fell off some scaffolding.'

'Any queries around that?' asked Boyd. 'Or was it nice and straightforward?'

Minter shook his head. 'His surveyor was with him at the time. He said that they'd gone to check that the site was still tight and secure after six months of being closed down and that it wasn't exposed to the elements. Clearly it wasn't all that secure, though.'

'Okay. What about his mum? Can we interview her?' Boyd asked.

'Not exactly, boss, no. She died when Leeder was young. From breast cancer.'

'What about other close family? Partner? Kids?'

Minter shook his head. 'None that we have found so far. Richard Leeder's a bit of a ghost. He's not listed as missing but it seems that he's completely vanished.'

Okeke stepped in. 'We managed to locate his profile on

LinkedIn. There was loads of professional bio stuff. He went to York uni and got a degree in economics. Worked for several finance companies in London. He seems to have done very well for himself. But his bio dries up in 2011. And nothing's been added to it since.'

'That's the same year that Meadows and Westfield went missing,' noted Boyd.

Okeke nodded. 'We've got his profile picture, although I'm not sure when it was taken.' She pushed a printout across the table for Boyd to look at.

He picked it up and found himself looking at a head-and-shoulders image of a man in his thirties. There was nothing particularly remarkable about him; he was a well-groomed man in a nice-looking suit, with a professional but friendly we-can-do-business smile, nothing too toothy. Perfect for LinkedIn. He bore a vague resemblance to the face on the scanned driving licence. But then, given the appalling quality of that image, so would a sizable number of white middle-aged, slightly overweight, slightly balding men.

'We searched all the socials,' added Minter. 'Tried all the variations on his name – Rick, Ricky, Dick Leeder et cetera – and came up with a Facebook account that is almost certainly our man. The profile pic, I'm positive, is the same bloke as the one on LinkedIn, just a bit older. We're going to need a warrant to send to Facebook for –'

'*Meta*,' said Magnusson. 'Keep up, sergeant.'

Minter pushed on. 'For a data dump from them.'

Boyd nodded. 'I'll talk to Sutherland.'

DSI Sutherland was searching through the drawers of his desk as Boyd entered, looking very frustrated. 'Where's my ruddy hole puncher gone? I swear that thing has legs.'

Boyd strode over and picked the hole puncher up from the top of the filing cabinet in the corner. 'The handle kept catching in the top of the drawer every time I opened it,' he explained. 'It was a pain in the arse.'

Sutherland took it from him. 'I said you could *use* my office, Boyd, not bloody *rearrange* it.'

Boyd sat down in the visitor's seat. 'I've got a couple of things for you if now's a good time?' he said.

Sutherland sat back down, placed the hole puncher back in its drawer, which he immediately shut. 'What can I do you for?'

'We need an application for a data dump from Facebook.'

He looked surprised. 'You've got a suspect already?'

Boyd gave Sutherland a non-committal shrug. 'Maybe. He's looking somewhat promising.' He updated the DSI with their leading theory that Leeder, Westfield and Meadows and the yet-to-be ID'd Robin had been involved with something serious.

'All right, email me the details and I'll fill in the request form before lunch.'

'Thanks. The other thing...'

Sutherland nodded at him to continue.

'I may need to take some sick leave. Pretty soon.'

Sutherland narrowed his eyes. 'How much and how soon?'

Boyd had been planning to share the news with Emma first. Emma then, unavoidably, Sutherland and finally, of course, his team. But he'd started now and asking Sutherland for sick leave without some kind of an explanation wasn't going to wash.

'I'm going to need to go into hospital in the next couple of weeks. For an operation.'

'Oh? What kind of an operation?' Sutherland asked.

Shit. It looked like he was going to have to spit it out. 'I've got cancer,' he said.

Sutherland's doughy face instantly folded into an expression of genuine concern. 'Cancer? Jesus Christ. Which one? Where?'

'Bowel cancer,' Boyd said. 'The consultant said it was a good one to have.'

'If there *is* such a bloody thing,' Sutherland commented.

'I'll need a couple of weeks. I'll be in hospital for a few days after the op and then the rest at home. I may need to have a course of chemotherapy after. But we'll cross that bridge...'

Sutherland got up out of his seat and came around the desk. For a horrifying moment, Boyd thought he was going to give him a hug. Thankfully he just perched on the corner of his desk. 'You take all the time you need, Boyd. I mean it. Just dial it in as you need it.'

'Thank you, sir.'

Sutherland shook his head and tutted. 'Bastard bloody cancer. Seems to be a lot of that going around these days. My brother-in-law, poor sod, had the prostrate one...' He was about to head off on a tangent, then stopped himself. 'Well, you probably don't want to hear about that.'

Boyd supressed a smile. 'I think you mean "prostate". Sir... I haven't told anyone else at work yet. It's all been a bit quick. I'm still trying to catch up with the news myself. Please... not a word to anyone. Not even HR. Not until I know how much time off I'm going to need.'

'Of course, of course! You'll keep me posted, right?' Coming from Sutherland, Boyd mused, that could easily have been to enable him to get ahead of the curve and the inevitable rota shuffling. But he was pretty sure he detected genuine concern for a friend in his voice.

'Yup. Of course,' he replied.

30

Emma brought the casserole dish in from the kitchen and plonked it down a little too heavily on the dining table.

'Chicken,' she announced tersely. She returned to the kitchen and came back with another steaming serving bowl, which she banged down beside the first. 'Mash.'

She pulled out a chair and sat down. It was just the two of them for dinner this evening. Charlotte was at the theatre; apparently they were a staff member down and dealing with a sold-out audience for some Eagles tribute band.

'You all right, there, Ems?' Boyd asked.

Emma reached for a serving spoon and *splashed* some chicken chasseur onto her plate. 'Not really.'

'Is it Dan?' Boyd guessed.

Emma skewered him with a glare. She reached for the wooden bowl at the end of the table, where car keys, house keys, junk mail and – for some reason, dead AA batteries – wound up. She pulled an opened envelope out of the bowl and set it down beside his plate.

'When, exactly, were you planning on telling me?' she spat.

He looked down to see it was a letter from Conquest Hospital.

'Ah,' was all he could think to say.

'You think I'm too dumb to have noticed you and Charlotte with your whispered conversations in the corners? I'm not an idiot, Dad. Do Grandma and Grandad know as well?'

'Nope,' he replied.

'Well, at least I'm not the *last* to find out, then.' She pulled the letter out of the opened envelope and slid it across the table to him. 'Why didn't you tell me you had an appointment this morning?' she asked. 'You're not supposed to keep things from me. Remember?'

'I'm sorry, Ems. I wanted to wait until I had something to actually tell you,' he explained.

'Well, do you? Have something to tell me? Do I get to know how that went?' She served herself another spoonful of the casserole. 'Or will I finally get briefed when your hair starts falling out?'

'There *is* a tumour down there,' he replied.

Emma's face began to soften. 'Is it operable?' she asked.

'That's the plan. Just a bit of colon splicing. I'll be in and out of hospital in a few days. It's going to be okay, Ems. A bit of surgery, then a bit of the ol' chemo if I need it.'

'Chemotherapy?' Emma said. The timbre of her voice raised a notch. 'I did some googling this afternoon. They do chemotherapy when they think there's a chance it's spread elsewhere. Dad? I want the whole truth. *Please.*'

'They also do it to be on the safe side,' he said. 'Kind of a "nuke it from orbit" approach.'

'Is that what *they* actually said?' She was getting angry

again. 'Because that sounds more like *your* expert opinion than theirs.'

He sighed. 'I'm due a CT scan on Monday,' he told her, and repeated what the doctor had told him.

She bit her bottom lip, reached out and grabbed his hand. 'Oh God, Dad...'

'If it has, you know... *spread*... it's early days, Emma. They've caught it nice and early.'

'No,' she snapped, squeezing his hand. 'No. No. No. You don't give me the baby version. You give me the shitty true version.'

'That's it,' he replied. 'Honestly. That's all I've got.'

'So, we'll know how big a deal this is on Wednesday, then?'

He nodded.

'I'm coming along.'

'It's okay,' he said. 'Charlotte's coming with me.'

'No. We're *both* coming with you,' Emma said firmly. 'No arguments. I'm not having you bullshit me on Wednesday. I mean it, Dad! I want to be there to hear for myself.'

He let go of her hand and raised both of his in surrender. 'All right. All right. There's no need to do Mrs Arsey at me.'

'Well, I *am* pissed off. I learned about this entirely by *accident*!'

'By snooping, you mean.'

Her brows locked together.

'Nuh-uh,' he said. 'You can't bollock me any more. New rules.'

'Huh?'

He shook his head officiously, then mimed pulling out a referee's red card and waving it around for all to see. 'You can't do angry at me. You have to be all sweetness and smiles with me from now on.'

She raised an eyebrow. 'Oh, I do, do I?'

'Yup,' he said, pocketing the imaginary red card. '... because I've got cancer.'

31

Boyd climbed out of his Captur and crossed the station's car park to find Okeke finishing a cigarette outside the main entrance.

'Morning,' he called out chirpily as he approached her.

She had a face like thunder. 'When exactly were you going to tell me?' she said, glaring at him.

'Oh, for Christ's sake, not you too. Who told you?'

She stubbed the cigarette out. 'The late starts. The groaning like an old fart every time you get up from your chair? I worked it out.'

He wasn't buying her detective skills at all. 'Was it Sutherland?'

'Sutherland knows?' That seemed to make her even angrier.

'I had to tell him to organise time off, for fuck's sake, Okeke.'

'We're meant to be... friends. Share things, you know?'

He raised a brow. 'Emma? Was it?' he asked.

Okeke's mouth clamped shut.

He sighed. He should have sworn Emma to secrecy. For

what good it would have done. She and Okeke were as thick as thieves.

'How's Charlotte?' Okeke asked, looking to change the subject.

'She's fine,' he replied. 'She's a trouper.' He pushed the door open. 'Tell me it's only you who knows.'

'It's just me... unless Sutherland's been blabbing.'

'Right, well, can we keep it that way for now?' Boyd asked. He beckoned for her to lead the way in. 'Since you're in the know... what happened to "How are *you* coping, guv?"'

'Fine. How *are* you coping?' she asked.

He shook his head but smiled. 'You blew it. Too little, too late, Okeke. Come on, get your arse inside.'

MINTER WAS LOOKING ENERGISED this morning, fresh faced, hair still glistening wet from his post gym-session shower. 'Morning, boss,' he said cheerily.

'Morning,' Boyd replied, dumping his jacket on the back of his chair.

'I've got some good news for you, boss,' Minter said. 'Facebook... sorry...I mean, Meta have delivered on the data request already.'

'That was bloody quick,' Boyd said, astounded. These things usually took weeks or even months.

Minter nodded. 'Very cooperative indeed. The email arrived overnight. They've sent an unlock link to the Facebook page and we've got full access.'

That was also new. The last time they'd applied, Facebook had simply given them a confusing dump of data, cloned from the page, complete with endless strings of gibberish HTML headers for them to pick their way through.

'What, we can just log in and look?' Boyd asked.

Minter nodded.

Boyd suspected that the collective social-media monster was upping its game to appear more cooperative. There'd been plenty of noise in the news recently around making them all – and, more importantly, their CEOs – personally liable for the toxic content that proliferated across their various platforms. The recent revelations about the Met and the widespread exchanges of unacceptable comments and images through Facebook, WhatsApp and the rest had stoked that debate to the point where virtual pitchforks and flaming torches were amassing.

Of course Facebook was being super helpful.

'Excellent. Well, guess what we're all doing this morning.' Boyd nodded at the double doors off the CID floor, leading to the stairwell and the canteen above. 'Coffee first, though, eh?'

Boyd waited until after lunch to gather them all into the Incident Room for a mutual show and tell. Minter had taken on Richard Leeder's Messenger history. Warren and O'Neal had been given his extensive friends list to work through, and Okeke was sifting through the various status updates that 'Rleeder' had posted from 2007 when he'd set up his profile until 2011 when it all seemed to have gone quiet.

'Right then,' said Boyd. 'So what have we learned about Mr Leeder this morning?'

Minter began with the Messenger history. 'There's a lot of old chatter with various people about investment opportunities – derivatives, futures, sub-prime baskets... whatever the hell those are.'

'Ah,' cut in Magnusson. 'So he's one of those lovely people who helped tank the world stock market.'

'I don't know,' said Minter. 'But there's a lot of that stuff and it's very boring to wade through, I can tell you.'

'Right. Is there anything case relevant, though?' said Boyd.

'Yes, boss.' Minter raised a finger. 'There's an interesting chat history with one MarkyMark.'

'That's Mark Meadows,' Warren said. 'He's on his friends list.'

Boyd nodded at Minter. 'Go on.'

'It seems that Meadows reached out with a friend request back in 2008, which Leeder accepted. There's not a lot of exchanges between them in the early days. Just a few "how're you doing" pokes from Meadows here and there that Leeder doesn't seem to have responded to.'

'Yeah, that was during the early days of social media,' said Boyd. 'I'm not sure any of us knew what to do with Facebook back then.'

'Right,' said Minter. 'They would probably have been in touch by phone at that time. Anyway, not much happens in the messages until 2010. Then it gets a little more interesting... This is one dated twenty-first of February, 2010.' Minter cleared his throat.

MarkyMark: Rick, we really need to talk about Andy. Urgent.

Rleeder: What about him?

MarkyMark: He's pretty much hit rock bottom.

Rleeder: Not my concern. He's a pisshead. I try to have as little to do with him as possible.

MarkyMark: He's been tapping me for money.

Rleeder: Ignore him.

MarkyMark: It's not that easy. He's got a mouth on him.

Rleeder: So you need to fucking remind him.

MarkyMark: I have. But he knows I've got money. And more to the point, he knows you've done particularly well, mate. Just saying...we need to be careful, yes?

MINTER LOOKED up from his notes. 'There's no further response from Leeder. Mark nudges him a couple more times in that particular exchange, but Leeder's silent.'

'*We need to be careful*,' repeated Okeke. 'That's pretty telling.'

'There's more,' said Minter. 'This exchange is from September twenty-third, 2011...'

MARKYMARK: So, still no sign of Andy. I can't believe he didn't turn up for the reunion this time. I can't get hold of him. It's like he's vanished. Has he contacted you? Or Robby?

Rleeder: He's probably drunk himself under a bus, the useless twat.

MarkyMark: You didn't answer me. Has he contacted you or Robin?

Rleeder: No. And, look, don't contact me again. I think I'm about done with these reunions.

. . .

Minter looked up. 'That's it as far as messages goes. Mark doesn't contact him again.'

'Does Richard Leeder have a Robin in his friend's list?' asked Boyd.

O'Neal shook his head. 'But there were two Robins in that school registration list. We can see if Meadows was friends with a Robin on Facebook, though.'

'Okay, look at that, asap,' said Boyd. He turned to Okeke. 'Does Leeder's profile info give us anything?'

She spread her notes out in front of her. 'He's pretty lean with his bio stuff, guv. He's male, single, UK based. There's mention of a couple of previous city employers but nothing about school or uni. It's pretty much the same stuff as his LinkedIn profile.'

'And what about status updates?' Boyd asked.

'The usual "how cool am I?" posts, showing off nice cars, nice places, nice bling. But then come 2011 there's nada. No updates or no responses to any other posts. He doesn't even share a funny cat meme. From summer 2011 onwards it's just a dead page.'

'And that was about the same time that Meadows went missing?' said Boyd.

'Right,' she replied.

'Okay, thoughts, people, please?' Boyd prompted.

'He's body number three?' volunteered Magnusson.

'He killed Westfield and scarpered?' offered Warren.

'Maybe Westfield found Richard Leeder, confronted him for whatever reason, then Leeder killed Westfield to shut him up? And he went on to kill Mark Meadows too?' suggested Okeke.

Minter looked at her. 'Maybe he felt that Meadows knew too much? Was Leeder getting twitchy? Maybe he dealt with them both. One after the other. Job done?'

'Then Leeder seems to have vanished,' said Boyd. 'Like Magnusson said, he could be our last John Doe.'

'Or he's left the country,' added O'Neal. 'Or just gone to ground?'

'That's what I said,' Warren reminded them.

'Yes, Warren. Duly noted,' said Boyd. 'However, it still leaves us Robin. Okay, Boy Wonder, we have two Robins on the school list. You're with O'Neal. I want them tracked down asap. All right?'

They nodded in unison.

'Right, team, if we find the correct Robin and he's alive and well...' Boyd shrugged. 'Then quite possibly the remaining Doe sitting on the slab is Leeder. If we've got a missing Robin on our hands... then the more recent body, presumably, is his.'

He pushed his chair back. 'So let's find Robin.'

32

'We have Robin James Mitchell and Robin Whitehead,' began O'Neal. He and Warren were standing side by side, both equally eager to present what they had.

'Whitehead's the interesting one, chief,' said O'Neal.

Boyd closed the 'side effects of chemotherapy' tab on his browser. 'What have you got on him?'

'He's a misper, sir,' said Warren. 'And a relatively recent one at that.'

'Reported when?'

'Two years ago.' Warren indicated Boyd's computer. 'Have a look.'

Boyd pulled up LEDS, navigated his way to the missing persons database and tapped the name in.

A recent picture of Whitehead popped up. He was a well-tanned man in his mid forties, his sandy-coloured hair whipped up by a stiff breeze and revealing a pronounced widow's peak. He was wearing a T-shirt with some indecipherable sports logo on it. It looked as though he was sitting in the cockpit of a yacht, a can of beer in one hand, the wheel of a helm in the other.

'Looks like he's living the good life,' said O'Neal. 'Or he was anyway.'

'He'd been living abroad for the last fifteen years or so,' said Warren. 'In Qatar.'

Boyd scanned the report quickly. 'He was reported missing by...?'

'His sister. Caroline Hussain,' replied Warren. 'She lives out there too. She's married to a local and sells property. Robin had been out there since 2006.'

'Doing what?' Boyd asked.

'Working for Caroline, selling apartments. According to the report, she said that in 2021 he was offered a job in London. He flew back to start work and she'd not been able to get in touch with him for several months after that, so she reported him missing to the Met.'

'And we know for sure he arrived in the UK?'

'There's been no follow-up by the Met,' said O'Neal. 'It looks as if they just logged it on the system and let it sit.'

'Why doesn't that surprise me?' Boyd grunted. 'All right, thanks, you two.' He dismissed them with a nod. 'Good job.'

He read through the misper report again. It was light on detail and he decided it would be quicker and more efficient to contact this Caroline Hussain directly. He guessed Qatar was around four or five hours ahead, so it was okay to call, and he dialled the contact number given.

The phone rang half a dozen times before the call was picked up by a smooth-sounding female voice.

'Good afternoon. Hussain-Whitehead Real Estate, how can I help you?'

'I'm after Caroline Hussain,' he said.

'Speaking,' she replied.

'Ah, Hello. I'm DCI Boyd from East Sussex CID,' he said.

'I'm following up on the missing persons report you made for your brother.'

He heard a sharp intake of breath. 'Well, it's about bloody time. It's been two years!'

'Yeah, sorry about that, Ms Hussain...' Boyd began, inwardly cursing the Met.

'*Sorry?* It's absolutely bloody disgraceful! I've had no updates from you. No one's reached out, nothing. Not that I'm surprised given what I've read about the London police recently.'

Her accent was a polished version of London estuary, but Boyd noted a few transatlantic vowels creeping in. The American accent, Boyd mused, was like a cold; rub shoulders with too many Yanks and, before you know it, it's a 'sidewalk' and not a 'pavement'.

'I'm with Sussex Police,' he replied. 'I'm not from the Met.' He resisted the urge to apologise on their behalf. The Met was a mess right now, fighting fires over frequently surfacing reports of misogyny, abuse, racism... and more. 'As I said, I'm calling to talk to you about your brother, Robin.'

'Have you found him?' she breathed.

The third body hadn't been officially ID'd yet. He strongly suspected it was either Richard or Robin – but... 'No, I'm afraid not,' he said. 'I just want to go over the report with you. Get a fresh take on it.'

He heard her huff on the other end of the line. 'It's a bit late for a fresh take, isn't it? Have you people done *anything* to find him yet?'

Boyd pulled a face. From the look of the case file, not a thing had been done. And, by the sound of it, Ms Hussain was still convinced she was talking to someone from the Met. He doubted mentioning, yet again, that he was calling from a different force would do much to win her round.

'I've been tasked with working on a couple of cold cases,' he lied. 'Can we review the details of your initial report and go from there?'

'It's all there in front of you, isn't it?' She sighed. 'Or have you lot lost the paperwork too?'

'No, it's right here, on my screen,' he replied. 'But since it's been a couple of years, maybe between us, we can pull out some fresh, helpful details? See if we can make some headway?' He was hoping the collaborative approach might mitigate things.

'Okay,' she said reluctantly. 'All right. Let's do this *again*. What do you want to know?'

Half an hour later, after assuring her they were now actively investigating Robin's disappearance, he hung up and reviewed the extensive notes he'd taken. He'd probed further into the past than the previous investigating officer had, back to Robin's childhood. Caroline hadn't queried that; on the contrary, she'd seemed encouraged that someone, at last, was taking her brother's disappearance seriously.

'ROBIN WHITEHEAD LEFT Harsham Grammar in 1993 and spent a couple of years doing the gap-year thing and travelling extensively,' Boyd began. 'He visited Bali, India and the Philippines before coming back to the UK to begin a business studies degree at Warwick. In '98 he got a job working as a sales rep for a print supplies company based in Reading. He became an office manager there in 2001... which was all very exciting stuff, but he was getting itchy feet.'

Boyd looked up from his notes and glanced around the table. They all gazed dutifully back. Satisfied, he continued.

'He stuck with that until 2006, then he contacted his sister, Caroline Hussain. She'd gone out to Qatar a couple of years earlier and was doing pretty well for herself. She offered to put him up, introduce him to some people and get him a job. So out he went, hoping to better his luck.'

'You can't go wrong out there,' said O'Neal. 'Everyone makes a fortune.'

'Well, he joins her and tries out a number of different jobs before settling on crewing and maintaining luxury yachts, which he did for about ten years...' Boyd pulled out the misper photo that showed Whitehead helming a boat with the can of beer in his hand.

'So, he's out of the country when Meadows and Westfield go missing?' said Minter.

'Right. But,' Boyd cautioned, 'we can't yet rule out that he didn't go back and forth for a few days during that period. Anyway...'

'We can track his Facebook page,' said O'Neal. 'Who doesn't post about where they're flying off to, right?'

'I'll come to his Facebook page in a moment,' said Boyd. 'It'll be going on our action list.'

So, anyway... according to Caroline, in 2018, he told her he wanted more of a career.'

'Was he nuts?' O'Neal chipped in. 'He was living the life out there!'

'Well, he asked if he could work at Caroline's real estate company,' Boyd continued. 'She agreed to take him on but, in her words, that turned out to be a bit of a disaster. He was her employee, but also her older brother, so, as you can imagine, the sibling rivalry kicked in and she says he became difficult to manage. They kept having rows in front of the other staff; it wasn't working out, et cetera, et cetera.'

'Then, in 2020, she said an old friend of his had

offered him a "decent opportunity" back home in the UK. She said he got a flight to London in July 2021. And he *did* make a bit of a thing of it all on Facebook, according to her.'

Boyd glanced down at his notes again. 'She said he put up a nasty post about how shitty it had been working for her, used some vaguely racist language about her husband and said that he was "itching to come home and make a new start with a proper job". She was pretty pissed off about that, and quite rightly so.'

'Where was his new start?' asked Minter.

'She doesn't know. Just that it was some job in London. A proper one, he told her,' Boyd said.

'I can see why she was pissed off,' said Okeke.

'So he packs up and prepares to head back to the UK, posting on his page about a "coming home" party at an Aussie pub in Shepherds Bush: the Walkabout. She said she remembered that because she'd visited it with him the previous time they were both in the country together. The last posts he made on his page were from this party.' Boyd placed his notes down on the conference table. 'And that was the last she heard from him.'

'How long after the party did she report him missing, boss?' Minter asked.

'A couple of months,' Boyd replied. 'She said it took her a few weeks to calm down before she tried reaching out to him. When she didn't get an answer and there were no further posts on Facebook, she became worried and made the call.'

'And the Met didn't follow it up?' asked Minter.

Boyd shook his head. 'I can understand why. He wasn't a minor. He wasn't female. He was clearly pissed off with his sister and therefore not a priority.'

'Just another family row, it'll sort itself out,' said Okeke. 'No further action.'

'Exactly,' Boyd said. 'And she said that she's contacted the Met a number of times over the last two years, but they've more or less fobbed her off with similar reasoning.'

'So, sir? What about the new job opportunity?' asked Warren. 'Are there any details at all?'

Boyd shook his head. 'Our next step will have to be another data request from Facebook. Meta... whatever they are. We need to find out who might have turned up for the gathering at the pub. Presumably those in the know would be on his friends list.'

'What about their parents?' asked Okeke.

'I've got their details. According to his sister, they're just as worried as she is. They've also been nagging the Met and got nowhere. Maybe you can have a chat with them, Okeke?'

'Where are they?' she asked.

'Sevenoaks, Kent, I think she said,' said Boyd, looking down at his notes. 'See if you can visit them this afternoon. Get a DNA swab for us will you and dig up some more details from his school days?'

He turned to Minter. 'And we need Westfield's, Meadows' and Whitehead's phone records,' he continued. 'I've got a strong suspicion there's a lot of back-and-forth communication over the years that we're missing out on. We don't know which service providers any of them used but, if we can track them down, they might still have the data.'

'On it, boss,' Minter replied.

'Right,' Boyd said, standing up. 'Let's get to it, people.'

33

Okeke set her beer down. 'When?'

Jay picked up a spiced drumstick and took a hearty bite out of it. 'Next month,' he replied, his mouth full. 'It's in Croydon, south London.'

She sighed. 'I know where Croydon is. How long for?'

Jay pulled a face. 'The training course is over three days.'

She looked at him. 'Why are you doing your guilty face?'

'What? I'm not doing a guilty face.'

'Yes, you are.'

He suspected she was probably right – it was one very good reason why Jay had never joined Poker Night with Louie and the other doormen at CuffLinks. 'See, the thing is I'll have to stay over a couple of nights.'

'You can get a train there and back each day, can't you?'

'There's some evening activities on the course.'

'Evening activities?' She raised a brow. 'Like going on the piss with your fellow PIs?'

He shook his head. 'No, I mean, proper in-the-field training.'

McGuire had told Jay about the course this afternoon.

The three-day event would cover a lot of theory, but during the two evenings the instructors would be getting them to put it into practice. Apparently McGuire had done the course several years ago, and the three instructors who ran it were ex-Mossad, ex-CIA and ex-KGB.

'We get to do a simulation,' Jay told her.' They call it Hunting the Bear.'

She rolled her eyes at the ridiculous name. 'What the bloody hell?'

'One of the instructors is the bear, right? And we have to tail him across London without being marked.' Jay grinned. 'McGuire said it's a real hoot.'

'Hoot?'

'You know, fun. We get to do "box pattern" tailing on foot like, you know, MI5 do. Use all the latest spy kit: bugs, thermal cameras an' shit.'

Okeke shook her head and chuckled. She looked around the Nando's restaurant; it was busy and noisy this evening. 'It's going to be one big party game for you, isn't it? Frickin' trip to Disneyland for three days.'

He nodded energetically. 'Can't wait. It sounds bonkers.'

'Do you get a nice shiny truncheon or something at the end of it? A goody bag?'

Jay looked at her. 'This is serious, proper-level training, Sam.'

'Covert surveillance. In just three days?'

He nodded. 'It's an intense course.'

She took a sip of her beer. 'What does your bro make of all this?'

Jay had had a beer with his brother a couple of weeks ago. His reaction to Jay's new career direction had been the same as Sam's: bemused scepticism.

'Karl?' he replied. 'He thinks it's all one big fucking joke.'

He sighed. 'Be nice to feel like at least one of you two believed in me.'

Okeke leant across the table and stroked his forearm. 'Babe, I *do* believe in you. It's just...'

'Just?'

'Well, I mean...' He could see she was doing her best to temper her words. 'What happened last year in Brighton was –'

'A wake-up call, Sam,' he cut in. 'A reminder that we can get busy dreaming or get busy *doing*.'

Okeke frowned. 'But you never dreamed of being a private eye before all that crap went down! Not that you said to me, anyway. You and Louie were all about upcycling furniture. Setting up a carpentry business. Not snooping into dustbins or sneaking around after unfaithful husbands.'

Jay dropped his chicken drumstick onto his plate. 'Louie's murder made me realise that I want to take down the bad guys. I want to help nail some well-deserving dick-heads.' He licked his fingers. 'And, as you've already pointed out, I'm never going to be police material... so this is the next best thing.'

'I never said that,' she replied.

'Not in those words. But you were pretty dismissive about it when I suggested joining the police.'

She winced, then rubbed her eyes, absently smearing the eyeliner she'd put on for this evening. 'It's not that I don't think you could hack it as a police officer. It's just...'

'*Just*.' He smiled. 'That word again.'

'Look, being in the police involves following rules, protocols, obeying orders, heaps of paperwork... and exams – and that just isn't you, Jay.'

'I've just done six months of exams, Sam. And passed them.'

'I meant the obeying orders bit. Mostly. You can't just take off and go rogue in the middle of a case when it suits you.'

'Why not? Boyd does.' Jay had her there. And she knew it.

She looked around her, then lowered her voice. 'He didn't have much choice at the time, if you recall. Not with the Nix case, and not with what happened to you.'

'But he does go rogue. You've told me God knows how many times, that he –'

'Yeah, but that's his look-out,' she snapped. 'He's my boss, right? It's on his head if he gets caught out cutting corners or breaking rules. Personally, I don't. I play by the rules. Which probably makes me a bit boring, but it means I get to keep my job, the wage that pays our bills, and the pension that will come at the end of it.'

She realised she'd come across too harshly. Once again, she reached across the table. 'You and Boyd are the same kind of bloke.'

Jay raised a brow, wondering where she was going with that. 'Which is?'

'*We'll bloody wing it*,' she said, doing a fair job of mimicking Boyd. '*Don't worry – we'll just fudge the paperwork, Okeke.*'

Jay nodded approvingly at her impersonation. 'How is he, by the way?'

'Boyd?' She hunched her shoulders and shook her head. 'He's...' She paused, took another slug of beer, then swilled it around her mouth. 'Yeah, he's okay. Same old, same old.'

Jay narrowed his eyes. 'That's called a displacement tick.'

'A what-the-what?'

'What you just did. Hitting the beer. It's a stalling tactic.'

'What are you – a psychologist, all of a sudden?'

'I read it.' He smiled. 'In an actual book, with pages and everything.' He leant forward. 'So, have you two fallen out over something?'

'No!' she replied quickly. 'It's just...'

'Ah, there it is.' He grinned, pleased with himself. '*Something*.'

'It's none of your business is what it is, babes.'

'Are him and Charlotte having problems?'

'No, they're fine. Look, Jay... stop trying to be a private *dick*! It's none of your business. It's a personal –'

'He's unwell?' Jay cut in.

She rolled her eyes. Not at him, he suspected, but at herself for giving too much away in what she *wasn't* saying.

'Is it something serious?' he pressed.

Okeke looked away, her eyes picking out things to distract her. She cleared her throat. 'It could be.'

'Shit,' muttered Jay. 'It's not something like cancer, is it?'

She cocked her head as she looked back at him. The answer was pretty much stamped on her face.

He let out a heavy sigh. 'Fuck. A bad one?'

'It's an early diagnosis,' she added. 'He seems to think it's no big deal.'

Jay shook his head. As far as he was concerned, Boyd was a brick wall that no one could knock down, a local piece of towering geology that you could drive around or over, but certainly not miss. He was Charles Bronson and Sherlock Holmes blended together and smothered in concrete. Not that he was going to share this with anyone – even Sam – but Boyd was someone who Jay felt he *could* be. One day. If he put his back into it.

'Shit. That's really shit.'

'Well, we'll see,' she added. 'It's early days. And cancer isn't the inevitable shitshow it used to be, right?'

He nodded. 'Fingers crossed, eh?'

Their conversation died out for a few minutes as they pushed chicken wings and fries around their plates, then finally Okeke spoke again. 'Actually, thinking about it... maybe you're right.' She sighed. 'Maybe this *is* the right job for you.'

'It is,' Jay replied. 'And I'm going to do well at it. I'm going to learn everything I can from McGuire while I'm working for him. And then...'

'And then?'

He shrugged. 'I'll go it alone, of course. Be my own boss.'

She hesitated for a moment, then picked up her beer bottle and raised it for him to clink his against. 'To that, babes, to being your own boss... one day.'

He clinked his bottle against hers. 'Damn right.'

34

Monday morning, and Boyd really wasn't in the mood for banter. And Sully, of all people, was back from his week's leave and full of himself. In the Incident Room, he was telling the team how he'd spent the week in Cornwall at some gathering of Dungeons and Dragons nerds, cosplaying in the countryside, playing the role of some spell-casting mage. Boyd could see a few faint flecks of face paint clinging to what remained of the frizzy blonde hair on his head.

'Anyway,' said Sully, concluding his detailed account of his adventures in the Cornish countryside. He gently patted one of Magnusson's broad shoulders. 'How did my stand-in perform while I was away?'

Magnusson looked at him and raised her brows. 'Incredibly, Kevin, we actually managed to cope without you.'

'I'm sure you did your best,' Sully replied. 'You got an interesting one, I see. How typical. I turn my back for two minutes...'

'You've read up?' asked Boyd.

Sully nodded. 'I spent the weekend catching up on

things. Chopped-up bodies in boxes, Karen, you jammy bugger.'

'Well, if you do choose to bugger off and play wizards with your little friends...' Magnusson said, patting his head.

The others laughed.

Boyd sighed, relieved. *Well, at least he's caught up. Good.* He wasn't going to have to waste an hour of this morning's meeting getting Sully up to speed and fielding his questions. He really, really wasn't in the mood to joust with him today.

The CT scan that was supposed to be scheduled for this morning had been bumped to Wednesday. According to the technician who'd rung him apologetically this morning, the large doughnut-shaped machine at Conquest Hospital needed to be recalibrated. Or something. Whatever the reason, it meant another forty-eight hours of wondering whether he was riddled with secondary tumours or not.

'Right, that's enough,' he said. 'Settle down, kids. Let's get straight to business.'

The Incident Room fell silent.

'Okeke, where are we with Robin Whitehead's parents?'

'I spoke to them Friday afternoon, guv, and I got a swab from both of them.'

'And I had that sent over to Ellessey,' Magnusson added. 'They said they'd fast-track it for us. Hopefully we'll have a result today or tomorrow.'

'The last time they saw Robin,' Okeke continued, 'was the day before his welcome-home bash in London. It was a brief visit. They said he was too busy to stay long as he had things to sort out.'

'Things to sort out?' Boyd pressed.

'He didn't say. They presumed stuff to do with accommodation and starting his job.'

'Did he tell them anything about his new job?' Boyd asked.

'His mum said she thought it was something to do with finance,' Okeke replied. 'A "fancy city job" were her words. She said he was excited about it and keen to get started.'

'Did he mention who he was working for?'

She shook her head. 'He did say, but she couldn't remember the name. It wasn't a recognisable name like, I dunno... Lloyds, Barclays, Goldman Sachs.'

'Did he not use their address for post?' asked Boyd. 'As he was just moving back? His new employer would have had to have somewhere to send his paperwork? His contract and all that?'

She shook her head again. 'Sorry, guv. It would probably have been emailed to him anyway.'

Boyd shook his head, then looked at Minter. 'Any luck tracking down the phone records?' he asked.

'I've contacted all the big providers, boss: Vodafone, O2, EE, Three. They were all pretty cagey about handing over confidential customer data.'

Boyd sighed. 'Of course they were. Well, we'll need to warrant the buggers. *All* of them.'

'However, I got lucky straight off with NeomCom,' Minter said. 'They're Saudi based. The chap there said they have a lapsed phone contract for Robin Whitehead, which they'd be happy to –'

'Lapsed?' Boyd cut in. 'Does it match our timeline?'

Minter nodded. 'It didn't get renewed. And the account was frozen. They're happy for us to take a look as long as we use the Interpol Request Portal.'

'Just a thought, ladies and gents...' said Sully. 'Did you show that scanned Alan Smithee driving licence picture to Whitehead's parents?'

'No,' replied Okeke defensively. 'Because the quality's so shit it could literally be anyone.'

'You mean you forgot to?' said Sully smugly.

She shot him daggers. 'No, as I said...'

'Easy mistake,' he said, smiling patronisingly. 'But it might be worth doing?'

'It might be worth a punt, actually,' agreed Boyd. 'While we're waiting on the phone data. You okay heading back over to Sevenoaks, Okeke?'

She nodded, reluctantly. 'Sure.'

O'Neal laughed. 'Doh, sorry, it's me again,' he yawped with a village idiot's singsong voice. '*Oi faw-got to show you this...*'

Magnusson, Sully and Warren chuckled.

Okeke shook her head. 'It's fine. I can hack it.'

35

The oak front door opened. 'Hello, Mrs Whitehead,' said Okeke. 'It's me again. I've got a couple more follow-up questions for you if that's all right?'

Mrs Whitehead nodded and beckoned her to step inside.

'I hope I'm not disturbing anything,' Okeke asked politely.

Mrs Whitehead shook her head. 'Oh no. We're just having elevenses with *Pointless*. Jeremy loves the old ones... you know, with Alexander Armitage and Richard Oswald.'

Okeke smiled, the old woman had managed to get *both* surnames wrong. Mrs Whitehead led her slowly across the entrance hall and into their lounge. This time around, Okeke knew which floral armchair was specifically for visiting guests.

'Hello again,' she said to Mr Whitehead as she took a seat.

He reached for the remote on the coffee table and

paused the recorded show. 'Again, Detective Obama? Is there some news?'

'Okeke. I'm afraid there's nothing new since yesterday.'

'Oh, right,' he said, visibly wilting.

'Would you like a cup of coffee?' asked Mrs Whitehead as she sat down on their faded chaise longue.

'No, thank you. This won't take long,' Okeke replied. She reached into her bag and pulled out a blue cardboard folder. 'I have a picture I want you to take a look at. The quality is awful, but, anyway, I'd like to know if it's anyone you recognise.' She pulled out the photocopied scan of the driving licence and handed it to them.

They both squinted at the image for a while. 'Sorry,' said Mrs Whitehead eventually.

'Who's Alan Smithee?' Mr Whitehead asked.

'The name's an alias,' Okeke explained. 'The man pictured, we believe, might have been a friend of your son.'

'No, I'm very sorry,' he said. 'I don't recognise him.'

'That's all right.' Okeke took the photocopy back from him and tucked it away in the folder. 'That was it, actually. I'm sorry to have bothered you both again.' She got up.

'Do you think my son's dead, detective?' Mr Whitehead asked as she was about to excuse herself.

Okeke paused, wondering how best to answer that. 'According to your daughter, Caroline, he's more than able to take care of himself. There are any number of reasons why he could have gone missing. It doesn't necessarily mean that he's –'

'Oh, crikey,' said Mrs Whitehead, interrupting her. 'You mentioning our Caroline has just reminded me. There was something I should have told you yesterday!' She got up off the chaise longue.

'What is it?' Okeke asked.

'A few weeks after Robin came back from Qatar, Caroline sent over a box of things he'd left behind.'

'Do you still have them?' Okeke held her breath.

'Of course, I do! They're up in his old bedroom. Do you want to...?'

'Have a look?' She nodded. 'If that's okay?'

Okeke followed Mrs Whitehead back into the hallway, then up a creaking staircase, painfully slowly, the old woman's knees clicking with every step. She led Okeke along a hallway and finally stopped beside a closed door.

'This is Robin's old room,' she announced. 'I always hoped he might stay with us for a while when he was back in the country, but he's always had, what I like to call, the wander bug.'

'So I heard,' Okeke said. 'Did he travel a lot?'

She nodded. 'He was always off backpacking and the like. He's always had itchy feet.' She opened the door. 'The things Caroline sent are still on his bed. Some clothes, some souvenir knick-knacks. A shaver. I think it's broken.'

Okeke inspected the items that were spread out neatly on the duvet. She suspected his mum had arranged them like this, ready for the next time he dropped by... to tell her what he wanted to keep hold of and what could be thrown away.

Mrs Whitehead picked up a sweatshirt that had an anchor logo on it with the name Sea Lotus underneath. 'He liked crewing on those big luxury boats out there...'

Beneath the sweatshirt was an iPad. Okeke bent down to touch the screen lightly, hoping there might be a residual charge. But it was dead. Obviously. She reached into her jacket and pulled out some nitrile gloves. 'The iPad might be helpful,' she said. 'Would you mind if I took it away with me?'

Mrs Whitehead shook her head. 'Take whatever you think might help.'

'You'll get it back when we're done with it,' Okeke said, carefully lifting it up. 'Do you have a carrier bag I can put it in?'

'I'll go and get you one.' She went to go.

'Do either you or your husband use an iPad or an iPhone?' Okeke asked on a whim.

'Jeremy has an iPad,' Mrs Whitehead replied. 'He plays Solitaire on the silly thing.'

'So you've got a charge cable?' Okeke said.

'Yes, in the kitchen. Do you want me to bring it up?' she asked.

Okeke nodded. 'Please.'

Once Mrs Whitehead had disappeared downstairs Okeke looked around Robin's bedroom more carefully. It was frozen in the nineties; there were several framed movie posters on the wall: *Reservoir Dogs*, *Terminator 2* and the like. There was a bedside table with a dusty lava lamp on it, and an even dustier CD player. She glanced out of the window at a garden that was way too big for the old couple to maintain. Tufts of nettles were in danger of overtaking the shaggy lawn, and unruly brambles choked what were once flower beds round the edge. A collection of CDs lined a shelf beneath the bedroom window – mostly nineties bands, she noted. She was carefully flicking through them when Mrs Whitehead returned.

'Here you go. A plastic bag, a cable and the plug it came with,' she announced.

Okeke checked the end of the cable – luckily it was the right one. She plugged it into the iPad and after a few moments the screen came to life, revealing a wallpaper image of a marina filled with ridiculously large pleasure boats. The screen showed a request for a four-digit code to unlock it.

'You wouldn't happen to know what his PIN was, would you?' she asked hopefully.

'Good God, no. I've got no idea,' Mrs Whitehead replied.

Okeke tried a couple of obvious ones without any luck. 'What was Robin's date of birth?' she asked.

'Fifth of August, 1975,' Mrs Whitehead replied.

Okeke tried it without success. 'Never mind,' she said. 'We have techies back at the station who will know how to get in.'

'Do you think there might be clues about where he is on that thing?' Mrs Whitehead asked.

'Maybe,' Okeke said. 'If we're lucky. Apple devices link together. If he's bought a new one and taken any pictures or downloaded anything on it since he's been missing... this may well tell us.'

'Oh God, I hope so.'

Okeke unplugged the iPad and bagged it. 'Like I said, you'll get this back after we've cloned the data.'

'Thank you, love.'

Okeke left the Whiteheads feeling guilty that she'd left behind a thread of hope for Robin's parents. Because it was looking increasingly likely that John Doe number three was going to be their son.

She was halfway back to Hastings when a thought occurred to her. She pulled her Datsun into the next layby she came across and pulled out her phone. She scrolled through her 'recent calls' list and found the number she was after.

The phone rang several times before it was answered.

'Hello?'

She tried to recall the woman's maiden name. It came to

her just as the protracted silence pushed into spam-call territory. 'Marjorie Barlow? It's DC Samantha Okeke. I came to see you the other day about your... about Mark?'

'Oh, yes,' came the reply.

'I've got a quick follow-up question, if that's all right?' Okeke said. 'You mentioned that Mark used to have a once-a-year reunion with his old schoolmates.'

'Yes?'

'Was it on the same day each year? The same *date*... I should say,' Okeke asked.

'Yes. Always,' Marjorie replied.

'Could you remind me what that date was?' Okeke held her breath.

'August twenty-first,' Marjorie said.

Okeke thanked her and hung up. 'It's worth a go,' she muttered, pulling on her gloves and easing the iPad out of the plastic bag. She tapped the screen. It had gained enough of a charge for it to reluctantly stir to life.

She tapped in the numbers 0, 8, 2 and 1.

The unlock screen disappeared to reveal a screen full of icons.

'Bingo.'

Before she could do anything else, it went blank again, the residual charge now exhausted.

36

Okeke placed the iPad on Boyd's desk.

'What's this?' he asked.

'Robin Whitehead's iPad,' she said smugly. 'It was in a box of stuff he left behind in Qatar. His sister sent it on not long after he came back to the UK.'

'Great. Well, let's get Sully to crack it open,' said Boyd, reaching for his desk phone.

'No need,' she said with a grin. 'I guessed the PIN. But it needs charging. It's dead and they wouldn't let me have the cable – Mr Whitehead needs it to play solitaire on his.' She rolled her eyes. 'Do you happen to have an old-style Apple cable on you?'

Boyd shook his head, then stood up. 'Anyone in here got an old-style Apple charging cable?' he called out.

A few heads turned in response. DI Abbott raised his hand. 'I have.' He rummaged in a desk drawer for a moment and stood up triumphantly, dislodging a small avalanche of pastry flakes from his shirt. He walked over to Boyd and Okeke, a kinked cable dangling from one fist like a cornered and captured grass snake.

'Here you go, sir.'

Boyd nodded a thanks, then plugged in the cable, careful not to smudge his fingers on the screen or the sides. He popped the USB connector into a port in his computer's docking station, and after a couple of seconds the screen blinked to life.

Okeke, gloves on, typed in the PIN and the screen changed to reveal the app icons that she'd glimpsed earlier.

'How'd you get the PIN?' Boyd asked.

'It's their reunion date. A wild guess,' she said.

'So that date was clearly significant to Robin,' he mused. 'Interesting.'

The email, phone and message icons all showed red dots, indicating hundreds of unread messages and missed calls.

'Nice one, Sam,' he said.

'Oh, so it's Sam when I do good, is it?'

He looked up at her with a faint smile. 'Okay, Sully's lot can fingerprint it, swab it and clone it –' he looked at his watch – 'over lunch, then we can get stuck into those messages this afternoon.'

THEY RETURNED from lunch to find that Sully had returned the iPad with a Post-It note stuck on the evidence bag it was sitting in.

Prints and swabs done. Data backed up. (Emailed you the link.) All yours, Boydy. Hope you enjoyed your lunch – I'm charging mine to your account. Thanks. S

Boyd picked it up, along with Abbott's cable, then called out to Minter, Warren and O'Neal to join him and Okeke in the Incident Room. Five minutes later, he had the iPad plugged in and connected to the projector and the station's Wi-Fi. The window blinds had been pulled down to kill the worst of the daylight, and his team were sitting around the conference table gazing up at the washed-out projection on the whiteboard.

'Let's start with the texts then,' Boyd said.

Okeke tapped the icon. The most recently active thread was titled 'Sis'.

'Okay. So that's Caroline Hussain,' said Boyd. 'Let's have a look at those first.'

Okeke opened the thread. The projection screen displayed a stack of unanswered blue speech bubbles on the right. Okeke scrolled up to start with the earlier ones. These were long and mostly Caroline venting her anger at her brother. As she scrolled down to the more recent ones, the tone changed from anger to growing concern. The last dozen or so had tumbled in once the iPad had detected the Wi-Fi over in Sully's domain and were dated after she had reported him missing. The very last of them was short, to the point and achingly futile: *Robbie, please... just let us know you're alive.*

'All right then, let's see who else has been messaging,' said Boyd.

Okeke returned to the list of message threads; the next one down was 'RickMeister'.

'Looks promising,' said Minter.

The thread appeared on the screen. This one was a balanced exchange of blue bubbles on the right and white bubbles on the left: an active conversation with timestamps above each message, indicating that this was a thread that had been ongoing in the weeks leading up to Robin's disappearance.

'Scroll back as far as it goes,' said Boyd.

Okeke swiped the screen downwards and after a moment's hesitation the message thread updated, jumping back in time. She swiped again, then again, taking them to August 2010.

RickMeister: Was good to see you, mate. You get your plane back okay?

Robbie: You too. Yeah. Still fucking hungover. Good to be back in the BIG HOT.

RickMeister: Ha. Nice one. We're the ones that got away.

Robbie: Unlike some. Christ, speaking of which... Andy's a shitshow, right?

RickMeister: M says he's a right fucking alcoholic now. I knew he was always going to end up like that.

Robbie: Mark needs to watch him. He's a loose cannon.

RickMeister: Indeed. I reminded him. Told him to keep his shit together. Don't end up like Andy.

Okeke scrolled down. There was a further, brief exchange on New Year's Eve: just the usual bland messages about the year past and the year ahead. The next back-and-forth was on 7 August 2011.

Robbie: Won't make it this year.

RickMeister: Shit. Why not?

Robbie: Client's booked a yacht for the week. It's a 'do it or pack your bag' scenario.

RickMeister: Great. I'm stuck with dumb and dumber then.

Robbie: Lol.

. . .

THE NEXT EXCHANGE was from 22 August, 2011.

RICKMEISTER: Just me and Mark bothered to turn up this time.

Robbie: And then there were two. Why the no-show from Andy?

RickMeister: No idea. Mark said he was after some money a few months ago. But nothing since.

Robbie: You'll find him in the bottom of a wheelie bin, no doubt.

RickMeister: LOL. Probably. Mark was worried. Said Andy been getting stupid ideas in his head.

Robbie: What do you mean?

RickMeister: Well, for one thing, he was thinking of tapping me for money.

Robbie: Shit.

RickMeister: Right.

Robbie: That's mental. Blackmail? We're all in this.

RickMeister: But I suppose he thought he had less to lose if it all came out.

'PAST TENSE,' noted Boyd, breaking the protracted silence. '*Had*... not *has*.'

'Right, guv, I spotted that, too,' said Okeke. She picked her phone up and took a picture of the projection on the whiteboard.

'Scroll on,' said Boyd.

. . .

ROBBIE: What are we going to do?'

RickMeister: Well... maybe he's walked in front of a bus. Or his liver's exploded or something. If he reaches out to you, I'd recommend you block him. Don't give him the space to make a threat.

'WELL, now Rick's talking like Andy's still alive,' said Minter.

'He's arse-covering,' said O'Neal. 'He knows he slipped up in the previous message and now he's trying to make it look like he's none the wiser.'

There was no reply from Robin Whitehead, and no exchange between the men until six months later.

ROBBIE: Mark's missing.

RickMeister: What?!

Robbie: I tried getting in touch. Got hold of his missus. Said she'd reported him missing months ago.

RickMeister: Fuck. What happened?

Robbie: She said he didn't return home from work one day.

RickMeister: Shit. That's weird.

Robbie: You think it might have something to do with Andy?

RickMeister: Maybe. Maybe he came asking for money again.

Robbie: What. And he killed him. Lol

RickMeister: Wouldn't be the first time things got out of hand. Especially if Andy was pissed out of his little skull at the time?

Robbie: Shit. That's making me feel twitchy mate.

RickMeister: Look on the bright side. If one of them did the other, then that's one less moron to worry about.

Robbie: Do you really think...?

RickMeister: Andy's always been a weak link. If he's done something stupid we're best keeping our distance. I'd lie low if I was you.

Robbie: What about you?

RickMeister: I'll be watchful. I don't have any links with him. I might block him/switch my FB page to private. Might even delete it. You should probs think about doing the same thing, mate.

'So, looking at the timeline,' began Sully, 'we know that both Andy and Mark are dead and boxed up at this point?'

Boyd nodded. 'Yes. And our RickMeister is beginning to look decidedly suspect.'

Okeke backed out of the thread and looked at the other chats in the log. The next one down was a conversation with someone called Captain Jack. She tapped on that. It appeared to be a conversation between Robin and some other expat friend, bitching about the building work going on everywhere in preparation for the looming World Cup. She returned to the log and spotted an interesting-looking thread further down the list. The date on the first entry was 5 May 2021.

RPL: Hello mate. It's me. New phone number. Been fucking ages, eh. You still in the Land of the Living?

Robbie: Ricky? Shit. Yeah it's been a while. How the fuck are you and where the fuck are you?

RPL: London, still. Kind of. Moved out of the city to the burbs. Fancied getting myself someplace bigger, more kerb appeal.

Robbie: Things going well then?

RPL: Really well. Set up my own business. It's hay-making time for investments. How're things with you?

Robbie: Working for my sister now. In real estate.

RPL: Carol? I remember her. Cute with a fucking big gob right!

Robbie: Lol. Caroline yeah. It's a fucking nightmare having your little sis as your boss! Tbh... I'm thinking of knocking it on the head out here.

RPL: In the land of milk and honey?

Robbie: It's not all that, mate. It's getting harder to get a toehold. She married some local Emirati with 'family connections' so it's all good for her. I'm her fucking lackey now.

RML: You seriously thinking about coming home?

Robbie: Yup.

RPL: Then maybe this was good timing.

Robbie: How do you mean?

RPL: Things are going well. Better than well, mate. I need more bums on seats here. Smart people with a bit of nous. Most important, people I can trust.

Robbie: You offering me a job?

RPL: If you want it.

Robbie: Doing what?

RPL: It's Richard Ledger Investments Ltd. Cold-calling granny investors to shovel money into my big fat investment pot.

Robbie: Lol. I don't know shit about that sort of thing.

RPL: It's piss easy. I can get you up to speed in an afternoon. Any muppet can do it.

Robbie: Flattered. Lol.

RPL: Good basic. Great sales commission. It'll be fun.

Robbie: How much?

RPL: Basic 50k plus commission. My lesser-performing bods pull in another 100k PA. My superstars do way better.

Robbie: I could live with that.

RPL: You wanna talk about it? I can skype you.

Robbie: Sure. My name plus 2108 at the end.

'TWO, ONE, ZERO, EIGHT,' said Minter. 'Again.'

'The reunion date,' said Okeke. 'It seems to have been big deal to Whitehead.'

'Hmm,' muttered Boyd. 'Is there any more?'

Okeke swiped the screen. That was it for the thread. Boyd got up and wandered over to the half of the white-board that wasn't being used to project onto. He grabbed the marker, put a line through '*Leeder*' and wrote '*Ledger*'.

He smiled. 'There we go, then. Richard Leeder didn't vanish; he just changed his name.'

So, we've finally found you, Mr Richard Ledger.

37

'Here it is...' said Okeke. 'The website.'

She had the Richard Ledger Investments page up on her phone within about a minute of them pushing back from the conference table. Sully and Magnusson excused themselves, with Sully announcing that they needed to have a department meeting of their own and pointedly reminding them all that Boyd's case wasn't their only one.

Okeke texted Boyd and Minter the link so they could pull it up on their phones too.

'What about us?' complained O'Neal.

'It's RLedgerInvestments.com,' she replied. 'Google it.'

O'Neal tapped the name into Whitehead's iPad and the webpage appeared on the whiteboard. He smirked at Okeke, who glared back.

Boyd swiped through the various pages: 'What We Believe', 'What We Do', 'How We Care', 'Meet the Team' and so on. He clicked on the latter and they found themselves looking at a page of smiling, friendly faces. At the top of the page was 'Richard Ledger, founder and CEO'. It was unmistakably Richard Leeder, a little older, a little greyer and somewhat paunchier than his old LinkedIn profile picture.

'That's definitely him,' said Okeke, looking at the same page on her phone and zooming in on his face.

'Ledger,' Minter said with a sigh. 'Just a couple of bloody letters.'

'Don't beat yourself up,' Boyd said. It was all too easy to do: throw a smokescreen up by changing your name. In Richard Leeder's case, it seemed, with the minimum of effort and imagination.

'I'll hit Facebook and the other socials again,' said Warren. 'See if I can find any accounts under *that* name.'

Boyd nodded. 'You do that. O'Neal? Can you chase up Whitehead's old phone records on the Interpol portal?'

'Yes, chief.'

He beckoned Okeke and Minter over. 'We need to reach out to Leeder. But softly, softly. Let's not spook him with any "you're the prime suspect" stuff. If he's rich, then he could be very, shall we say... *mobile*.'

'So likely to rush to the Bat Cave and make off and away in his Bat-copter?' said Minter.

Boyd gave him a look that wiped the grin from Minter's face. He still wasn't in the mood for banter. 'All we need to share with him is that we're looking at an old misper case,' he said.

'Which one do we pick?' asked Minter.

'Robin Whitehead,' Boyd replied. 'The most recent one and the one that we're most likely to be looking into. We don't mention the lock-up; we don't mention Meadows or Westfield.'

Minter nodded. 'Do you want me to make the call, boss...?'

Boyd was tempted to do it himself, but decided not to for

a couple of reasons. His head wasn't fully in the game with the make-or-break CT scan due in a couple of days. He wasn't sharp enough to make a call where he was going to have to judge every word he uttered on the fly. Also, given that he'd just recommended both Minter and Okeke for promotions, it made sense to take a step back and give them the space to prove themselves.

'Yes. Okay, Minter, you make the call. Woo him with your Welsh charm.'

Okeke looked disappointed.

'We'll need you when we bring him in, Okeke,' Boyd said. 'You're more of a Rottweiler.' He glanced at Minter. 'He's more approachable Lab.'

She nodded. 'Fair.'

He looked at his watch. It was approaching 5 p.m. Richard Leeder/Ledger would be in his London Head office, winding down from the day's work, perhaps a little tired, perhaps thinking about what he was going to get up to this evening, certainly not expecting an out-of-the-blue call from the police.

'MAY I SPEAK TO RICHARD LEDGER?' Minter asked.

'Who can I say is calling?' replied his PA.

'It's Steven Minter.' Minter decided to keep his CID rank out of things until he'd been put through.

He had to endure several seconds of Coldplay while on hold before the call clicked through.

'Richard Ledger speaking.'

Minter had the call on speakerphone so that Okeke and Boyd could hear the exchange and jot down any prompts or notes.

'My name's Steven Minter and I'm a detective sergeant with East Sussex CID,' he said.

'Okay,' Leeder replied. 'How can I help you?'

'I'm looking into a recent misper case...' Minter began.

'Miss-per?' Leeder asked.

'Sorry.' Minter mustered a relaxed laugh. 'It's our shorthand for "missing persons".'

'Right, I see. Okay?' Leeder sounded guarded. 'Who are you looking for and how can I help?'

'We're investigating the disappearance of a Mr Robin Whitehead,' Minter said. 'I believe he's an employee of yours?' The error was deliberate.

'Nobody works here, or should I say, *has* worked here by that name, I'm afraid,' Leeder said.

'My mistake,' Minter said. 'I think, looking at my notes, he was due to start at your company, but never turned up?'

He heard Ledger take in a deep breath. This was followed by a long pause. 'Ahh, right... yes. I do recall. Yeah, if I remember correctly, I offered him a sales job, but he didn't bother to turn up. I'm not a big fan of unreliable people. If you can't even make your first day on time, then I'm afraid you're not going to be any use to me.'

'Did you attempt to contact him?' Minter asked.

'I honestly can't remember. I might have had someone from HR chase him up and tell him not to bother coming in the next day, but... no. I'm afraid beyond that I don't think I can tell you anything useful. Is there anything else? Because... I'm actually getting ready to go home.'

'I've just got a couple of other questions, if that's okay?'

'Sure,' Leeder replied.

Okay. Careful now, Minty boy.

'So, we managed to access Robin Whitehead's Facebook page and found your name among his friends list...' Out of the corner of his eye he could see Boyd nodding. *So far so good.*

'Really?' Another pause. 'Well, I suppose, I'm not that surprised. I use my page to promote my company, as a sort of calling card if you will. If someone makes a friend request, provided it's not another Lucy Lastique or Pamela Randerson or...'

'Rhea Rend,' suggested Minter. 'Alotta Winkie...'

Boyd frowned. *Get on with it.*

Ledger laughed. 'Exactly. It's good to know these sexbots reach our law enforcement's Facebook pages too.'

Minter laughed along with him. 'Well, anyway, Richard... I was talking about your personal page... the one under your original name. Richard *Leeder*.'

There was a protracted silence from the other end.

'Mr Leeder?'

Finally... 'Yes, that's my *old* page. I haven't used that one in years.' The easy *bonhomie* had gone now.

'Robin Whitehead appears to have been a Facebook friend of yours going all the way back to 2010,' Minter remarked.

'Really? Wow. Time flies, doesn't it?'

'Yes, it does. So apart from this Facebook connection, did you have any other association with Robin Whitehead at all?'

'Uh... let me think...'

Boyd scribbled something down on a pad and turned it round. *He's stalling. Give him some time.*

Minter nodded and waited patiently.

'I... I think... yes, I think he possibly went to the same school as me. That's it. He must have looked me up or recognised me. Then later he approached me for a job.'

'And how did he approach you exactly?' Minter asked.

'Oh, I don't know. I get CVs all the time. I must have liked the look of his; I vaguely recall there was a brief chat over Skype. He seemed like the right kind of stuff. It's all about personalities here, DS Minter. People skills, right? He obviously managed to charm me.' Minter heard him sigh. 'More fool me, eh? Anyway, look, I've got a train to –'

'Can I ask you one last question?' Minter asked.

'Go on. If it's quick.'

'Why the name change, Mr Leeder?'

Leeder sighed. 'It's a brand thing. Optics right. "Ledger" scans better than "Leeder". Looks better on a business card, looks better over the front door of my offices. This business is all about appearances and confidence, you understand?'

Boyd scribbled down another message. *Wrap it up, now.*

'All right, well, I think that's all we need for now,' Minter said. 'Thank you for your assistance, Mr Ledger.'

'I hope you find him,' Ledger replied, and the call disconnected.

Minter let out a huge sigh of relief.

Okeke was the first to speak. 'Well, now, that was clearly a load of evasive BS, wasn't it?'

Boyd nodded.

'So what next, boss? Because he's going to be on high alert now,' Minter pointed out.

Okeke agreed. 'He's a flight risk, for sure.'

Boyd disagreed. 'No, not necessarily. If he bolts, then that really is evidence of guilt. And I think you sounded woolly enough on the phone to make him think we're a way off pinning anything on him just yet.' He looked at Minter. 'Nicely done, by the way.'

Minter beamed.

'The problem is,' Boyd continued, 'we don't have enough yet to get a thirty-six-hour detention or charge him.' He stroked his chin absently. 'But I reckon Leeder... *Ledger* will definitely be weighing up whether or not to *appear* to be fully cooperative.'

Boyd checked his watch – it was five past five. He suspected Leeder was probably not rushing for a train but sitting behind his desk pondering his next move, as was Boyd.

'We need him face to face,' he said.

'Then he really will think we've got something on him,' said Okeke.

'Well, let's play dumb. Let him think we're after someone else. Minter, get him back on the phone with a "just one more thing".'

'Which is?' Minter asked.

'Tell him we have someone we think may have something to do with Whitehead's disappearance. Alan Smithee. Tell him we've got a photo of this chap and we need him to pop down and take a look at it. If he's keen to make a show of being cooperative, he'll hopefully jump at the chance. Then while we have him with us... we'll ask him for a DNA swab.'

'Well, that will definitely mean the game's up,' said Minter.

Boyd nodded. 'Yes, but if he refuses the swab, that'll be enough of an *evasion* for us to apply for thirty-six hours' detention.' He smiled. 'Then we can hit him with everything we've got.'

38

Boyd lay perfectly still as the bed of the CT scanner slowly entered the doughnut-shaped cocoon.

'Now please relax and no moving around,' came a voice from a speaker inside the unit.

'Not that I've got much choice,' he muttered. He gazed up at the smooth white plastic hood, only a half a dozen inches above his face.

The speaker crackled again. 'We're ready to start, William. This won't take long. Just listen to the instructions coming from the machine, all right?'

A few moments passed, then a pre-recorded female voice, with an unexpected Lancashire twang, told him to 'breathe in and hold'.

He took a deep breath, wondering for how long exactly he was supposed to hold it.

Last night he'd managed to successfully argue Charlotte and Emma into *not* coming with him. If he was going to get bad news this morning, he wanted a chance to process it alone. And if it was bad news, he didn't want to break down in front of Emma. Because he couldn't very well tell Emma that Charlotte could come but not her, he'd made the case for going alone. He'd also stressed that he needed to hurry straight into work afterwards as he had an important interview to lead – which was true.

Five minutes later it was all done and he was back in the control room putting his jacket back on and lacing up his shoes.

'So when will I know the results?' he asked the radiographer – Stewart, according to his name badge.

'It'll go straight to the oncology department for analysis and they'll be in touch once they have the results for you,' Stewart told him.

Dammit. He'd been hoping for some answers this morning. Now he had another bloody wait to contend with. He looked at the young man who'd been operating the scanner, with his threadbare hipster goatee, a topknot of hair tucked away beneath a hairnet.

'You must have an idea whether I'm riddled with tumours or not, right?' he asked.

'I'm sorry,' Stewart replied. 'I'm not qualified to give you a clinical analysis.'

'But you've got an idea, right?' he repeated. 'I mean, you must have done a fair few of these...'

Stewart shook his head. 'I'm really sorry, I can't tell you. You'll get a call from the oncology department very soon.'

Boyd finished double-looping his laces and looked up at the young man; his patience was beginning to wear thin. More to the point, the gnawing anxiety that he'd been doing his best to keep a lid on for the last week was beginning to cause him stomach pains. The last time he recalled having 'tummy worry' to the point of feeling sick was when he'd been under threat of expulsion from school for bringing in a pack of B&H fags.

'Please,' he said. 'Just an indication... A smile or a frown would do it...'

Stewart gestured towards the door. 'Take care now,' he said as he walked Boyd over.

As Boyd stepped out of the control room, he thought he caught the faintest glimmer of a smile on Stewart's face as he closed the door on him.

Whether that was an answer or a response to his pleading, Boyd couldn't tell.

Dammit. He was taking that as a positive sign.

He rang Charlotte as he traipsed around the hospital car park, trying to remember where he'd parked his bloody Captur.

'They didn't say anything?' she repeated.

'Nope,' Boyd told her. 'Not a word.'

'Oh, God. More waiting.' She sounded as fed up as he felt. 'How are you doing, Bill?'

'I'm okay... I'm okay, actually,' he said.

'It's just such a wretched nightmare,' she murmured. He could hear her herding her own emotions into something that sounded vaguely positive. 'Look. Whatever the result, remember, the consultant said that staying positive is really important.'

'Right.'

He finally spotted the cobalt-blue hood of his car and clicked the key fob. The lights blinked a 'hello there' in response. 'I know. I've got a good feeling about this. I badgered the poor techie,' he confessed.

'And?'

'He couldn't say anything officially, but he gave me a smile.'

'Oh God... that's a good sign!' Charlotte said.

'It is.'

'Just a bit longer, Bill. Then we'll know what we're dealing with.'

'I know,' he replied, pulling the door open and climbing in. 'Onwards and upwards, eh?'

'Onwards and upwards,' she repeated. 'I'll let Emma know.'

He ended the call and slumped in the seat. 'Oh, for fuck's sake...'

He'd forgotten to pay for his bloody parking ticket.

BOYD DUMPED the car keys on his desk and his jacket on the back of his chair. 'Has Ledger arrived yet?' he asked.

Minter and Okeke came over, both carrying their notes. 'I just plonked him in Room Two with a coffee and a Twix, boss. We're good to go when you are,' Minter told him.

Interview Room Two was the only one with a mirrored observation window. He was going to watch through that while Minter and Okeke ran the interview. Minter was going to buddy up to Ledger, while Okeke was going to go in harder when the time was right. He would prompt them both by text message, if needed.

'Good. Then let's crack on,' he said.

Minter led the way. Okeke drew up beside Boyd. 'You seem in a better mood this morning,' she said softly. 'Good news?'

He nodded. 'I think so.'

39

'All right, then,' started Minter. 'First of all, thanks for coming all the way down from London this morning, Richard. I know it's all a bit of a faff.'

Richard Ledger nodded. 'You could say that.'

'So, this is DC Samantha Okeke. And, of course, I'm DS Steven Minter. We both work on missing persons cases. In this instance, the person missing is Robin Whitehead.'

'Business is slow down here, I'm guessing, eh?' Ledger said.

'Sorry?' Minter asked.

Richard smiled. He'd obviously decided to go with easy, convivial confidence. 'Working on missing persons, I mean? Rather than, I don't know, knocking down doors, arresting drug kingpins, that sort of thing.'

Minter laughed. 'Oh, it's not like that down here in Hastings, is it, DC Okeke? There's never much going on here. Maybe the occasional pinched handbag.'

Ledger sipped his coffee. The Twix remained untouched.

'Well then, Richard. The first thing I have to do is a bit of box-ticking, see. I'd like to reassure you that you're not a suspect in any crime and you're not under caution. We just want you to have a look at that photograph I mentioned yesterday.'

'Right. That's no problem,' Ledger said, settling back in his chair.

'But, before we get to that, there are just a couple of little things I want to get clear in my head... if that's all right with you?'

Boyd shook his head and smiled. Minter must have watched a few episodes of *Columbo* last night, he thought.

'You told us that you and Robin had no history together,' Minter said.

'I said we went to the same school. Harsham Grammar,' Ledger corrected.

'Right, yes you did. You did say that,' Minter agreed. 'But – and here's where the confusion lies – we recently interviewed Robin's parents and they mentioned that you and Robin were pretty good friends at school. Is that right?'

It had actually been Meadows' wife and Westfield's mum who'd mentioned the name Robin. But the plan was to hold their names back for later.

Ledger shrugged. 'You know what... it's a long time ago. Friendships tend to come and go during your school days, right? We might have hung out once or twice. I honestly can't remember.'

'But during your Skype interview with him, he must have reminded you that you went to school together?' Minter pressed.

Ledger's face creased as he made a show of casting his mind back. 'He may have done. Yes... come to think of it... yeah, we might have talked briefly about Harsham Grammar.'

'Right.' Minter jotted that down, keeping up the pretence that this was all new info. 'But, and again, I only want to clear up any confusion, can I ask why you didn't think to mention that yesterday?'

'Because I just remembered.' Ledger adjusted his position. 'It was a long time ago. You know, ancient history. To be honest, I didn't have a great time at that school. There was a bit of bullying going on back then... and I was on the receiving end of some of it. So, no, I don't tend to dwell on my school days that much.'

Minter nodded. 'Well, that's understandable.' He glanced down at his notes. 'Now, you told us that you offered Robin a job at your firm. Can I ask why?'

'Because I could,' was Ledger's self-assured response. 'Because it's my firm.'

Minter cocked his head, waiting for a bit more. 'Was it because you and Robin actually were very good friends?'

Ledger stiffened and crossed his arms. 'All right... look, Robin was my only real mate at school. He was a decent bloke. He stood by me. We got in touch via Facebook a while back. You know how it is... Folks look up folks from back in the day, right? Just out of curiosity to see how they're doing. Anyway, having reconnected, I found out he was struggling a bit. So, I suppose, out of a sense of gratitude – misplaced in hindsight – I offered him a job. He said he was up for it. He was coming back to the UK anyway, so... why not?'

Boyd texted Okeke. *Push him on the job offer. Why him? No relevant experience.*

Okeke looked up from the phone on her lap. 'But, as far as we're aware, Robin has no experience in finance, does he?'

Richard chuckled. 'Like I said to your colleague yesterday. It's not rocket science.'

'What *is* your business exactly?' she asked him.

'Financial management and advice,' Ledger replied promptly. 'There's not much to it, to be honest. We reach out to retired investors who are looking to make their pension pots do a little more for them. The money goes into our fund, which is, in turn, managed by an investment broker that I trust. We've got three funds: low, middle and high risk. We give our clients the advice to come in on low risk. Then, when they feel confident they're in safe hands, we look at encouraging them to step up.'

'To high risk?' Okeke asked.

'To high*er* risk,' Ledger replied. 'But, honestly, it's all pretty safe really. Post Covid, the areas we invest in are all steady.'

'So how do you make your money?' Okeke asked him.

'A handling fee and a slice of the appreciation of their value. They do well; we do well.'

'So what was the job you offered Robin?' Okeke asked.

'Financial planner. Which is to say, glorified telesales. My team cold-call potential investors. It involves a bit of hand-holding, a bit of trust development. We let them know that we're not sharks; we're here to work together, to help them leverage that pension into something more useful. That kind of thing. Nothing that requires expert knowledge of the markets, just a nice manner... and a lot of patience.'

'So then,' resumed Minter, 'you offered him the job. And what happened after that?'

'I gave him a start date,' Ledger replied. 'I explained that when he turned up I'd give him some training, get him settled in and at the same time we'd sort out his paperwork and so on.'

'And when he didn't show up for work?' Minter asked.

Ledger shrugged. 'To be honest, I let it go. I guessed he got cold feet, or maybe he found a better offer elsewhere.'

'You didn't chase him up? Call him? Send him a text asking what was going on?' cut in Okeke. 'Since he *was* an old friend.'

'No. Contrary to current appearances, I'm extremely busy most of the time. I threw him a bone for old times' sake. If he couldn't be bothered to turn up, or at least out of courtesy send me a text and say why he wasn't there...' He spread his hands. 'Well, I can't be doing with time-wasters. I offered to help him. I did my bit.'

Minter nodded. 'I can understand that.'

'So...' Ledger looked at his watch. 'You wanted me to look at some photograph, didn't you?'

'Yes, we did.' Minter reached into his folder and pulled out the scan of the driving licence. The name and details on it had been blacked out with a marker pen, only the small, head-and-shoulders picture was visible.

Ledger squinted at the picture for a moment. 'Sorry, mate, I've no idea who that is.' He passed it back. 'Should I?'

'It's someone we think might have known Robin,' volunteered Okeke.

'How?'

'I'm sorry, we can't say.'

'Right. Well, I honestly don't recognise that bloke. Sorry. So... is that us done then?' He checked his watch again. 'I've got an unsupervised sales team waiting for me back in London. For all I know they could be sitting around with their feet up on their desks and drinking coffee.'

Boyd texted Okeke. *DNA swab.*

'Almost,' said Okeke, looking up from her lap again. 'We'd like to take a DNA swab from you before you go.'

'DNA?' Ledger looked surprised. 'Why?'

'It's just a routine thing, Mr Ledger, while you're here.'

He narrowed his eyes. 'You're talking about forensics, aren't you?'

Okeke remained tight-lipped.

'Wait...' He looked from one detective to the other. 'If you're talking forensics... you've actually found him, haven't you?'

Good Cop Minter nodded. 'I'm afraid so.'

'He's not a missing person any more?' Ledger sat back down. 'He's dead?'

'We have recovered a body, yes,' replied Minter. 'And it has recently been identified as Robin Whitehead.'

'Shit,' he uttered. To Boyd, who was sitting next door, he seemed genuinely shocked.

'But why the hell do you need *my* DNA?' Ledger asked.

'As a matter of procedure,' said Okeke. 'We need to work through everyone he might have encountered once he had returned to the UK.'

'I spoke to him over Skype. Over Facebook. That is literally it,' Ledger said. 'We never actually had a face-to-face encounter.'

Okeke offered him a firm but placatory smile. 'As I said, it's routine procedure. We just want to rule you out of things so that you can get back to your business.'

Ledger took a moment and shrugged. 'Fine. If that's what you need, you'd better get on with it.'

Inside the viewing room, Boyd could feel himself wilting as Okeke snapped on a pair of gloves, pulled out a testing kit and came around the table to take a mouth swab.

Ledger hadn't refused. Which wasn't the response he'd been hoping for.

'That's it?' said Ledger after she'd capped the cotton bud.

'That's it,' confirmed Okeke.

'I'm free to go now?'

Boyd quickly texted. *Yes.*

She nodded.

'And thanks again, Richard, for coming down,' said Minter, getting up. 'My colleague will show you out.'

THE FEATHERED chavs were being particularly bold today, swooping and diving at anyone daring to emerge from the pier café with food in their hands. Boyd chose a picnic table as far away from the overflowing bin as possible. The gulls had staked a claim around it, making it their centre of operations, and were busy pulling everything out from it and onto the decking.

Boyd watched Warren and O'Neal queueing inside the café for their lunch order.

'So, what were your impressions, boss?' Minter asked.

Boyd gathered his thoughts. 'One thing I did notice is that Ledger seemed genuinely surprised at the news that Whitehead's dead. That – plus the fact he seemed willing to do the swab – makes me think we *might* be barking up the wrong tree.'

'Maybe he was just shocked that we'd found the body he thought he'd safely stashed away?' suggested Okeke. 'And the willingness to be swabbed... was just an act.'

'He could easily have said no,' said Minter. 'He wasn't under arrest.'

'But if he'd refused, he'd know that *we'd* know he had something to hide,' she replied. 'He's not an idiot.' She turned to Boyd for support. 'Come on, guv.'

'It's possible,' said Boyd. 'He may have guessed that we were hoping he'd refuse. But...'

'Which makes him a very clever, very slippery bastard,' said Okeke. 'He's bought himself a bit of time. Time to get his story straight. Time to lawyer up... Maybe even time to flee the country. We should have hit him with everything we had.'

Boyd shook his head. 'He'd have clammed up and "no commented".'

'But what if he does flee?' Okeke said.

'He won't. An attempt to leave the country would just add weight to his guilt. That's usable in court.' Boyd looked at her. 'We have to play the long game, Okeke. You know the drill. We've got to give the CPS as much as we can.'

Every move Richard Ledger made from now on could potentially be admissible and usable. If he was guilty of murdering his three friends, then giving him enough rope with which to hang himself was the smart move.

'We'll get his swab over to Ellessey. Hopefully we'll have the results by tomorrow. If it's a match with the coffee cup, then we can get CPS to greenlight an arrest-and-charge. Until then, whatever he's up to over the next twenty-four hours... any calls he makes, anything he googles on his phone or laptop, becomes ammunition the prosecution can use. If he's panicking right now... he's going to be building up a mountain of evidence for us further down the line.'

'Hey! Watch your heads!' said Minter.

A gull swooped down over them and landed on the end of their table, beady eyes searching it thoroughly before it changed tack and interrogated them for scraps.

'Go on, bugger off!' said Minter, waving his hands at the bird. It eyed him defiantly for a moment, then leapt off the table and down onto the decking to check the planks for pickings.

'Bloody gulls!' grumbled Minter. 'It's all these flaming holidaymakers that attract them.'

'Nah,' said Okeke. 'It's just Boyd. He's their secret deity. They just want to commune with him.'

'Commune?' Boyd lifted a brow. 'I'll give them bloody *commune*.' He swung his foot at the bird, which hopped back a few steps and carried on eyeballing him from a safer distance.

40

Boyd returned home to an unusual silence. Where, he wondered, was the deafening canine welcoming committee beyond the front door. He let himself in, bemused by the calm. He walked down the hall and was about to call out that he was home, when he heard the pleasant sound of Charlotte and Emma chatting in the dining room.

He tiptoed to the dining-room door and peered in. It was empty. They were both in the tiny kitchen prepping dinner. He lingered.

'Oh, but, you know, he's going to love being Grandpa Bill, Emma.'

'God. That's what concerns me. What the hell's he going to be teaching my offspring?' Emma replied with mock horror.

'What was he like with you when you were a little one?' Charlotte asked.

A pause. He could hear chopping. 'Well, he taught me to swear. My first word, apparently, was "bloody".'

Charlotte laughed. 'Oh God, I bet your mum wasn't too pleased.'

'Nope. She wasn't. My first actual phrase was "bloody scrotes".'

They both chuckled.

'How was he with your little brother?' Charlotte asked.

The sound of chopping paused. He could imagine Emma cocking her head, recalling a very different time, a different life. 'I remember him and Noah on the floor wrestling. They had their own little game: Poison Ivy.'

The name of the game stung him. He'd forgotten all about it. He used to lie on the floor, coiled up in a foetal position, and the game was for Noah to step stealthily past him. If he made too much noise, Boyd would spring to life and snatch Noah into his arms. The more he struggled, the tighter the grasp; the less he struggled, the looser it got until he could worm his way free, giggling as he did so... and the game would start all over again.

'They played soldiers too, setting up little plastic men and pew-pew-pewing them until they were all knocked down. They made little Lego forts... you know? He was more hands-on with Noah than me,' continued Emma. 'I think he knew what to do with a boy.'

'Well, whether this little one is a boy or girl, I'm pretty sure they'll have him wrapped around their little finger from day one,' said Charlotte.

There was a long pause as Emma resumed chopping. Boyd was about to announce his presence when she spoke again. 'I hope so. I really hope so.' He could hear raw emotion surfacing in his daughter's voice. 'I need him. I need him to be around, to be a grandad... to be *my* dad... to...'

Her voice died away and he heard Charlotte offering murmured words of comfort.

'No, it's fine,' said Emma. 'It's fine... I'm good. It's just the onions.'

I am going to be here for you, Ems, Boyd answered silently. He'd walked away from the scan this morning feeling positive. That parting I'm-not-saying-anything smile from the radiographer, he convinced himself, had been answer enough. He was going to be around to make sure Baby Boyd learned a whole load of godawful language.

He felt his phone buzz in his pocket. He quickly shuffled up the hallway before they noticed the noise. He opened the front door quietly and stepped outside.

'Bill Boyd speaking, who's this?' he said.

'It's Dr Chudasama, your oncologist,' came the reply.

'Ah, hello there!' Boyd said, closing the door noisily behind him as he stepped back into the house. A moment later Ozzie and Mia were dancing circles around his feet, jumping up at him. 'That was incredibly quick!' he said loudly.

'Yes. It was quick. I received your scan results this afternoon,' Dr Chudasama continued, his tone flat and neutral. 'I have some news for you...'

41

Boyd went into work the next day nursing, what O'Neal would call, a bitch of a hangover. A stupid, ill-advised, middle-of-the-working-week one. He made a beeline for the kitchenette and slapped the kettle on. He needed coffee. A strong one.

Last night at the Pump House he'd sealed his fate by ordering that second bottle of merlot. Emma wasn't drinking for obvious reasons and Charlotte had barely helped him out at all. He'd had the best part of two bottles all to himself. Emma and Charlotte, he vaguely recalled, had had to steer him up the hill as they'd walked back home.

He smiled to himself as he watched the kettle boil.

It had been a celebration. A well-deserved one.

The news from his oncologist had been Bloody Good News, in his humble opinion. There were no signs of any secondary tumours in the scan. It was all clear, except for that gnarly-shaped twiglet protruding from his bowel. Dr Chudasama's call had been carefully measured to manage Boyd's expectations; of course it had. But, essentially, the tumour was stage two and operable. Surgery was needed asap – in the next couple of weeks if Dr Chudasama could find a spare slot in his theatre schedule. And, yes, unfortunately there would be six months of chemotherapy afterwards to make damned sure no rogue cells had begun to set up home elsewhere in his body.

But, as far Dr Chudasama was concerned, it was all very treatable and Boyd had a very high probability of experiencing a full recovery.

So, naturally, in light of that, he'd decided to take 'the girls' down to the Pump House for some pub grub – sod their half-prepped dinner – and now he was paying the price for it.

'Boss?'

It was Minter, standing in the doorway, looking fresh-faced and particularly energised. 'We've got us a match on Ledger's DNA.'

~

THE CID POOL cars were available once again, to Minter's profound relief. With Okeke back behind the wheel of a car that wasn't hers to crash, she was inclined to drive more conservatively.

'What time are we rendezvousing with them?' she asked.

'Eleven thirty. Outside,' Minter confirmed.

He noticed her check her watch. 'We've got loads of time, Okeke, don't worry.'

'I hate driving into central London,' she replied. 'Flippin' Deliveroos and those stupid hipster scooters are everywhere.'

Minter had the warrant for Ledger's arrest freshly signed and sitting on his lap. He was a little surprised that Boyd hadn't opted to come along with them. He was usually after any excuse to get out of the station.

'So, what's up with the boss, then?' he asked after a while. 'Sam?'

She shrugged. 'What do you mean?'

'You know him best,' he replied. 'You must have noticed he's been very cranky of late, out of sorts?'

'He seemed fine this morning,' she replied, keeping her eyes on the road for once.

'Yes, oddly enough, this morning he's been in a much better mood, even though he's hangin' like a sign. But he's been a grumpy bugger recently and he's been late in a few times.'

She remained silent.

Which, to Minter, meant she probably knew something. 'Samantha?'

'It's personal,' she replied eventually.

'Ah. So you *do* know what's up with him? Is he ill? It's not cancer, is it?' he guessed.

She nodded.

'Ah, man, you're shitting me – that's bloody awful, that is,' said Minter.

'Look, he doesn't want anyone to know. Emma told me; it wasn't him. He doesn't want a pity party so keep schtum, okay?'

He nodded. 'Don't worry, I'm not about to run up to him and give him a big sloppy *cwtch*. Just keep me in the loop, all right?'

She nodded. 'Okay.'

They parked up outside Stern House on Charter Street: a Jenga brick tower of glass and cladding, dwarfed by the much larger looming glass-and-steel structures all around it. They were five minutes late and a patrol car was already there, waiting for them. Minter went over to introduce himself.

'Hello, I'm DS Steven Minter from East Sussex CID and this is DC Samantha Okeke,' he said.

'Morning,' the officer replied. 'So... who are we arresting?'

Minter handed him the warrant. 'One Richard Ledger,' he said.

42

Boyd started the recorder and waited for the test bleep to finish. 'The date is the fifteenth of June, 2023, and the time is three thirty p.m. Present in the interview room are DCI William Boyd, DS Steven Minter, interviewee Richard Ledger, and his lawyer...'

'Graham Hart,' the lawyer supplied.

'Ledger has been cautioned,' continued Boyd, 'and, Mr Ledger, you understand the caution?'

Richard Ledger nodded.

'Aloud, please, for the tape,' Boyd told him.

Hart nodded at his client.

'Yes, I understand,' Ledger replied.

'Right then.' Boyd opened the folder on the table in front of him. 'I'm going to begin with the forensic evidence that makes you our prime suspect, Mr Ledger. Just so that we're not wasting each other's time.'

He pulled a printed photograph out of its plastic sleeve and slid it across the table for Ledger and his lawyer to see. 'This is a picture of a Nesso paper coffee cup, recovered from within Unit Thirty-Seven at Best Price Storage.'

He pulled out another sheet of paper and slid that across too. 'And this is a DNA chromograph of a sample taken from that same coffee cup.' He took out a third piece of paper. 'And this is the chromograph of your DNA, Richard. For the record, the two chromographs match.'

'Also, for the record, my client willingly submitted to a DNA swab,' said Hart.

'Indeed he did.' Boyd settled back in his seat. 'So, can you provide us with an explanation as to why your DNA might have found its way into this storage unit?'

Ledger glanced at his lawyer, then back at Boyd. 'No comment.'

'Have you ever visited Best Price Storage, near Little Fritton?' Boyd asked.

'No,' Ledger replied. His lawyer gently nudged him. 'No comment.'

'All right.' Boyd gathered the sheets of paper and tucked them back into their folder. 'Do you recognise the following names, Mr Ledger? Robin Whitehead. Mark Meadows. Andrew Westfield.'

'No comment.'

'Well, let me help you out. Those three people are friends of yours that go all the way back to your time at Harsham Grammar School. They are your old school buddies. Do you recognise their names now?'

'No comment.'

Boyd pulled a few sheets of paper out of the folder. 'For the record, I'm showing Mr Ledger and his lawyer printouts of several texted exchanges between Mr Ledger and Robin Whitehead.' He slid them across the table and sat back, giving both men a chance to read the back-and-forth on the pages.

'Mr Ledger,' he said, 'we obtained these conversations

from Robin's iPad. It's quite clear from these that you've been in touch with not only Robin Whitehead but Mark Meadows and Andrew Westfield too. Spanning a number of years, in fact. And since you left school the four of you were in the habit of meeting, every year, on the twenty-first of August, according to these texts.'

'No comment,' Ledger repeated.

'Can we have a copy of this?' asked Hart.

'You can take those copies, if you like,' Boyd told him.

Hart nodded, then resumed scanning them more closely.

'So the four of you met once a year, Richard, to discuss something. The four of you shared a secret, didn't you? And it seems, looking at that exchange between you and Robin Whitehead, that you shared a concern that your mutual friend, Andrew Westfield, was in danger of letting it slip.' Boyd raised a brow.

'No comment.'

'He was an alcoholic, wasn't he? He was after money. He'd approached Mark Meadows for money a number of times, and... it seems that he was thinking to coming to you – presumably threatening to use this secret as some sort of leverage. How did that make you feel?'

'No comment.'

'But then... this Andy Westfield went missing in 2011 and Meadows a few months later. Do you know what happened to them?'

'No comment.'

'In a previous interview, yesterday in fact... we revealed to you that Robin Whitehead was dead. That his body has been recovered. Now, I distinctly recall your reaction. You were surprised. I might even say... shocked.'

'That's right,' said Ledger. 'I was. I am.'

Got him talking... at last.

'Were you aware he was a missing person?' Boyd asked.

Ledger opened his mouth. It looked as though he was about to say 'yes', but then he stopped himself. 'As I told you... I'd offered him a job. He didn't bother to turn up for it. And that's it.'

'You didn't make any attempt to contact him?' Boyd said.

'Because I was pissed off he didn't turn up. Because, as I mentioned yesterday, I don't have the time to deal with time-wasters.'

'Right. Okay.' Boyd decided now was probably as good a time as any. He opened his folder again, pulled out a stack of evidence photographs taken from the storage unit and spread them out across the table for Ledger to see.

'These are the dismembered and desiccated bodies of Robin Whitehead, Mark Meadows and Andy Westfield,' Boyd said. 'They were discovered in that storage unit I mentioned earlier.'

He let that hang in the air as he studied Ledger's face intently, his eyes darting from one image to the next. His gaze settled on the image that showed the three heads nestling together on a blue tarp. He looked horrified.

'Oh... my... God...' he whispered.

You can't fake a reaction like that. Not unless you were a world class actor, thought Boyd. *Though he just might be.*

'All three were murdered,' Boyd said. 'They were hit from behind by a heavy weapon with a blunt edge. Then they were beheaded, dismembered and stored in crates filled with road grit.'

'Good God!' exploded Hart. 'I don't approve of this. Ambushing my client like this, and without warning I might add, with these awful –'

'Richard,' Boyd cut in, 'did you do this? Did you kill your friends?'

Ledger's mouth opened and closed silently.

'Did you kill them, Richard? Was there something the four of you knew. Some secret... some pact that they were in danger of revealing? Were they threatening to blackmail you?'

'I... I... didn't...' Ledger whispered.

His lawyer leant closer to him. 'No comment,' he prompted.

'Let *him* answer,' snapped Boyd irritably.

'My client needs a break,' Hart replied. 'And I insist we have one. Right now.'

Boyd ignored him. 'They were murdered. Dismembered... and before they were packed away in salt, one of *these...*' He pulled another photograph out of the folder and set it down in front of Ledger. It was a photo that Okeke had taken while Dr Palmer was walking them through her autopsy and it showed a pine cone, resting on the cold metal of the examination table.

'One of these was inserted into the rectum of each of your friends.'

Ledger lurched back in his seat. The disgust and horror on his face had turned to terror. 'Oh God. Oh God!'

'Right! That's it! This stops right now!' snapped Hart. 'I'll be taking this further; you can be certain of that.'

Boyd nodded. 'Interview suspended at three forty-nine p.m.'

'I DON'T THINK he did it,' said Boyd.

'Why?' Minter looked at him. 'Because he nearly shat himself over the pine cone?'

Boyd nodded. 'Partly. That... was a genuine reaction. I don't think I've witnessed a response like that in an interview room. Ever.'

They had the mini conference room to themselves. Three mugs of steaming coffee sat on the small round table in front of them, so far ignored.

Minter nodded. 'It did seem very real.'

'So what are you suggesting?' asked Okeke. 'Do you think someone else did it?'

Boyd nodded. 'It's feels that way to me. I think whoever rented that unit, whoever's face is on the driving licence is a fifth person here.'

'Who is Alan Smithee?' Minter murmured to himself.

'We'll let him have his half-hour rest break, then we'll go back in and focus on his reaction.' Boyd turned his mug round and round on the table absently. 'He's absolutely terrified of *someone*.'

Okeke sucked air through her teeth. 'Hold on. His reaction, just now... you're saying that *trumps* the forensic evidence on the cup?'

'Yes.' Boyd couldn't recall an interview he'd done, ever, with a reaction as sudden, as unrehearsed, as genuine and visceral as Ledger's had been. 'I am. It was the pine cone,' he said. 'That's what he responded to.'

'It's highly significant then,' said Minter.

'I'd say so. It definitely means something to him. We're going back in there with a conciliatory tone. We're his friends now. His best mates. We're there to help him. We need to find out who the fuck he is so bloody scared of and what the pine cone means.'

'And the coffee cup,' prompted Okeke again. 'We need to ask him about that.'

'I'm beginning to suspect that was put in there deliberately,' said Boyd.

'To frame him,' Minter added.

'Well, it certainly could have done,' replied Boyd. 'But the point here is that... if our killer, Mr Smithee, managed to find and place a coffee cup with Ledger's DNA on it in the lock-up, it means...'

'He's been stalking him?' said Minter.

Boyd nodded. 'Our killer's been watching Richard Ledger... and I expect Ledger's worked out that he could be next.'

MINTER LET the recording beep finish. 'Interview resumed at four twenty-five p.m. Present in the room are: DS Steven Minter, DCI William Boyd, interviewee Richard Ledger and his lawyer, Mr Hart.' He pushed a paper cup of fresh coffee across the table towards Ledger. 'It's from the downstairs vending machine, I'm afraid. It's not the best.'

Ledger took the cup and nodded a muted thanks.

'Now then, Richard... how are you feeling? Are you okay to continue?' Minter asked.

Ledger didn't respond. His swagger had gone. He looked hollowed out and haunted.

'Look, Richard, I think we all know that we need to track down the sick bastard who did this to your friends, okay? We're all on the same page here.'

Ledger managed a nod.

'So then...' Minter continued. 'No more photographs, for starters.' He pushed the folder to one side. 'We can see that you're afraid of someone. So, we'll begin with that, shall we? Can you think of anyone who would want all three of your friends dead? Someone who'd want to make us think that you killed them?'

Ledger shook his head.

'For the recorder, mate,' Minter said.

'No.' Ledger shook his head again.

'Can I throw a name at you?' Minter asked. 'It's someone that we're interested in.'

Ledger looked up. *Was that a look of hope on his face?* Boyd wondered.

'Does the name Alan Smithee mean anything to you?' Minter asked.

Ledger frowned for a moment. 'No... I...' He stopped. A faint flicker of recognition crossed his face. 'Oh shit,' he said.

'Richard?' prompted Minter.

'There was... shit. There was... someone...' His eyes darted around the room as he tried to dig up some vague memory. 'Someone I interviewed.'

'By the name of Alan Smithee?' Minter pressed.

Ledger nodded uncertainly. Then again, more forcefully this time. 'Yes. Smithee. Alan Smithee.'

'And when was that?' Minter asked.

'A couple of years ago, I think. Yes. That's... that's – shit – that was about the same time Robin was meant to start!'

'All right.' Minter nodded. 'Would you have any record of that interview? An application form? A CV?'

Ledger shook his head. 'He... He didn't get the job. I... He wasn't right. I would have just binned his CV.'

'How did he manage to get an interview with you?' Boyd cut in.

'I get cold-callers all the time,' Ledger said. 'Not just agencies looking to place people but walk-ins. The City of

London's a small place, okay? The building we're in... there's several other boutique financial companies like mine above and below. I get their sales people coming down, during a lunch break, discreetly you understand? Checking out whether there's a chance to jump floors for a better offer.'

'And you agreed to interview him?' Minter said.

'Yeah. It was just... a quick chat...'

43

'Come on in... Alan, isn't it?'

The man nodded as he stepped into Richard Ledger's office. He looked around. It was all glass walls, chrome and black ash. The enduring design scheme of the eternal Wall Street man-child. Richard Ledger was clearly another Gordon Gekko fanboy.

'Take a seat,' Richard said, setting his coffee and his chicken wrap down on the desk. 'I'll have a quick scan of your CV first, if that's okay?'

'Sure,' Alan replied, looking out of the window at the spectacular view of Canary Wharf.

He turned his gaze onto Richard Ledger, busy speed-reading the bogus CV that Alan had put together and sipping his coffee as he did so.

You don't recognise me, do you?

Of course he didn't. It had all happened so long ago. *Everyone changes with age*, he thought. *Apart from the eyes. They never change.*

Don't you even sense my rage, Richard? Clearly he didn't. Richard was clacking his tongue absently as he read the CV.

Mr Big Man. Weighing up the lies on the page and deciding whether or not Alan Smithee was worth his time.

You have no idea what I'm going to do to you. The thought made him smile as he studied Ledger's face. He looked up from the page and met his gaze. 'What're you smiling at?' he asked.

'Nothing – I'm just flattered that you're giving me your time, Mr Ledger,' he replied.

Ledger shrugged. 'It's a pretty decent CV,' he said, taking another swig of his coffee.

'Thank you.'

He couldn't take his eyes off Ledger's and the moment passed into something too uncomfortable for Ledger, who looked back down at the pages in his hand. 'Well, you've got enough experience, clearly,' he said.

Oh, I have. A lifetime of it. Thanks to you and your friends.

The compulsion to come to Ledger's place of work, to meet him, to *evaluate him* first, had become an overwhelming urge. It was perhaps a touch reckless. Truth be told. But, after so many years, he wanted to get an updated impression of the man. A genuine, uncontaminated impression of him. Not like the others, the whimpering wretches pleading for forgiveness as they struggled to free their hands. Oh, they'd discovered plenty of long-overdue contrition while staring at the sharp end of the bloodied knife.

I want to know who you are now, Richard. Are you the same person as you were back then?

There had been a small chance that Richard would have recognised him. But it had been a calculated risk. He'd looked very different at seventeen. He'd been lean and gangly, his hair long, dyed and backcombed like the Cure's Robert Smith. His face had been permanently clogged up with gothic make-up. Thirty years had turned him into a pudgy middle-aged man. His mane of thick dark hair was reduced now to a closely cropped stubble of silver with a pronounced widow's peak, inching its way to meet the spreading bald patch at the back of his head.

Nature and time – a ruthless couple.

'So, Alan,' Ledger said finally, picking up his chicken wrap and taking a bite out of it. 'My sales team are all a lot younger, to be honest. How would you feel working with people ten, fifteen years younger than you are?'

'Fine,' Alan said.

'You got family? Kids?' Richard asked.

'No. I'm single,' Alan replied.

'Well, that's good. We're a work-hard, play-hard bunch here. We work long hours. Very long. We're all here to make as much money as we can. so we make every office hour count...'

Ledger began to give his spiel. It sounded like something rehearsed, which of course it was. He would have uttered it a million times before, and Alan simply nodded along with the corporate-mission bollocks while he silently contemplated the man's fate.

You're going to get... special treatment... Richard, my friend.

The others had been a vaguely unsatisfying experience, all told. Of course there'd been some gratifying pleasure watching them squirm and struggle. Watching them choke on the leaves and twigs that he'd rammed into their mouths before gaffer-taping them shut. The conversation with all three of them had been limited, reduced to head nods and headshakes. They had all been very, very sorry for what they'd done, obviously. Oh yes. All three understood completely – by their vigorous nodding – that what they'd done was vile, brutal and cruel. They understood that it had ruined his life. They were less in agreement however, that, the balance of justice needed to – finally – be settled.

He'd been too impatient, he reflected. Too hasty to end their lives to really get what he needed out of the experience. Answers to questions like... Why? Why did you do it? Why me? WHAT THE FUCK WERE YOU LITTLE BASTARDS THINKING?

As grown men, they must have thought back to that day. Thought about what had driven them. They must have contemplated the evil they'd demonstrated... Perhaps even confronted it? Atoned for it?

But gagged and screaming, their mouths clogged with forest floor, there hadn't been the opportunity for a nuanced conversation, a shared victim–perpetrator therapy session.

So his knife had settled the matter.

However, this time, with Richard, maybe there was room for a more meaningful encounter. A chance to find out whether or not his conscience had troubled him through the years. To see if any part of him had tried to make amends.

He'd come to meet Ledger firmly intending to kill him. Not today, obviously; today was all about sizing him up. But... as Ledger spoke at length about the pile of money he was making, about his reputation being his brand, another possibility began to form in Alan's head. How satisfying it would be to take it all away from him? To destroy his life, rather than simply take it?

He became dimly aware that Ledger's spiel had come to an end and that he'd asked him a question.

'I'm sorry?' he said. 'I missed that...'

Ledger's face flickered with irritation as he downed the last of his coffee and tossed the paper cup into the bin beside his desk. 'I said... do you have any questions?'

Alan looked down at the cup. 'You really should recycle that, Richard.'

'What?' Ledger now looked both irritated and confused.

'Your cup. It's designed to be recycled, not just tossed away. Got to save the planet, right?' he said, staring at it. 'Or don't you give a shit?'

'I'll tell you what, Alan...' Ledger reached down into the bin, grabbed the cup and handed it to him. 'Why don't you take the fucking thing with you? On your way out?'

44

'That explains it!' said Ledger. 'That explains your paper cup with my DNA on it! The son of a bitch took my cup and planted it!'

Boyd nodded slowly. 'Well, that's certainly possible,' he said.

'*Possible?*' Ledger repeated. 'Are you joking? That's obviously what fucking happened!'

'So then,' Boyd continued, 'the obvious question is why. Why would he do that, Richard? Why would he want to frame you? Why would he kill three of your childhood friends and then try to make it look as though you had done it?'

'No comment,' prompted Hart.

'I don't... for Christ's sake... NO COMMENT!' Ledger said, banging the table.

'All right.' Boyd opened his folder. 'Let's talk about something else, shall we?' He shuffled the pages until he had the transcript he wanted before him. 'We interviewed Mark Meadows' wife,' he said. 'She told us about the annual reunions: Mark, Robin, Andy and you would meet up every year on the same day... the twenty-first of August.'

Ledger sat back in his seat and folded his arms. 'No comment.'

'She told us that she overheard Mark and Andy talking about some secret between the four of you. A secret the four of you shared. What can you tell us about that?'

Ledger shook his head. 'No comment.'

'Something happened in the past, didn't it?' Boyd said. 'Something involving all four of you. Something bad enough, that if it came out, even now, thirty years later... it would ruin you.'

Ledger kept his mouth firmly clamped shut.

'So, given that we only have your word that this interview with Smithee took place, I think we're looking at –'

'Alan Smithee's real!' said Ledger. 'I told you what happened.'

'I think,' Boyd continued, 'we're looking at one of two possible scenarios. Either something happened between you and your mates and you killed them to keep them quiet, or...' He paused, watching Ledger's face intently.

Ledger kept silent.

'Or... the four of you did something to someone else. To this Alan Smithee, perhaps? If he exists.'

'He's not made up,' Ledger said.

'So then who is he?' asked Boyd. 'What's he got on you and why would he want to frame you?'

Ledger looked as though he was almost ready to crack.

'Who is Alan Smithee?' asked Boyd again. 'He's someone you know, isn't he? Someone you remember?'

Ledger closed his eyes and kept them shut for a moment before finally opening them. 'Can I talk with my lawyer?' he asked.

Boyd shrugged. 'Sure.'

'Alone.'

Boyd looked at Minter and nodded. 'Interview paused at four fifty-two p.m.,' he said hitting the machine and switching off the audio feed to the observation room. He picked up his mug of coffee. Both Boyd and Minter pushed back their chairs, stood up and headed for the door. 'You've got five minutes,' Boyd said, closing the door behind them.

Okeke emerged from the observation room. 'Oh, he's about to spill, guv,' she whispered.

'I think so too,' he replied, glancing at the closed door to Interview Room Two. 'Right now, I'll bet he's asking his lawyer how much he can safely say.'

'What's your best guess?' asked Minter.

Boyd chewed his bottom lip as he pondered the question. 'My gut says Smithee is real.'

Okeke pulled a face. 'That interview story sounded like complete BS.'

'Maybe. But like I said... that look on his face when he saw those autopsy photos *wasn't*.' He sipped the tepid dregs of coffee from his mug. 'I think he's genuinely rattled now.'

'Scared of what... the cones?' Okeke frowned, unconvinced.

'Afraid of what they imply. What their message is.'

'Which is?' she asked.

Minter leaned in from behind her and hissed into her ear. 'You're next.'

She jumped. 'Fuck off, Minter!'

The door opened and Ledger's lawyer poked his head out. 'My client's ready to resume.'

They filed back in and Okeke returned to the room next door. Boyd pressed the button to restart the recording and enabled the audio link. 'Interview resumed at four fifty-eight p.m.'

'Okay, Richard...' he said. 'Are you ready to tell us what the hell is going on?'

Ledger nodded. 'None of it was planned. It just... Well, things just spun out of control...'

45

Richard spotted him sitting alone on a bench, on the other side of the playing field: a lanky, fluttering crow of a figure. 'Check out the freak show over there,' he said to the others.

His friends turned to look where he was pointing.

'What the fuck?' gasped Mark, bringing the squeaking swing he was idling on to an abrupt halt. 'Is it even human?'

'It's a goth,' said Richard. His expensive boom box was busy pumping S'Express out across the play area. He turned the volume up full whack so that the speakers began to distort as they blasted across the playing field.

The goth looked their way for a moment, then slowly, derisively, shook his head.

The gesture irked Richard. Irked him *a lot*. 'Did that wanker just diss us?' he asked stepping off the roundabout.

The others looked his way. 'Are you gonna sort 'im out then?' asked Andy. 'Or do I have to help you out again?'

Andy was the biggest of them. And dumbest. At fourteen he was already sprouting a faint halo of bum-fluff on his chin. Richard Leeder – true to his name – was their leader, the smart one, the rich one. But Andy was always there, waiting in the wings... challenging him, goading him, waiting for Richard to screw up and lose face.

'Fuckin' right I am,' said Richard, tossing the last half inch of his Marlboro to the ground and striking out across the playing field towards the boy on the bench.

As he neared the lone figure, he realised that the goth was a few years older than him. But he was committed now. He reassured himself that all goths were basically pussies. They were just hippies in black. This one had taken it to the next level: his long, dark hair was a frizzy, backcombed mess. His face was covered in make-up, including a stick-on beauty spot that made him look like a pantomime dame. He was wearing what looked like a crushed-velvet corset around his narrow waist, and a white shirt with ruffles around the neck and cuffs that reminded Richard of Mrs Slocombe from *Are You Being Served?* His parents loved that programme.

Richard drew up in front of the bench and the goth removed a pair of headphones.

'Yes?' he said coolly.

Richard glanced back at his friends. 'What the fuck are you?' he said, loudly enough, he hoped, for them to hear. 'A tranny granny?'

'Oh, go away,' replied the goth. 'Little boy.'

Richard took a defiant step forward. 'Go on. Piss off out of our park, gay boy.'

The goth looked up from his hands, his face as pale as a ghost, his eyes rimmed with dark smudges. He smiled sarcastically. 'You know? Your music's really shit,' he said.

'I'll fuckin' slap you up!' Richard snarled.

He laughed. *'I'll fuckin' slap you up,'* he repeated, mocking the squawk of Richard's just-broken voice. 'Why don't you go back and play Top Trumps with your monkey friends over there?'

Richard could feel his cheeks flushing with rage. 'Suck my balls!'

The goth laughed again.

Richard clenched his fists.

'Ooh!' The goth laughed at him and mock-shivered. 'Scary.'

Richard was well aware that all eyes were on him. His friends were watching the exchange from afar. Andy, no doubt, hoping he was going to return red-faced and humiliated.

The goth noticed him glancing back. 'Oh, I get it... This is about looking tough, right?' He chuckled. 'Well, this isn't working out too well for you, is it? What are you going to do now?'

Richard wished he'd brought his flick knife with him; that would have scared the goth off, he was sure. But he hadn't. All he had were his balled-up fists. 'You'd better fuck off or we'll kick your head in,' he tried.

The goth sighed. 'I'll leave when I'm good and ready,' he said, leaning back on the bench and spreading his arms out along the backrest. 'It's a nice day.' He winked. 'Go on, piss off back to your little friends.' He put his hissing Walkman headphones back on and closed his eyes.

Richard considered his options: he could step forward and smack his smug fucking face. But what if this freak decided to fight back? His mind conjured an appalling image of himself being knocked down by a pussy in girls' clothing. Pinned to the ground before being released to walk back across the playing field with grass stains on his shirt and his tail between his legs.

They'll laugh at me. His role as leader would be over. Andy would step up, turn the others against him, and it would be game over. He'd be Andy's little bitch forever.

He decided to cut his losses. He turned round and headed back. No grass stains. No knock-down, but pondering, as he walked over, how to turn the situation round, quickly... How to save face.

Richard returned to his squad, waiting to hear what he had to say.

Andy was grinning, awaiting his imminent coronation. 'Aw, what's up, Ricky boy...? Did he scare you?'

Richard slumped down onto a swing, rehearsing the response in his head.

Mark was emboldened by Andy's challenge. He got up. 'You wimped out.'

Richard looked up at him.

Make it good. Make it gross.

'He asked me if he could suck me off,' he said.

The look of horror spread across Mark's face like ink across blotting paper.

'He said we could go in there and do it,' Richard added, pointing to the tree line beyond the playing field. That wood – as every boy at Harsham Grammar swore blind – was where all the gays communed at night.

'Fuck off!' gasped Andy. 'You're fuckin' jokin' me, right?'

Make it convincing.

Richard shook his head.

Mark pulled a face. 'Ah, man... that's fucking gross!'

Robin glanced across the field at the goth. 'Should we go and tell someone there's a perv in the field.'

The goth got up off the bench.

'Shit... he's coming over!' hissed Mark.

The goth walked slowly away from the bench, and away from them, in the direction of the woods. 'He's definitely a homo,' said Andy, any doubts he might have had about Ricky's story evaporating.

Richard sighed inwardly. The trick had worked. The mood of disgust and horror had successfully eclipsed the fact that he'd returned humiliated.

And that, really, should have been the end of it.

'SO, WHAT HAPPENED NEXT?' asked Boyd.

Ledger shook his head. 'I... It's... It was a long time ago. But I'm sure it was Andy who suggested it.'

'Suggested what?' Boyd asked.

He looked down at his hands. 'That we should follow him. He was always trying to impress the others. To take control of things.'

'And did he say what his intention was?' asked Boyd.

'He just said we should follow him into the woods and maybe scare him... a bit,' Ledger replied.

'Scare him?'

'You know... make some creepy noises, spook him.'

'Is that what Andy *said*...?' Boyd pressed. 'Or is that what you thought he meant?'

Ledger shrugged. 'I can't remember. It's what I *thought* we were going to do. Just creep him out a bit.'

'And did anyone disagree with his suggestion?' Boyd asked.

Ledger paused for a moment, looked down at his hands and then shrugged. 'I think Robin said we should leave it. I agreed.'

'But you all went into the woods together?' prompted Boyd.

Ledger looked up at him. 'I had no idea what was going to happen... I was... I was just going along with the rest of them...'

46

'There he is,' whispered Richard, pointing.

The other three huddled close to him and followed the direction of his finger through the undergrowth. The goth was sitting down, his back against a tree, fumbling in his pockets for something, before finally producing a packet of tobacco and some Rizlas.

'Fucking hippy pothead,' muttered Andy.

'Maybe we should head back?' said Robin. 'It's getting late.'

'It's four.' Richard sighed derisively. 'Nearly your bedtime, is it, mate?'

Robin shook his head defensively. 'No. I'm just sayin'... there could be others out here.'

'Other homos?' Andy chuckled. 'They only come out at night, Robbo. So they can bum each other by moonlight.'

The others sniggered.

'We should spread out,' said Andy. 'Surround him.'

Andy was taking over again. Trying to take charge. Richard wasn't having that shit. 'No, you idiot. We'll make a ton of noise all moving around.'

'Then what, smart-arse?' replied Andy.

Richard thought quickly. 'Let's just rush him.' He played it out in his head. He'd lead the others in a charge out of the undergrowth. The goth – startled like a deer – would scramble to his feet and bolt. Job done. They could all go back to his place, play pool on Dad's table and congratulate each other.

He relayed this to the others, who nodded. 'Good plan,' whispered Robin.

Richard held his fist out and counted down three-two-one with his fingers. Then they emerged from the undergrowth, all four of them screaming like banshees.

The goth, startled, dropped the roll-up he was making into his lap and attempted to get to his feet.

'GRAB HIM!' screamed Andy.

Unthinking – in the moment – and reacting instinctively to the command, Mark leapt forward and rugby-tackled him to the ground. A second later Andy was astride him, sitting on his chest and holding his arms down.

'Get the fuck off me!' the goth screamed.

'Fucking bender!' snarled Andy.

'WHAT THE FUCK?!' the goth bellowed loudly.

'Someone gag him!' snapped Richard. 'Quickly!'

Mark reacted first, grabbing a fist full of fallen leaves and twigs and shoving them into the struggling goth's open mouth. He immediately tried to spit it all out. Andy tore a strip from the boy's shirt.

'Hold his arm!' Andy ordered Mark. He looked up at Robin who was watching, slack-jawed and useless. 'Hold his other arm down, you prat!'

Robin did as he was told. Andy tied the strip of material around the boy's head, pulling it up over his mouth and nose. The goth's screams were immediately reduced to a gurgling moan.

Mark and Robin, both kneeling on an arm each, looked up at Richard, clearly wondering what they were supposed to do next.

Richard was aware that standing there with his mouth flapping open and closed like a goldfish was, in effect, transferring leadership to Andy. Unless he took charge now, he was done.

~

'So, you had him gagged and pinned down on the ground...' prompted Boyd. 'Go on.'

Now that Ledger was talking freely, allowing him the time to pause and think his way ahead was not a good idea.

'Come on, mate,' coaxed Minter, his voice light and friendly. 'You've started; you might as well get it all out.'

Ledger nodded. 'I just wanted to scare the crap out of him. You know? But...'

'But what?' Minter asked.

'Andy...' he began, looking first at Boyd and then the recording machine. 'Andy was going batshit crazy.'

'What do you mean?' asked Boyd.

'I mean... exactly that. He was big. The biggest and the strongest. And, to be honest with you, he was beginning to scare me.' Ledger shook his head, his face crumpled with emotion. His voice began to quiver. 'He... he was out of control. I couldn't rein him in. He took over...'

~

'He looks like a ladyboy,' said Richard. He grinned. 'You reckon he's got one of each, lads?'

Andy laughed. He loved the idea. 'Shit, yeah. I gotta see this...' He got up from the boy's chest and grabbed hold of the waistband of his jeans. The goth squirmed violently kicking out at him.

'Let's have a butcher's, shall we?' He jerked the boy's jeans down to his knees and stared at the Y-fronts revealed beneath. 'Shit, that's disappointing. I was expecting lady panties, or are they under those?'

He grabbed the boy's Y-fronts and jerked those down to his knees too. All four boys stared at his exposed genitals.

Andy staggered back, disgusted. 'Ah, fuck! So he's just a normal bender, then.' He looked down at him. 'You lot like it up the arse, don't you?'

He looked around, searching for something.

'What are you doing?' Robin asked.

Just then the goth worked an arm free from beneath Mark's knees and started flailing.

'Shit! Get his arm!' snapped Andy. He looked at Mark. 'Grab it!'

Mark did as he was told, dropping his weight down on to the boy's arm and pinning it back down to the ground once more.

Andy resumed his search.

'What are you doing?' asked Robin again.

Andy hurried across the clearing to a spot beneath the drooping bough of a pine tree and began kicking through the dead leaves and nettles.

'What the fuck are you doing?!' snapped Richard.

'Just a sec...' Andy replied.

As far as Richard was concerned, they were finished. He could see that the poor bastard on the ground was swivel-eyed with fear. They'd scared him and humiliated him. Job done.

'Let's go,' he said to the other two, 'before someone comes along.'

'Wait!' Andy emerged from beneath the low-hanging branch and back into the waning sunlight, holding aloft a large fir cone and grinning as though he'd just pulled a rabbit out of a top hat. He stepped over the goth and sat down heavily on his chest. He waggled the cone in front of his wide, make-up-smudged eyes.

'Looky-look what I've found!' he whispered menacingly.

Richard advanced. 'What the fuck are you doing with that?'

'We're gonna give him a bit of what he wants, right?' He got up from the boy's heaving chest and circled around to study his squirming bare legs, bound together at the knees by his jerked-down pants and jeans. He pulled them down further, down to his ankles.

The goth clearly understood what he was intending and started to wildly thrash his bound legs.

'Hold his legs down!' Andy snapped.

Richard remained where he was.

'Ricky! I said, HOLD HIS FUCKING LEGS!'

For the first time since they'd first bumped into each other at Harsham Grammar, on day one of the first term in their first year... Richard was genuinely afraid of him. There was missionary zeal on his face; he had his Big Idea and he was going to damn well see it through. His size and strength had made him a handy addition to Richard's little gang – the biddable attack dog who'd do what he was told because he liked hanging out with the smart, rich kid and playing pool on his daddy's full-sized table. But now Andy was a vicious, untrained dog that was out of control.

Richard found himself kneeling down and settling his weight on the goth's drumming feet. He realised his lie had set all this in motion. The goth had told him to piss off back to his little friends, that was all. There'd been no gayness. No bender talk. And now he was trapped by his own bullshit. If he wimped out... or, worse, told the others he'd made it up... all the pent-up adrenaline that he could see on Andy's flushed face would swing round and be directed at him.

Andy held up the cone and the goth screamed through his mouthful of leaves, twigs and the cloth gag.

'OKAY,' said Boyd. 'You'd better take a moment.'

Ledger's account had emerged in garbled pieces. His eyes were red-raw with tears, his nose streaming. His shoulders shuddered as he heaved in air and rattled it out. 'I... I... couldn't... s-stop him...'

Boyd was damned if he was going to comfort the man with some supportive platitude.

'So, what state did you all leave this boy in, Richard?' he asked.

Ledger dipped his head.

'I think that's enough now,' Hart said. 'You can see he's clearly distressed and unfit to continue.'

Boyd ignored him. 'Richard?'

Ledger continued to sob into his hands. Boyd could see dabs of moisture trickling down onto his knuckles. Tears weren't an easy thing to produce at will from his long experience of interviewing 'remorseful' perps over the years. The hitching breath, the endless eye-rubbing, the cry-baby voice – he'd witnessed those many times.

'Richard? How was he left?' he repeated more softly.

Ledger shook his head in response. He did his best to dry his eyes and wipe the snot from the end of his nose.

'Andy...' he began, then paused. He took another long, steadying, deep breath. 'Andy smashed a rock down onto his face.'

'A rock?!' Boyd asked, shocked.

Ledger nodded.

'Was he attempting to kill him?'

Ledger nodded again.

Boyd wanted that clarified for the tape. 'You left him in the woods... believing he was dead?'

'Oh God... I... We all just panicked... and ran...'

Boyd had heard more than enough for now. He reached for the machine. 'The time is five forty-seven p.m. Interview terminated.'

47

'Joint enterprise?' repeated Lesley Lloyd. Her voice filled Superintendent Hatcher's wood-panelled office. They'd managed to catch her before she'd headed home for the day and, by the sound of her voice over the speakerphone, she wasn't too thrilled about it.

Boyd had given the CPS lawyer a bullet-point overview of the case and the evidence they'd gathered against Richard Ledger, including the gist of his detailed statement. Joint enterprise was what he was pinning his hopes on as the line they needed to cross to detain him.

'No, sorry,' she replied. 'That's a dirty term these days. It doesn't sit well with jurors. They see it as, at best, lazy policing… and, at worst, a police-state catch-all. It just won't stick.'

Boyd let his head drop to his chest.

'Plus, he was a minor when the incident took place,' she continued. 'That'll be a mitigating factor. It was 1989, you said?'

'Yes,' replied Boyd.

'So no hate-crime legislation at that time, I'm afraid.

Homophobia wasn't a crime back then, just an attitude. Bloody dark ages. Anyway... it sounds as if you've got bigger fish to fry with this Smithee character out there – who you're presuming is the victim of that assault *and* your serial murderer?'

'Yes,' said Boyd.

'Well... seems to me that he should be your focus, DCI Boyd. We can loop back and deal with this Ledger chap later.' She paused. 'Are we good? I really have to go.'

'All right. Thanks for hanging on for us, Lesley,' said Hatcher.

'No problem.' The call ended.

Hatcher sat back in her chair and looked from Boyd to Sutherland. 'So...?'

'It sounds like you're going to have to let him go for now,' said Sutherland. 'Is he a flight risk?'

'He's got money. But...' Boyd shook his head. 'I get the impression he's more interested in us finding this Smithee than worrying about any charges.'

Hatcher stroked her fountain pen, which she'd been using to take notes during Boyd's update. 'He volunteered that statement. His lawyer will make that point if this assault ever gets to court.' She absently doodled a spiral in the margin of her notepad. 'Plus, he'll know that fleeing the country would imply guilt later down the line. So, you're right – I shouldn't imagine he'll be a flight risk.'

Boyd nodded.

'I do have a couple of thoughts,' said Hatcher. 'We're *assuming* this Smithee is the victim of the assault?'

'Aggravated sexual assault,' Boyd added. 'And attempted murder, according to Ledger's account.'

'Right. But we're currently assuming Smithee's the victim? And those three bodies from the storage place were the perpetrators of the assault? That's the prevailing theory, right?'

'Yes,' replied Boyd.

'Although we have no proof at all that he even exists yet. Correct?'

'Yes, ma'am.'

'So...' She looked at her notes again. 'This entire statement from Ledger could be something he made up? There's nothing, so far, to corroborate any of it?'

'No. Not yet.'

'Then it's entirely plausible he's got you looking for someone you'll never find. In fact, he could be this Smithee, who's been paying for that lock-up – and who, for whatever motive he has, is responsible for the murders of the other three. And everything he told you this afternoon was about explaining away his DNA on a coffee cup?'

'That's possible, yes, ma'am,' Boyd agreed.

'But I'm getting the impression you're not buying that? He's obviously had time to think up that very detailed story, Boyd.'

'But I honestly think he was surprised that his DNA was in the lock-up. We sprung the deaths of his friends on him and he was, in my opinion, genuinely shocked. I just don't buy that this was a previously rehearsed story. I'm not saying we take everything he said at face value. He may have been more involved in the assault than he's letting on. After all, none of the others are going to say any different, are they?'

'But if this goth was killed...'

'He said they left *thinking* he was dead, ma'am.'

'All right, but if he was dead, there'd have been a body. And if there was no body, then presumably someone would have found him and called an ambulance... There'd be a record of that somewhere, surely.'

'I've put Minter and Okeke on it,' Boyd said. 'But it was 1989...' He pulled a face. 'All paper records. And I doubt any paramedic or A & E doctor will recall treating a specific head injury thirty years ago.'

Hatcher sighed. 'Then we have to hope the assault was reported to the police. And if you don't find anything?' she pressed. 'What then? Are you still going to assume Smithee is real?'

'That paper cup feels planted. It was the only other item in the storage locker, apart from the crates. We found no prints or DNA from Ledger on the crates themselves. Which suggests he would have been very, very careful. Then... to casually leave behind a cup that he'd been slurping from ...' Boyd shook his head.

Hatcher sighed. 'Fine. Well, make sure you keep me up to date, Boyd.

'Yes, ma'am,' Boyd replied.

'There's a question that begs to be asked,' said Sutherland. 'Is Richard Ledger at risk? At the moment? I mean, if this Smithee exists and killed the other three, why not finish the job, hmm?'

'That might have been his plan,' Boyd agreed. 'But we think the storage unit being auctioned and the bodies being discovered has thrown a wrench into it.'

Hatcher tutted and looked at her watch. It was getting late. 'There's one other scenario to consider,' she said.

Both men looked at her.

'What if his account is, essentially accurate, but... Ledger himself was the victim?'

48

Minter returned to them with a tray of food. It had been Okeke's suggestion to indulge in a McSupper.

'A Big Mac meal for the boss,' he said, handing it over. 'A McFishy meal for you...'

'What's yours?' asked Okeke.

'I've got a McPlanty,' he replied. He passed out the fries, sauces and coffees, and then slipped the tray onto an empty table next to them.

'Of course you do,' she muttered, looking at his McSalad side and bottle of water.

'I'd have thought you'd be all about the protein,' said Boyd.

Minter shook his head. 'No gym tonight, boss. I'm done in. It's been a long day.'

Boyd nodded. He felt the same. Ledger had walked out of the station half an hour ago with his lawyer with what looked, to Boyd, like a smirk on his face.

'I still can't believe there wasn't enough to hold him,' said Okeke.

'CPS calls it,' said Boyd, digging into his fries. 'No point cracking the eggs if they can't make the omelette.'

'So what's our next move, boss?' Minter asked.

Boyd had relayed his conversation with Hatcher to them while they waited for Ledger's release paperwork to be processed. 'We'll have to dig around a bit more to corroborate his story. If it's true, then presumably a 999 call was logged. If Smithee made a full recovery, then did he report the incident to the police? And if he didn't recover, or if he was left brain-damaged,' continued Boyd, 'then wouldn't someone related to him have called the police about his assault?'

'There was nothing on LEDS,' said Okeke.

'It'll be somewhere in the paper records, I bet,' said Boyd.

Every police station in the UK had a bank of dusty filing cabinets full of handwritten statement forms and case files... still waiting to be manually entered into the system. It was one of those tasks that could be chipped away at during a slow, empty in-tray day. But, of course, in-trays were never empty.

'You two should head over to Harsham police station and ask – very politely – if you can dig around in their legacy cabinets tomorrow,' he said. 'And I'll get Warren and O'Neal to trawl through local newspaper archives. The *Argus* might have written up something about the incident.'

'If... it happened,' said Okeke.

'Are you buying Her Madge's suggestion?' asked Minter.

'Hatcher could be right,' Boyd conceded. 'If we draw a complete blank, then I suppose we're unlikely to ever find out what really happened.'

'And of course Ledger'll walk,' said Okeke.

Boyd nodded. 'We only have the one piece of forensic

evidence and Ledger has provided a plausible explanation for that. His defence would argue that the cup was not found on the first sweep of the lock-up. Suggesting, at best, incompetence on our part; at worst, an attempt to plant evidence.'

He took a bite out of his Big Mac and spoke with his mouth full. 'We'll need to build a credible timeline running from 2011 to the present that would indicate Ledger could have been responsible for their deaths. Phone records might help. Particularly his.' He took another bite of his burger. 'I keep replaying his reaction to the photos in the interview, though. That was one of the most convincing responses I've ever seen in an interview room. He was genuinely shaken.'

'He certainly didn't seem overly concerned at the idea there was someone out there who might want him dead, though,' said Minter.

'Hmm. He didn't, did he?' agreed Okeke. '*I'd* be bloody well begging for police protection if that was me.'

49

Richard Ledger, parked his Land Rover in his basement garage and switched the engine off.

'Graham, you're sure there's no chance of a joint enterprise conviction?'

'I'm sure.' His lawyer reply came out of the car's sound system. 'Yours is the only account of what happened back then. And, like I said, judges and magistrates are exceedingly twitchy about the police using joint enterprise these days.'

'Right.'

'Added to that... you were a minor at the time. You also volunteered to give your account when you didn't have to. That'll play in your favour, Richard. Particularly if I request the interview recording be played to any jury. You were clearly distressed. Traumatised by what you witnessed as a boy.'

Richard settled back in the seat. 'It was difficult. Reliving that.'

'It sounded horrific.'

'It was. It really was.'

'Look, Richard... I'm concerned for your safety. We should probably have asked for some kind of protection. This Smithee chap obviously knows how to find you...'

'I think he was actually sussing me out when he came to my office.'

He heard his lawyer suck in a breath. 'I thought you said it was just some weird interview?'

'It was a little more than that. I realise that now. I think he wanted to see if I recognised him. Maybe he was trying to figure out if I was worth blackmailing.'

'Why the hell didn't you mention that?'

'I... well... I was concerned that it might look as if I have something to hide. Some involvement. I didn't do anything. I mean... I should have done something. I should have tried to step in and stop what was going on. But... shit... Christ... I wish –'

'All right, all right. It's okay. Take a moment.'

Richard took a deep breath. 'It looks as though he killed Andy, Mark and Robin, right? They got the special treatment because they all played an active part in the assault. But because I held back... I think, somehow, he sees me as less culpable, deserving a lesser punishment, maybe.'

'Look, Richard. I think, if the police pull you in again for interview, you should consider mentioning all that. The fact that he hasn't treated you the same way as the others clearly suggests, as you say, that he blames you less. That's another win if this ends up in a court.'

'Right.'

'I mean, did he *specifically* ask you for money?'

'It was... I can't recall exactly. At the time... I thought something very odd was going on, but... Christ, it was over a year ago. It only came back to me after those detectives told me Robin and the others had been murdered.'

'You didn't think about it before? I mean, before today's interview?'

'No. Because I thought that goth boy was long dead. I...'

'Jesus!' hissed his lawyer. 'Okay, you don't ever say *that* again, right? You say you suspected he was hurt badly that day... and you wished you'd called an ambulance at the time, but you didn't because... you were in shock. Afraid. Scared that your friend Andy might do the same to you.'

'I should have, though! Jesus. I should have done something...' Richard could hear the raw emotion rising up in his own voice.

'All right. All right. Just take a breath.'

He sucked in a couple of deep, ragged breaths. 'I'm okay. It's...'

'You were a minor. You witnessed a violent, sexualised assault. You witnessed Andy attempt to kill that boy with a rock. And it's something you've repressed. You've struggled with it for all these years and felt guilty that you didn't do the right thing at the time. Is that a fair representation?'

Richard rubbed his eyes and sniffed. 'Right. Yes.'

'And all those annual reunions of yours – that was all about processing that guilt, yes? Trying to make sense of what happened that afternoon?'

'I suppose so. Yes.'

'Right. Then that's what we should probably share with the police. I think the smart move would be for me to arrange for a follow-up interview where you can tell all this to them. We can also ask for some sort of protection. Because... if he's still out there, then –'

'Okay. Good idea,' Richard said.

'All right. One last thing, Richard. And I need you to be honest with me... Has Alan Smithee attempted to make contact again with you since?'

'No. It was just that one time.'

'Okay. So you're back home now?'

'Yes. I'm home.'

'Good. Lock your doors and get some sleep. I'll call you tomorrow morning.'

Richard bid him goodnight and ended the call. He closed his eyes and let out a sigh of relief. The tears over the phone, the tears back in the police station really hadn't been that hard to produce. It looked as though those two detectives – the friendly Welsh one and the bearded grump sitting beside him – had both lapped them up.

But the fact remained... the crowlike figure who had haunted his dreams for the last three decades and become a ghostly raggedy caricature – the pale face, the smudged eyes, the wild black hair clogged with drying blood and spattered brains – hadn't died in the woods. He'd survived. He'd remembered. He'd somehow tracked down the other three and killed them. And two years ago he'd come knocking on Richard's office door with a fake CV and that stupid alias.

If he doesn't want me dead... what the fucking hell DOES he want from me?

50

Alistair sipped his coffee through the plastic lid, sat back on the park bench and studied the empty playground. At eleven o'clock at night – bathed in a sickly sodium light and absent of little toddlers bustling from the swings to the climbing frame and back again – a playground could be a forlorn place. The daytime cries of joy and excitement covered the creaking of rusty swing chains, the rattle of old bearings beneath the roundabout, the rustle of wind teasing empty crisp packets across the soft-play tarmac.

His eyes lifted from the fenced-off play area to the gated mews beyond. Those were nice houses and apartments in there. A nice little dormitory mews for the rich, close enough to central London to make for an easy commute, far enough from London to almost feel like a cosy rural hamlet – if you could ignore the light pollution, the distant twinkle of Canary Wharf and the faint, ever-present hum of traffic.

They were a mixture of mock-Tudor and modern houses, refurbs and new builds, ring-fenced with wrought-iron swirls and peppered with CCTV cameras to keep the plebs at arm's length.

He knew which one belonged to Ledger. It was the modern-looking slate-grey two-storey house. All floor-to-ceiling windows and mood-lighting within.

He knew Ledger was home. He'd watched him pull up at the gates in his Range Rover and wave a key fob at them. The gates slid to one side and he'd watched as Ledger had driven along the mews to the end and down the ramp into his basement garage. And now, every so often, through the slatted blinds he detected movement as the man went about his solitary evening routine.

I'm just here, Richard. Just here... sitting in the playground.

It had been two weeks now since the bodies had been discovered. The female superintendent had made a good effort at giving the impression – from behind her nest of microphones – that they were on the case and had a number of leads to follow. But in these two weeks there had been no more news.

He had no idea how fast a police investigation worked on a newsworthy case like this one. Did they work around the clock? Did they work in bleary-eyed shifts through the night? Blitz through weekends? Or was it like any other job...? Tools down on Friday and everything could wait until Monday morning.

Were they closing in on him now? Had his name been scrawled on some whiteboard at police HQ?

Alistair doubted it. What had occurred had happened a long time ago, before the internet stored every little thing in its vast digital cloud.

He'd been found in the woods by a woman walking her dog and rushed to hospital. They'd managed to save him, but he'd been told later that it had been a close-run thing.

The police were called to his bedside – and he'd been asked if he wanted to report a crime. His nose had been broken, an orbital socket had been crushed, his skull had been badly fractured, he was missing four teeth at the front, his jaw had been broken in three places... and his rectal passage stitched where it had been torn. He was never going to be a pretty boy again... and he was destined for a lifetime of discomfort. Not to mention the crippling anxiety and the traumatic flashbacks that would plague him years later.

At the time he'd genuinely wanted to help the police identify who'd done this to him, but the last thing he'd been able to recall was listening to the Cure on his Sony Walkman as he'd headed towards the playing field.

His ex-foster parents had visited a couple of times during his rehabilitation. That was nice – they didn't have to... He'd been a difficult foster child. And then, six months later, when he'd just turned eighteen, he'd been discharged, looking very different. His hair, which had been shaved off so that they could operate on his skull, had grown back to a short patchy fuzz; his face was no longer something anyone would want to frame with long wild locks and highlight with make-up.

He'd emerged from hospital a very different person. And with a different name.

Whereas before, his first name had suited his effete, Byron-esque image and aspirations, his middle name now suited him better. No longer wearing crushed velvet and jangling bangles, he looked like a borstal bruiser – the world's least successful boxer... so why fucking bother? These days it was jeans and trainers from Primark and a long list of casual labour jobs booked through an employment agency.

But twenty uninspiring years later everything changed once again...

~

'*Go on, mate... Shove it in there...*'

An innocuous phrase that he must have heard a thousand or more times in his life: helping a friend pack and move house; on the telly as some Albert Square trader in *EastEnders* shoved potatoes into a bag; a customer at the checkout in Aldi; the lady at his local post office taking parcels from him over the counter.

But on this occasion – with the 'maaaaate' drawn out – it triggered a panic attack, taking him back to the moment twenty-two years ago.

He glanced up from the till at the face of the customer; it was a man with blotchy red skin and a mop of greasy brown hair, who was holding open a canvas shopping bag. No one he knew. Just a random customer who'd selected half a dozen old eighties action movies from the stock-clearance dumpbin and was waiting patiently for him with his bag wide open.

All of a sudden he felt sick, ready to hurl his Greggs breakfast all over the counter.

'Are you all right?' asked his colleague.

He felt dizzy, breathless. His chest felt as though it was collapsing in on his lungs, squeezing the air out of them. 'I... I need a moment,' he managed.

He stepped back from the counter, clumsily, supporting himself by holding onto a shelf behind him. Somehow he made it all the way to the back of the store, through the staff door and into the toilet cubicle. He slammed the door shut behind him, collapsed onto his knees and threw up his breakfast into the toilet bowl.

He heard the word again, in his head.

Maaaate.

He wasn't seeing the mess in the toilet bowl now; he was seeing something from a long time ago. A bed of brown leaves and twigs. Right up close. He could actually feel them pressed against his face... but far worse was the excruciating agony as he felt something jagged and sharp... *violating* him.

And, behind his back, the whooping of delight. The chorus of young male voices, all barely broken, goading and egging each other on.

And that phrase: '*Go on, mate... Shove it in!*'

He retched again, but his stomach was empty. He wiped his mouth and collapsed onto his behind in that small cubicle. It was the eyes... He remembered now. Those wide-excited, gleaming eyes...

The man he'd just served... had been one of them.

Unmistakably.

'*Maaaaate.*'

51

'Ahoy there!' called out Sully. 'This is very interesting!'

There was no reply.

He turned in his seat to see that Magnusson had her headphones on and from the faint trilling female voices leaking out from them he recognised Léo Delibes' 'Flower Duet'. He pushed his chair so that it rolled across the linoleum floor and tapped her shoulder. 'Karen?'

'Jeepers!' She lurched in her seat and dropped the breakfast bap she'd been chomping on into her lap.

Sully raise a brow. 'Jeepers?'

She removed her headphones and retrieved the bread roll, sausage and fried egg from between her thighs and rebuilt it. 'Yes, *jeepers*... you made me drop my bloody breakfast.'

'Who says *jeepers*... apart from Thelma and Shaggy?'

She picked at the crumbs in her lap. 'I do. What do you want?'

'To show you something.' He curled a finger, inviting her to slide her chair over with his, back to his desk.

They both rolled gracefully across the floor like chair-bound figure-skaters and Sully pointed at his monitor. He'd been reviewing the forensics that Magnusson and O'Neal had collected from the lock-up. On the screen were a number of open image files: photos taken at the scene, along with several images of the fingerprints lifted from the crates, enhanced for clarity with digitised markers identifying various significant whorls and curls.

'So... I've just been reviewing the prints you managed to lift from those plastic crates.'

She looked at him guardedly. 'And?'

'Worry ye not, a splendid job was done...'

'And yet I sense a "but" is on its way.'

'So...' He grabbed hold of his mouse and minimised the photos taken from the scene, leaving just the fingerprint images open. 'This print, which was taken from the lid of one of the crates,' he said, pointing, 'is identified as matching one of those two panners.' He checked his notes for the name. 'Sid Beckett.'

'Right.'

He pointed to another image. 'And this one, also lifted from the same lid, matches up with...'

'Colin Holmes,' she supplied.

'All right. So, according to the interview notes, they both went in, opened up just one crate, the top one in the stack, found the human remains inside and then immediately backed away and called it in.'

'Right,' she said.

'But their prints are also on some of the other crates too.'

'Yes. They must have touched several of them beforehand. Maybe straightening them up... or...'

'No, that's fine,' said Sully. 'They walked in expecting to

find a bunch of resalable bric-a-brac, not a crime scene. So I'd fully expect to see their prints all over the place.'

'Then what?' she prompted.

Sully pointed at another fingerprint image. 'So... this one was taken from the light switch inside the lock-up. From the side of the switch's plastic case, to be precise.'

She nodded. 'Yes... they would have had to turn the light on when they stepped in. Obviously.'

'Obviously.' He smiled. 'So far, so good. Right?'

She nodded.

Sully clicked on two of the prints lifted from the lock-up and set them side by side. He pointed at the one on the left. 'Thumbprint from the lid of the plastic crate.' He then pointed at the one on the right. 'Print from an index finger on the side of the light switch.'

She nodded again. 'Right.'

'Obviously different digits, one thumb, one index finger... but comparing them side by side, what do you notice?'

She leant in to look more closely. 'Umm... the thumbprint from the lid looks a little sharper. Tidier.'

He nodded.

She looked at the print from the light switch. 'That one's less defined. But that would probably be down to the amount of finger pressure applied and the motion at the time. He casually reached out to flip the switch... but with the lid he would have had to prise it off.'

'True. But look at the centre area of both prints... where we have enough detail to make comparison markers. What do you see?'

She frowned and pursed her lips. 'Well... I'd say the print from the lid is a tad sharper, more defined. But, like I said, he'd have applied more pressure there.'

Sully nodded. 'Yes, I take your point, but... look more closely at the prints' ridges.'

She peered at the screen. 'Well, the ridges from the lid are... thinner, I suppose, than the other one.'

'Fatty acids,' said Sully. 'Present on our skin and deposited in the print. Over time the fatty acids tend to flow down into the "valleys" between the ridges, creating thicker-looking ridge lines.'

She looked again. The difference in thickness was there, subtle, but – now that Sully had drawn her attention to it – noticeable.

'There's a research paper on this, by the way, on the migration over time of heavier biomolecules in a fingerprint.' He pulled it up. 'It's not a precise way to age a print. We all have slightly different chemical compositions on our skin, so there's no constant yardstick to judge the age of a print, but...'

'But...' She nodded slowly; she was getting his point now. 'You're saying the print on the light switch occurred...'

'A lot earlier than the print on the lid.' Sully grinned. 'Our lucky auction winners

appear to have had access to the lock-up a significant time period before they should have. And both prints belong to the same person.'

'Which one?'

He pointed to one of the print cards that Magnusson had made when both men had come in to give their statements. 'Him...'

52

Okeke blew dust off the top box file and immediately regretted it. She sneezed, six times in a row, each one escaping like a Chihuahua's *yip*.

Each one counted by Minter. 'Bloody hell, Okeke, are you going for the world record?'

She casually flipped a finger at him as she wiped her nose and eyes with a tissue. 'Bloody dust,' she croaked. She carried the stack of box files over to a collapsible table that the station's sergeant had set up for them down in the basement.

Minter pulled up a chair for her and she sat down next to him. 'LIO files 1988 to 1989,' she said as she set them down. The sergeant had explained that half of the filing cabinets' contents had been entered into the old Holmes system some years back when they'd had funding for a couple of civilian admins to help. The priority had been to enter the intelligence gathered on the 'frequently active scrotes' in the area: known aliases, known associates, book-ing-in forms, statements that included references to them, arrest photographs and the like.

The lesser priority had been everything else.

She opened the first box file and sighed at the disorganised stack of papers: 'everything else' included everything from written statement forms to stacks of clipped receipts, photocopied photo-ID album pages to old dog-eared PC notebooks. None of it categorised or chronologically ordered; the only common denominator was that somewhere on each faded piece of paper was the year 1988 or 1989.

'It's a bloody shambles,' grumbled Minter as he stared at the bulging contents of his box file.

The sergeant, a grizzled old sweat who looked as though he was just a year or two away from collecting his police pension, had promised to bring them a coffee. An hour later they heard him clomping down the stairs, the sound of jangling keys on his belt and accompanied by asthmatic wheezing.

'Here you go,' he said, setting down a couple of chipped mugs on the camping table. 'Sorry about the delay... we just had a D and D brought in.'

'Bit early in the day for that, isn't it?' asked Okeke.

He sighed. 'Roger's one of our regulars. He drinks in the local graveyard; this morning he was caught pissing on the graves.' He lingered beside the table. 'So what are you two looking for?'

'An incident that happened locally... quite a while back,' offered Minter.

The sergeant noted the year on the box spines. 'In 1989?'

'Right.'

Okeke looked up from the stacks of paper she'd sorted

into various piles. 'Any remote chance you were stationed here back then?'

He nodded. 'Aye, as a matter of fact. Never been rotated anywhere else; I've worked my entire career out of this old building.'

She smiled. 'The police force forgotten all about you?'

He laughed. 'Feels that way.' He pulled up a stool and settled down on it. 'Mind you, I've got no complaints. Harsham's hardly crime central. The only hotspot is Coleman Road Estate. Got a couple of families down there that account for about half the petty crime in these parts.'

He scanned the piles of paper spread out. 'So what's the incident? I might remember it.'

'A violent sexual assault of a male teenager,' she replied. 'It happened in the woods next to the playing field.'

'Oh, that's all gone now,' he replied. 'It's all new builds. A hundred or so identical red-brick homes packed in with tiny gardens overlooked by everyone else.'

'But does that ring any bells?' she prompted him. 'You said Harsham's a quiet place...'

He stroked the tip of his nose absently. 'You know... I think it might do.' He clenched his eyes shut as he concentrated. She waited for him to say something, and was beginning to suspect he'd dozed off when he finally spoke again.

'The lad was found in the woods. Barely alive. Awful head injuries, if I recall.'

'That sounds like the one,' said Minter hopefully.

'What happened?' asked Okeke.

He clenched his eyes shut again. 'The lad... survived as far as I remember. I think my sergeant at the time – David Wood – tried to get a statement out of him after he was out of danger, but nothing doing.'

'No descriptions? No likely suspects?'

He shook his head. 'Woody said it was a dead end. The boy was next to useless as a witness.'

'Uncooperative?'

He shrugged. 'No, not uncooperative. I think he just couldn't remember anything about it.'

'I don't suppose you could recall the boy's name... could you?' asked Okeke hopefully.

He screwed up his eyes again and grimaced. 'I'm pretty sure his first name... began with an A.'

'Alan?'

He shook his head.

'Andrew?' tried Minter. That prompted another head-shake from the sergeant. 'Andy? Arthur?'

'No,' he replied. 'Longer. Sort of... like a posh-sounding name.'

'Alexander?'

'Archie. Archibald?' offered Okeke. 'Albert?'

He opened his eyes. 'Alistair. His first name was Alistair.'

'It was a serious assault,' said Minter. 'An attempted murder. It must have been passed up to your local CID?'

'You know... I don't think it actually was,' the sergeant replied.

'What?' Okeke said, incredulous. 'Are you serious?'

The man hunched his shoulders. 'Well, there was nothing much to work with. The lad recovered. I mean –'

'It was a sexual assault and an attempted murder, and your sergeant didn't pass it up?' Okeke shook her head.

'It was in those woods, see?' the sergeant replied. 'All sorts used to congregate down there. It was full of local druggies, alcoholics, perverts... you name it.'

'Perverts?' Okeke raised her brows.

He winced guiltily. 'Well, you know... men... benders...

Sorry. I know that's politically incorrect lingo now. But, you understand, back then...'

Okeke shook her head again. 'Not really. I do believe there was a correct term to use in those days as well.'

The sergeant's mottled cheeks burned red. 'Times change, all right?' He spread his hands. 'The lingo changes.'

She was about to respond but Minter nudged her foot with his under the table and cut in: 'Well, your Sergeant Wood... he must have logged *something,* right?'

'Yes. He obviously opened a file but...' The old man got up off his stool. 'Hold on. Give me a minute...'

Minter watched him head back to the stairs. 'Where are you...?'

'Upstairs. Top floor. We've got a rainy-day cabinet for some of the old cases. Let me see if I can dig it out.'

They watched him clomp wearily up the steps again, keys jangling, wheezing with the effort as he went.

'Jeez,' uttered Okeke once they were alone again. '*Benders*. Let's hear it for the Good Old Days.'

53

'Chief?'

Boyd looked up from the keyboard he'd been stabbing at, slowly transcribing the Ledger interview, one finger-pecked character at a time. He was never going to be one of those clatter-clatter types like Okeke who could type with all ten digits without even looking at the QUERTY arrangement of the alphabet *and* hold a conversation at the same time.

'O'Neal?' he replied. He was holding something he'd printed out in one hand.

'I've got something, sir. From the *Argus* news archive.' He handed it to Boyd.

It was a clipping, dated 22 August 1989.

Yesterday, local police announced they were investigating a serious violent assault that occurred in Thatcham Woods, Harsham, a local 'trouble spot' according to community officer PS David Wood. The victim of the assault, Alistair Muldoon (17), was sexually assaulted, bludgeoned and left for dead, and was discovered by local dog walker Mary Carlisle.

'I thought the poor lad was a dead body when I first saw him,' she claimed. 'But when he started groaning, I realised he needed urgent help.'

An ambulance was called and Muldoon was rushed to hospital. Police are currently working on the theory that Muldoon, a foster-care teenager, may have randomly encountered a sexual predator in the woods. Thatcham Woods is known as a gathering place for 'gay swingers', and police are hoping that Alistair Muldoon will recover from the serious head injuries he sustained and be able to provide an account of what happened and a description of his assailant.

Boyd looked up from the printout and smiled. 'Finally. A name! Nice one, O'Neal.'

'Thank you, sir.'

Just then his phone buzzed on the desk. Boyd picked it up and saw it was Okeke calling. He swiped to answer. 'Yup?'

'Guv, we got lucky. The local police sub-station have some paperwork on an open-ended investigation into an assault that occurred...'

'On August the twenty-first, 1989. The reunion date.'

'Huh? How do you know?' she asked.

'O'Neal has literally just handed me a clipping from the *Argus*. Our victim is Alistair Muldoon.'

'No. That's his foster family's surname. The paper must have got that detail muddled. His name is actually Alistair Holmes.'

'*Holmes?*' The name jangled in Boyd's head. 'Hold on... Wasn't one of those two lock-up bidders called Holmes?'

He heard her huff a laugh. Not in humour but giddy excitement. 'The victim's full name, guv?'

'Go on...'

'Was Alistair *Colin* Holmes.'

'Shit. That's...'

'Our auction bidder,' she jumped in. 'Colin Holmes. His age tallies as well. Late forties, early fifties, isn't he?'

It was something like that he vaguely recalled. Although he'd looked older. Life clearly hadn't been kind.

He spotted movement from the corner of his eye and looked round to see Sully and Magnusson hurrying over, weaving through the cubicle farm towards him.

'Hold on,' he said to Okeke, 'it's like London buses here. Sully looks like he's got something.'

Sully drew up beside O'Neal. For once his dry sardonic demeanour had been supplanted by the wide-eyed glee of someone who'd just found a tenner down the back of an old sofa.

'You've got something?' asked Boyd.

'Oh yes indeedy, Boyd. I've got your killer for you. It's Colin Holmes,' he announced. 'He's one of those two panners who "found" the bodies.'

BOYD ASKED O'NEAL TO DRIVE, and Warren was seated in the back. He tapped the address they had for Colin Holmes into the satnav. Holmes lived over in Bexhill-on-Sea, which was just over five miles away.

'Uniforms are going in first,' he said. 'If he's there, O'Neal, as you were first to ID him, *you* can do the arrest and caution.'

O'Neal nodded, looked pointedly at Warren in the rear-view mirror and grinned. 'Cheers, chief.'

'Do you need an idiot card or can you remember it?' Boyd asked him.

O'Neal glanced across at his boss as he turned out of the station's driveway and left onto Bohemia Road. 'What? Of course I –'

'I'm pulling your leg,' said Boyd. However, he recalled, a botched caution had been used as part of a defence from his time in the Met. Not that it had particularly impressed the judge as a defence, but it had thrown a shadow over the competence of the MI team involved at the time.

'But you might want to run through it,' he said.

'Okay...' O'Neal began. 'You do not have to say anything –'

'In your head,' added Boyd.

As O'Neal turned right down at the front, Boyd glanced towards the White Rock Theatre hoping to catch a glimpse of Charlotte in the lobby. She was preparing for an event tonight, a shadow-theatre dance troupe who were over from France. He had no idea at all what the hell that involved, but the event board outside the entrance indicated that the tickets were all sold out.

His mind switched back to Sully's discovery... and the very lengthy technical explanation about old versus recent fingerprints. That would be crucial evidence further down the line. Motives and opportunities aside, that was one piece of evidence they had in the bank that would be hard for any defence to sidestep. How could Colin Holmes' older fingerprints be in the lock-up unless he'd been there before?

As for the motive... If Ledger's account was credible, then – simply put – it was revenge. Colin Holmes had been assaulted and tortured by those boys, before they'd bashed his head in with a rock. Although he'd survived, he'd been unable to help the police at the time, according to Okeke.

Shock or traumatic disassociation could explain that. Even brain damage. But at some point in the last decade or two, the memory of the incident must have come flooding back to him... and the rest of the story was his very carefully and patiently deployed campaign of retribution.

Also, if Ledger's account was accurate – and he'd taken a step back that day and not actively participated in what had been done to Colin Holmes – then perhaps that explained why his body hadn't been found along with the others.

Revenge, he pondered silently, could be argued as a form of therapy: a rebalancing of cosmic karma, but it wasn't a cure. It was a painkiller. A temporary one. Revenge had been something Boyd had considered during the three dark years after Julia and Noah had died. They'd been brutally snatched away from him, because the driver of the truck behind their car had been arsing about on his phone. The driver had been charged with manslaughter and given a twelve-year sentence. In just three years' time, the man who'd all but bisected his wife's torso and removed the top half of his son's skull could be let out on parole. And, yes, during those dark years he'd considered the long wait, and the chance he'd eventually have to 'rebalance' matters.

Given the opportunity, back then, he might just have taken it. If the man hadn't received a custodial sentence and had walked free on some technicality, there was every chance he'd not be alive now. Boyd would have closed the circle, got his pound of flesh and presumably some temporary respite from the pain he'd been going through.

But it would only have been temporary.

The pay-off that came with retribution was only a

fleeting experience. And after it was done... what was there left to live for?

O'Neal followed the police van ahead of them as it turned right off the seafront onto De La Warr Road and onto Dorset Road, heading inland. It was flanked on either side by neat semi-detached houses that loomed high with their attic rooms. The van came to a halt and the officers inside piled out, wearing their stab vests and riot helmets. Dorset Road was deserted. It was gone ten in the morning so it wasn't that surprising. Everyone who had a job to go to was gone; everyone who didn't was probably in bed still and watching *This Morning*.

Colin Holmes lived in Flat 3a. Which would undoubtedly be one of those attic flats. Which meant two flights of stairs. The ever-present ache in Boyd's side – now he knew what it was and what the bloody thing looked like, even – would be there with him every step of the way.

Boyd turned on his radio and flipped to the ops channel. 'Bravo-Mike-Two-Two, this is Boyd. The target is Flat 3a, an attic room at the top, by the look of it.'

One of the officers looked his way and gave him a thumbs-up. 'Copy that.'

Boyd let the radio sit in his lap, crackling as they listened to the chatter. The good news was that there'd be no easy back-door escape for Holmes if he decided to bolt.

'I love this bit,' said O'Neal.

There was no messing around at the front door. The sergeant had been briefed that Holmes was a multiple murderer and the Big Red Key was already swinging into the front door beside the handle. After a couple of hefty smacks, the door shuddered inwards and all ten officers piled inside.

Over the open channel, Boyd could hear them all

barking 'POLICE!' like a pack of hunting dogs tearing across a ploughed field. He could hear their boots on the stairs, and probably Colin Holmes right at the top could already hear that too.

'Bravo-Mike-Two-Two... you said Flat 3a, right?'

Boyd confirmed and a moment later they heard the crash of the small battering ram again, and the officers all yelling their presence as they burst in. A succession of different voices shouted 'CLEAR!' and Boyd found himself wilting in his seat. Finally the sergeant in charge of the team announced that Colin Holmes wasn't there.

'All right...' Boyd sighed. 'Thanks, sergeant. You can stand down. Everyone back outside, please.'

A minute later they emerged from the battered front door, a steady stream, one after the other. Boyd opened the passenger-side door and climbed out. He approached the sergeant as he removed his helmet.

'Sorry, sir,' he said. 'It's a no-show.'

Boyd nodded. 'Your lads can head back to the station.'

O'Neal and Warren drew up beside him. 'Gloves on?' said O'Neal.

Boyd nodded. 'Gloves on.'

54

Richard Ledger slowly opened his eyes. Last night he'd poured himself a large 'therapeutic' gin and tonic. Which had been mostly gin, to be fair. He'd chased it down with another and may well have had a third before he'd checked the doors and windows and gone to bed... This morning he was paying the price.

His head was thumping mercilessly and he was pretty sure he was going to throw up unless he got some dry toast into him, sharpish. He turned to look at his side table. The alarm clock was showing 10.17 a.m.

Shit. He fumbled for his phone and dialled his office. Imogen, his PA, answered after the first ring.

'Are you all right?' she answered chirpily. 'I was expecting you in at nine. You had a conference call scheduled for –'

'I'm feeling really crappy,' he croaked. 'I'll probably be in after lunch. Can you bump anything else I have in my diary to this afternoon?'

'Of course. You caught a bug?' she asked.

'Yeah, something like that. Tell the sales team I'll be in later to check in on them.'

'Will do.'

He hung up and dropped his phone onto the pillow beside his head. 'Fuck...' he said, sighing heavily and blinking the sleep out of his eyes as he stared up at the ceiling, zebra-striped with sunlight spilling in through the drawn blinds.

He gave himself another minute or two to wake up properly, listening to the peaceful soundtrack of the gated mews: birds twittering away, the soft whine of someone's hybrid rolling off a gravel driveway, the sound of children in the school playground just a few hundred yards away. A soundscape he'd not had many opportunities to listen to since he'd moved in.

He let out a long groan, lifted his head off the pillow and sat up.

'Hello, Richard.'

He jolted at the sound of the voice and turned to find someone perched on a stool in the corner of his bedroom.

'Remember me?' said the figure. He stood up, knees clicking, weary bones creaking. He was holding a kitchen knife in his hands. Richard recognised the eight-inch stainless-steel Damascus boning knife from the block in his kitchen.

'I've been sitting here for hours,' the man continued, 'and I just can't decide what to do with you...'

Boyd did a brief three-sixty scan of Colin Holmes' lounge. It was something of a disappointment, to be fair. It was a small and well-kept living space with none of the telltale signs of a tormented killer's mind gradually unspooling.

It was a far cry from Ewan Jones's halfway-house lodgings in Dover, with its walls covered in haunting depictions of the girl he'd murdered in childhood. That had been every bit the Hollywood scriptwriter's take on a serial killer's sanctum.

Colin Holmes maintained a tidy home. One wall was filled with shelves that were laden with DVD cases. There was a mixture of sci-fi-nerd box sets: *Star Trek TNG*, the original *Star Wars* trilogy, The *X-Files* among others. Alongside these were a fair number of old black-and-white classics: *Citizen Kane*, *Rear Window*, *Peeping Tom* and the like.

Colin Holmes clearly fancied himself as a bit of a movie buff.

In the corner of the room was a tall, slim shelving unit, filled with vinyl LPs and beside it a record player. Boyd carefully leafed through the dog-eared record covers. Holmes's taste in music tended very definitely towards classic gothic: the Mission, the Cure, Bauhaus, the Cult.

On the top shelf of the unit Boyd found a small photo frame containing a faded Polaroid of a young man with long dark hair, spiked and tousled with gel, holding the camera in his hands. It had obviously been taken in a mirror – a selfie taken a long, long time before that word ever existed. Colin Holmes in this photograph was completely unrecognisable... if that was, in fact, even him: a lean pretty boy dressed up like an Adam Ant-styled dandy, all bangles and hooped earrings, wearing an extravagantly ruffled white shirt and tight leather trousers. A stark contrast to the scruffy older man with the boxer's nose that Minter had interviewed at the station a couple of weeks ago.

Boyd moved to his bedroom. Tidy again. Bed made. *His*

mother would be proud. On the walls were a number of artfully framed posters of classic movies from the seventies, eighties and nineties: *Chinatown*, *Seven*, *Dune* – the eighties David Lynch version, Boyd noted. His eyes were drawn to a poster for *Hellraiser IV*. He scanned the credits at the bottom... a name jumped out at him. *Directed by Alan Smithee.* That pseudonym again. Clearly that's what had inspired Colin Holmes's alias.

Alan Smithee who had rented a storage unit eleven years ago. And presumably same Alan Smithee who, according to Richard Ledger, had turned up one day at his work place for a little chat. Boyd hadn't really been sure about that part of Ledger's story. It had been a very convenient explanation for that coffee cup. But now, seeing that name on the poster, gave him the shivers.

Maybe he should have insisted that Ledger found somewhere else to stay last night, other than his home.

Shit.

He pulled his phone out...

'LOOK... MATE... COME ON...' Richard's voice was trembling, lacking any conviction. 'P-please... just put the knife down.'

Colin shook his head and smiled. 'It's a good job that you called work to say you'd be late. This might take a bit of time.'

'Wh-what are you g-going...'

'Going to do?' Colin shrugged, then stretched and yawned. 'Let's just say... my plans are in a state of flux. It's taken me a long time to piece together what happened in those woods. The memories were all jumbled and confused. Then... do you want to know what happened?'

Richard wasn't sure he did. But he nodded, because that's what his intruder wanted from him.

'I bumped into a friend of yours. In fact, I served him in a shop. And that's when all the random fragments of memory sort of... jiggled into place.'

Colin lazily dragged the blade of the kitchen knife across the bedsheet. It sliced through the silk with ease. 'This is very sharp, Richard. It's a quality knife you've got yourself here.'

'Jesus... please...'

'You have a very nice kitchen. A very nice home... and a very nice job. You've done well, haven't you? How did you manage that... or was it all down to Daddy?'

Richard shook his head. 'H-hard work. Lots of hard work... Discipline. Ambition.'

'Ambition?' Colin repeated. 'Yes. I had ambitions... once upon a time. Back then I wrote poetry – lyrics, actually. I suppose I wanted to form a band. Or join one. Become someone famous, see my face on the front of *Melody Maker*, *NME*. You know? I was a bit of a pretty boy. That was the big thing in those days, wasn't it? Image.'

Richard felt the smallest glimmer of hope. Maybe music would provide a much-needed common ground on which to build a dialogue. 'Right, yeah,' he said. 'It was. I mean, remember Duran Duran... Depeche Mode...'

Colin tutted. 'Awful bloody music. I was into the Cure, the Cult. *Decent* music, Richard. Not plastic pop.'

'Exactly,' Richard conceded. 'Back then... I... I was into acid house.'

Colin nodded. 'Oh yeah, some of it was bearable, I suppose. But not the shit you were playing that day. Do you remember, Richard?'

He did. 'Mate...' he tried. 'I was just playing the crap the others wanted to hear.'

'Mate?' Colin laughed. 'I fucking hate that word. You could at least use my name.'

Richard's mind was a blank. He knew it wasn't Alan Smithee.

'Oh, that's right, you didn't bother to ask, did you? Well, it was Alistair... at the time you attacked me. It's Colin now, though.' He leant forward. 'So, no more of this "mate" crap. All right? We're *not* mates.'

Richard nodded.

'And in the time we have left together... we're not going to become *mates*, either.'

'Wh-what are you going to do with me?'

'Oh, that question again.' Colin sighed. 'Well, it's the same answer as last time, Richard... I'm deciding.'

55

Boyd rang Okeke's phone. It was Minter who answered after the first ring.

'Boss?'

'Where are you?'

'We're on our way back to Hastings. You managed to pick up Colin Holmes yet?' he asked.

'No. We're at his place now,' Boyd explained. 'But he's gone. Look, have you got Ledger's phone number on you?'

'Just a sec, boss… Lemme check my call history.' He read out the number. Then: 'What's going on?'

'I think I fucked up,' replied Boyd. 'I think Colin Holmes may have already gone after Ledger.'

'Shit. Get the local nick to do a welfare check,' Minter suggested.

'I have. But I'm going to try and get hold of him myself, now,' Boyd said.

'Then tell him to get out of his house,' Minter said.

Boyd sighed. 'Yes, that's the plan.' He hung up and immediately dialled Richard Ledger's number.

RICHARD'S PHONE buzzed on the side table.

'Now, I wonder who that is? Could it be... the police?' Colin said.

From where he was, Richard could see 'Unknown Caller ID'. It wasn't his lawyer and it wasn't work. He suspected – hoped – that Colin was right. 'It's probably a client,' he said.

'Let it go,' said Colin. 'We're busy.'

The phone continued to buzz until it finally stopped and presumably flipped to voicemail. The room was silent once more.

'So...' Richard broke the silence. 'What now?' If, as Colin had said, he was genuinely undecided, there was surely room for persuasion, for a case to be made.

'Colin, mate...'

Colin raised a cautionary brow.

'Sorry. Colin... this d-doesn't have to end... with...' Richard paused.

'Me killing you?' Colin suggested.

'Look, Colin... I'm no legal expert, but I know that what was done to you, what we did to you, will be taken into account.'

'The pain, trauma, the physical damage and the severe psychological scarring, you mean?'

Richard nodded.

'I very much doubt it,' Colin said calmly. 'I didn't kill the other three in the heat of the moment. I tracked them down over a number of years. You could say I hunted them down. Then, of course, I interrogated and tortured them before I murdered them.' Colin smiled. 'I don't think teenage trauma would wash as a defence, do you?'

'I... I could be a witness... in your defence...'

'Really? And what would you say on my behalf, Richard?'

'I could describe how brutal the attack was. What horrific things they did to you...'

Colin waggled the knife at him. 'What you *all* did to me.'

'I didn't do anything!' Richard pleaded. 'I didn't hold you down. I didn't –'

'Shove a pinecone up my arsehole? Kick and punch my head until I stopped screaming? Smash my head in with a rock and leave me for dead?'

Richard shook his head. 'I was screaming at them to stop... You must remember that?'

'Do you know how life has been for me since that day?' Colin asked him. 'I can't eat properly. I have piercing migraines nearly every day. I have nightmares. Oh, yes, they come at me every fucking night. Every time I look in the mirror, I see what a bloody mess you made of me...'

'I'm so sorry,' Richard whispered.

'Oh no. *Don't you dare tell me you're sorry*. Not if you don't want me to stick this in your throat right now!'

Richard raised his hands. 'Okay. Okay... Okay.'

'And to answer your question, no,' said Colin. 'It might not have been you holding me down... but I don't remember you screaming at them to stop. I remember you all egging each other on.'

'What? I was trying to rein them in!'

'When I asked them if it was your idea, they all nodded.'

'Of course they fucking did! They were probably fucking terrified!'

Colin cocked his head thoughtfully. 'Yes, they were.' He smiled. 'Mark – I think it was Mark – actually shit himself in the chair he was sitting in.' He sighed. 'You know, all three of your friends were drunk when I snatched them. Alcohol, I think, lays bare who we really are, strips away the programmed personality. It unpeels the nurture, leaving only the nature, don't you think? Andy tried fighting back; he threw a few wild punches. But Mark and Robin took one look at the knife I was holding and they couldn't have been more helpful.'

Colin got up from the end of the bed, ambled towards the floor-to-ceiling window and parted a couple of slats to peer out at the leafy suburban cul-de-sac. 'But once I had them hog-tied... once they'd all sobered up a little... they all had the same little expressions on their faces.' Colin turned to look at him. His eyes rounded, swivelling manically, his mouth wide open. He chuckled. 'Like three little piggies.'

Richard's phone buzzed again on the side table.

56

Boyd hung up as the call flipped across to voicemail again.

O'Neal glanced his way. 'No answer?'

'Christ. Eyes on the road,' said Boyd. They were on blues-and-twos now, speeding westwards along the M25 towards Richmond, the traffic pulling over to make a run-through for them.

There was no point leaving a message. If Colin Holmes was there with him, it was too late to give Ledger any warning. The message itself, if Colin heard it, might only exacerbate things. He wondered now if it had been a smart move to send the local police around for that welfare check. The knocking at Ledger's front door might do the same thing.

He was also concerned that he'd not given the local police enough detail. If they'd sent over a couple of newbie coppers expecting nothing more than an irritated man in a bathrobe to open the front door... they could be in for a shock.

Shit.

He glanced at the satnav on the dash, according to the

screen they were still half an hour away. He dialled control again. The operator started to speak, but Boyd cut straight over her.

'This is DCI Boyd, East Sussex CID. I called five minutes ago for a welfare check on a house in Carlton Mews, Richmond.'

'Just a second...'

He heard a muted exchange between operators, then the voice came back to him. 'Yes, we've dispatched a patrol car. They should be there soon.'

He needed to elevate this and fast. 'It's a potential hostage situation,' he told the operator. 'The suspect is Colin Holmes, almost certainly armed and extremely dangerous. You need to stand that patrol car down.'

'Okay. Are you requesting an ARU?' came the calm reply.

'Yes. Absolutely,' said Boyd.

~

COLIN SAT BACK DOWN on the bed. 'I've got a nasty feeling the police are coming for me,' he said.

Richard felt both a glimmer of hope and a dawning realisation that the arrival of flickering blue lights outside might tip Colin over the edge.

Reason with him. Dammit.

'Look... Colin... that may well be. But y-you've got a chance here to... maybe leverage the situation.'

Colin rolled his eyes as though that was the dumbest thing he'd heard in his life. 'I'm not interested in leveraging anything,' he said. 'If they're coming, then they already know I've murdered three people and they know you're next on my list. To be honest with you, Richard, I don't really care whether my sentence will be reduced by going quietly.' He sighed. 'I'm not even sure I give much of a shit whether I'm alive at the end of the day.' He looked at Richard. 'It's not been a particularly wonderful life thus far.'

'You'll get help now,' Richard replied. 'Support.'

'Well, wonderful as that is to hear… I'm not really after help.' Colin studied the long glinting blade in his hand. 'I can't tell you how many times I've considered ending things over the last thirty years…' He pushed his shirt sleeve up to reveal a ridged pattern of scars, both old and more recent, along his wrist and forearm.

'Jesus…'

'Oh, stop it. As if you care. Do you know what's kept me going though?' He smiled down at the knife as he played with the blade in his hands. 'You, Richard. You and your little friends. Truth be told, Richard, tracking the four of you down has given me a reason to get out of bed in the morning.' He grinned. 'It's been like a game, these last twelve years. A bit of honest-to-God fun… watching you all from afar, planning, preparing.'

He looked up.

Richard could see blood dripping down his fingers.

'Have you ever watched *The Jackal*?' Colin asked.

Richard had once. The one with Bruce Willis. He nodded.

'It's been a little like that,' Colin said. 'Or it's felt like it, at least.'

'The killer… He fails in the end, though… doesn't he, Colin?' Richard said, regretting the words as soon as they'd left his mouth.

But Colin just hunched his shoulders. 'Yes. You're quite right. He did. But… I suppose, that's not really the point. It's all about the journey… The heroic quest.'

Again, a glimmer of hope.

'Right. Right. Well, you found me, right? You managed to find all four of us.'

Colin grinned. 'Just like Pokémon. *Gotta catch 'em all.*'

Richard forced a smile and laughed. 'Right. Colin, look... I was interviewed by the police yesterday. I... I made a full confession to them – about what we did to you. I'll... I'll probably end up doing time for it.'

'I'm not sure I really care that much about what happens to you.'

'Well then, if you don't care... Jesus... just let me go! Please!'

Colin cocked his head, thoughtfully.

Is he... considering it? Richard couldn't help but think.

A flicker of blue light danced through the blinds' slats. Colin got up again to look out. 'So... here they are at last...' He nodded as half a dozen vans and patrol cars slewed to a halt outside. 'God, it really is just like a movie, isn't it? Come and see.' He flicked the knife, beckoning Richard over to join him at the window.

'Colin...' whispered Richard, peering out at the scene below. 'Come on. It's over... Just put the knife down. Please?'

Colin turned to stare at him. 'Not quite yet.' He waggled the blade from side to side in a silent eeny-meeny-miny-moe.

'I think it's about time for me to make my mind up.'

O'NEAL SWUNG the pool car into the private estate. The gate was wide open, the leafy mews was packed with response vehicles: patrol cars, two police vans and a couple of ambulances – blue lights aplenty flickering unnecessarily in the mid-morning sun. He imagined, without the traffic, the uniformed coppers hurrying from house to house to clear the occupants and the paramedics busily preparing for casualties, it might have been a peaceful little oasis of calm amid the bustle of Richmond upon Thames.

O'Neal found a space on the kerb and parked up.

Boyd climbed out into the heat of the day, removed his jacket and tossed it back into the car. He was beginning to wonder now if he'd over-elevated the alert.

'You two stay with the car,' he said. O'Neal and Warren drooped with disappointment.

He picked his way forward through the vehicles, towards what appeared to be the epicentre of everyone's attention, a slate-coloured modernist cube of a building, wildly out of place, nestled among a crescent of mock-Tudor new builds. In front of it were two ARU vans parked at diagonals to provide cover for – he counted – twenty armed response officers who were currently checking their equipment.

He spotted the command point and hurried over.

'DCI Boyd, East Sussex CID,' he announced, waggling the ID tag on the end of his lanyard.

'I'm DSI Khan. You're the one who called this in?' replied the detective superintendent.

Boyd nodded.

'Can you give us a bit of detail?' he asked. 'Because all we have right now is "armed and dangerous" and –' he nodded towards an upstairs window – 'we've seen that for ourselves.'

'You've seen them?' Boyd repeated.

Khan nodded. 'Yes, and one of them is brandishing a knife. I've got a negotiator, Nigel Fuller – where is he?' He looked around, spotted the negotiator and waved him over to join them.

Boyd shook his hand and introduced himself. 'Our

hostage taker is Colin Holmes and it's the owner of that house, Richard Ledger, who is on the wrong end of the knife,' Boyd told him.

'So what do you have on this Colin Holmes?' asked Fuller, pulling out a notepad.

57

Colin surveyed the scene outside. So many vehicles, so many people. All of them here just for him. He smiled at the theatre and spectacle of it all. It was like a mini Nakatomi Plaza. But then what did that make him – John McClane or Hans Gruber?

Perhaps McClane, he decided. The hero. Kind of. They'd both relieved the world of some nasty people, hadn't they? Reduced the total sum of evil from the gene pool. But sadly, while the moral scales seemed to work just fine in the world of movies – the Avengers were allowed to wipe out thousands due to collateral damage in pursuit of justice – in the real world the same rules didn't apply.

He looked down at the bloodied blade in his hand.

He wondered if the problem was in the optics. If Captain America had had a face like his and emerged from the carnage of a final showdown wearing a blood-smeared Primark shirt and brandishing a smeared kitchen knife in one hand, would he have still had that hero's welcome?

Richard's phone buzzed in Colin's other hand. He looked down at the screen.

Unknown number.

He peered out through the slats of the blind and spotted a cluster of police officers gathered around a patrol car. One of them had a phone to his ear. Colin answered the call. 'Yes?'

'Richard?' a voice asked.

'It's Colin,' he replied. 'I'm afraid Richard can't come to the phone right now.'

'Okay, it's nice to meet you, Colin. My name's Nigel. I'm a –'

'Negotiator. Yes, I've got that.' Colin replied.

'Good,' Nigel said. 'I'm going to start by asking you... how's Richard?'

Colin turned to look at the superking-sized bed and shrugged. 'Well, he's here.'

'Good,' Nigel said again. 'That's good. Could I speak to him?'

'No. Not really.' Colin sighed. 'I thought the whole point of this... was to speak to *me*.'

'It is, Colin. It is,' Nigel assured him. 'I need you to understand... it may look intimidating outside. But we're not here to hurt you. We're only here to help you.'

'Help me?' Colin laughed softly. 'I'm beyond help, don't you think? Besides, I'm pretty much done here.'

'*Done here?* Can you tell me what you mean by that?' Nigel asked.

'I've done what I came here to do,' Colin said. 'It's not rocket science.'

'Have you hurt Richard?' Nigel asked.

'You could say that.'

'Does he need medical assistance?'

Colin looked back over his shoulder. 'Not really.' He could hear the voices of the other officers gathered nearby in the background. There were murmured exchanges.

'Colin, listen carefully. We have paramedics out here. If you've... done something to Richard, there's a chance he may still be alive. The quicker you and I can sort this mess out, the better for everyone, okay?'

Colin remained silent.

'Look,' Nigel tried again. 'You answered the phone. Which says to me, you want a way out of this situation.'

Colin sighed. 'I do.'

'That's good, Colin. That's... great. So, then...'

'Do you want me to come out?' Colin asked.

'I do. Can you do that for me?' Nigel asked.

'Sure.'

BOYD APPROACHED the negotiator as he lowered his phone. 'He's coming out?'

He nodded.

'And what about the hostage?'

Boyd could see the negotiator was troubled. 'Colin said he doesn't need medical assistance.'

'Which could mean the best case... or worst case?' said Boyd.

Fuller nodded. 'He said he'd done what he came here to do. I'm afraid that doesn't sound encouraging. Gimme a sec,' he said to Boyd. 'I need to quickly brief the tactical commander.'

Fuller hurried over to crouch behind one of the vans and exchange words with the sergeant leading the armed response unit.

'Shit,' mumbled Boyd to himself. If Ledger was dead, he knew he'd be piling some of the blame at his own front door. Christ, Sutherland had called it yesterday evening. He'd voiced a concern for Ledger's safety, and Boyd should have acted on that immediately.

If he was dead, then Boyd knew what the price tag would be: another regret held in a sealed box in his head. Another 'What if...' to trouble him during a sleepless night. The '*I got it wrong*'s massively outweighed the '*I got it right*'s when it came to career retrospection. They were splinters that protruded and they snagged painfully.

One of the armed officers called out, 'MOVEMENT INSIDE!'

The negotiator and the sergeant promptly ended their hushed exchange, and the sergeant started muttering instructions to his team across their radio channel.

Boyd turned to look at the grey slab that was Ledger's home: ugly to the point of being an eye sore. He thought he caught a glimpse of movement through the slats of a downstairs window. Then nothing.

They waited.

What the fuck's he up to? Boyd had heard the negotiator's side of the conversation: the clear instructions – front door, empty-handed, see you in a minute. And now five or more had passed. The tension was killing him. Even though Boyd was SIO, he was three rungs down the command ladder here: strategic – the DSI; tactical – the firearms sergeant and advisory; the negotiator. While this played out, Boyd was just a spectator.

'GARAGE DOOR!' one of the armed officers shouted.

Boyd's gaze switched from the front door and swept left to the driveway that ramped gently downwards towards the building's basement. The garage door, the same slate-grey as the rest of the building, began to slowly rise.

He stretched on tiptoes to get a better angle. The narrow space inside the garage had been revealed by the rising door. It was light and bright inside: a white-washed interior uncluttered with the usual dumping-ground detritus of a family home. There were spotlights in the ceiling, Boyd noticed. More car showroom than garage.

He could see the rear end of Ledger's Range Rover, its spare wheel perched on the back like a nautical fender.

'WATCH THE CAR!' barked the sergeant.

You've got to be kidding me, thought Boyd. *Surely he's not going to have a go?*

The sergeant in command of the tactical team had a loudhailer in one hand. He raised it quickly. 'DO NOT ATTEMPT TO USE THE VEHICLE!'

Boyd noticed a number of the armed officers stepping back from the vehicles they were using as cover. If Colin decided to reverse up the ramp and ram the patrol cars, the Range Rover would probably have the horsepower and momentum to shunt them aside with ease.

And he could see it in his mind's eye, like a scene from a movie. Every one of those armed officers letting loose, peppering the vehicle with bullets, windows shattering, sparks flying and the Range Rover kangarooing down the cul-de-sac towards the exit before finally coming to a lurching halt as it smacked into one of the red-brick pillars flanking the gate.

What a fucking mess that would be.

'COLIN!' The negotiator had the loudhailer now. 'JUST GET OUT OF THE CAR. HANDS EMPTY AND RAISED... LIKE WE AGREED...'

They waited for what seemed like another full minute before one of the armed officers barked out a sighting.

"EYES ON GARAGE. BEHIND THE ROVER!'

Boyd could see movement in the gap between the belly of the Range Rover and the floor of the garage. Legs. Only two of them, though.

A figure emerged from behind the vehicle, darkly clad, wearing what looked like a balaclava over his head, his hands behind his back.

'HANDS RAISED!' shouted the sergeant.

The figure slowly raised his arms out beside him as he stepped out of the garage and began to make his way up the gentle incline of the driveway. In his right hand was a bloodied kitchen knife and from the other hung a canvas shopping bag laden with something.

'STAY WHERE YOU ARE AND DROP THE KNIFE!' the sergeant shouted.

He carried on up the ramp until he reached the top. His arms still spread like Lady Justice above the Old Bailey: scales of justice in one hand, sword of retribution in the other.

'DROP THE KNIFE AND THE BAG!'

Holmes kept walking, approaching the patrol cars and the ARU's van, which were collectively blocking the drive-way. He showed no sign of slowing down or lowering his arms as he stepped off the kerb and onto the road, now just five yards away from the nearest unit.

'Take him down,' commanded the sergeant.

The quiet suburban mid-morning peace of Carlton Mews was momentarily shattered by the sound of a gunshot. The figure jerked and shuddered, his black hoodie puffing with exit discharge and a pink spray cloud of aerosolised blood as he collapsed onto the road.

The nearest armed officer hurried over, kicked the kitchen knife well clear of the body before reaching down to check for a pulse. A few seconds passed before he announced he was dead.

DSI Khan came up behind Boyd and nudged him out of his stupor. 'Can you ID him, Boyd?'

'Right.' Boyd hurried forward and squatted down beside the body. He lifted the balaclava and instantly recognised the flattened profile of Holmes's broken nose.

'It's Holmes,' he confirmed.

He got to his feet, his eyes drawn to the shopping bag, which was now lying on the pavement a couple of yards away. He could see the white plastic inner lining of a cooler-bag... with dark strands of something spilling out.

A choking realisation jolted him into action. He hurried down the ramp towards the open garage, the sound of the paramedics' footsteps behind him and DSI Khan's voice calling out for him to stay put.

Boyd crossed the garage floor, the cleanest garage floor he'd ever seen in his life, headed through a door at the back that led up a half flight of stairs and up to an open-plan living room of bleached pine, hard edges and dark granite, punctuated with ugly pieces of 'object d'art' sitting in up-lit display cases. He looked around and quickly spotted the stairs leading up to the first floor.

He climbed the steps three at a time, in his haste misjudging the first few strides and stumbling clumsily upwards. He paused at a midway turn, bathed in diagonal shafts of sunlight from a vertical window that appeared to run from the ground all the way up to a flat roof in one interrupted six-foot wide band of thick double-plated glass. He paused for a moment as he stared down at a sequence of dark, almost black, spatters of blood along the steps.

You really want to do this? Julia's voice. Funny how she still lingered after all this time. *You know what you're going to see, Bill.* He had a pretty good idea. But it wouldn't be the worst thing he'd ever seen. Noah held that particular badge.

He scrambled up the rest of the stairs onto a faux-marble mezzanine landing that overlooked the lounge below. His mental compass steered him right, as did the trail of dark droplets of blood, and he headed towards double doors that were swung half open. Through the doorway he could see ground-to-floor windows, striped horizontally by a ladder of slats. And the corner of a bed.

He ground to a halt. He could also see a bare foot protruding over the edge of the bed, perfectly still.

Lifeless.

From down below he heard the paramedics entering the house the same way he had.

'Up here!' he called down to them – *for what good it would do.*

He advanced slowly towards the room, each step revealing another few inches of the super-king-sized bed and a little more of Ledger's bare leg.

Finally, Boyd found himself standing in the doorway as the paramedics reached the top of the stairs and turned to hurry along the polished, shiny mezzanine floor towards him.

He let out the ragged breath he'd been unintentionally holding onto for the last half a minute.

The lead paramedic approached him. She was a short woman in her forties, shouldering a bag of equipment that looked almost as big as her. 'Please tell me that's not his head in the bag outside?' she said sombrely.

He stepped to one side to let her into the room.

She went in, caught one glimpse of Ledger, bound,

gagged and shuddering with sobs of relief, and hurried over to deal with him.

'Luckily not...' Boyd whispered under his breath. 'Thank fuck.'

58

'How am I doing?' Boyd stared down and swilled the dregs of his coffee around and around in its paper cup before finally chugging the last of it down. 'I'm shit scared.'

Charlotte reached across the picnic table, her index finger playing with his. 'It's going to be fine,' she assured him. 'Very "snippable", I believe, was the word the consultant used.'

He looked up from his lap and smiled at her. 'I know.'

'Well,' she said, 'you're going to have to put your feet up for a bit. You'll have me and Emma waiting on you.'

He turned to look across the decking of the Kitkat Café at the wide sandy ribbon of Camber Sands. Emma was down near the water's edge with both the dogs, their leads slung over her shoulder, her sandals in one hand as she kicked sprays of seawater up from a tidal pool for Ozzie to snap at and Mia to flee from. Even from this distance, her bump was visible.

'I feel old,' he said.

'You're still on the right side of fifty.' Charlotte laughed. 'It's all right for some.'

'No, but cancer... it feels like an old-person disease, well this kind, anyway,' he said.

'It's indiscriminate is what it is, Bill. You can make lifestyle choices that tinker with the odds, but at the end of the day it picks victims randomly... and unfairly,' she said.

He nodded as he watched Emma. His little Ems all grown up and having her very own rug rat. She'd stopped kicking up water for Ozzie and had stepped out of the tidal pool onto a low berm of wet sand.

Charlotte followed his gaze. 'You're going to be around for years to come, Bill. You're going to be able to teach Baby Boyd all sorts of deplorable habits.' She squeezed his hand and lowered her chin so that she was doing interrogative Lady Di eyes at him. 'Operation worries aside... how are you doing in there?'

'Fine.'

'*Fine*,' she mimicked his gruff voice.

He smiled.

'Are you still replaying the... you know?'

He nodded. It was hard not to keep seeing Colin Holmes twitch and jerk like some piñata donkey as the shot rang out. It was clearly what he'd wanted to happen, armed as he was with the bloody knife – they discovered later that he'd cut his own hand – and what had looked like a head in a shopping bag (it had turned out to be the head from one of Ledger's collection of tasteless 'art' – a grisly, wrinkled, faux Victorian taxidermic 'mermaid').

Holmes knew he'd be taken down.

Oddly, the nightmare Boyd was having was about what he *hadn't* seen. What he'd been expecting to find inside

Ledger's bedroom. The man's headless body sprawled across the bed; the sheets soaked in dark blood.

Over the last fortnight, he'd had time to dwell on Colin Holmes's mental state and the choices he'd made. Interviewing Ledger about it a few days afterwards, it had been confirmed that Colin had chosen to spare him because he believed Richard had played a lesser role in his horrific assault decades ago. But it had also been clear that he wasn't hoping or expecting to leverage that mercy into a marginally more lenient sentence. Truth be told, having murdered three people, even with the mitigating circumstances and last-minute act of compassion, at his age, prison would almost certainly have been for life.

He'd emerged from the basement garage *determined* to be gunned down.

There was a tragic logic to his thinking. He'd been assaulted, abused and nearly murdered three decades ago – his whole world had been shattered by the incident. And from the pieces he'd picked up in the aftermath, he'd built a directionless, meandering life. The local police had made less than a token effort to find his assailant, the local press had moved on to other more interesting things, and the world had shrugged its shoulders at Colin's misfortune.

Dying dramatically like that... his arms stretched out Christ-like and walking fearlessly towards the guns was his final '*screw you*'. And the more Boyd thought about it, it had been a justified 'screw you'. The police had let Colin down. Social services had let him down. The damaged young man who'd emerged from the hospital months after the attack had been left to deal with the post-trauma, his physical rehabilitation and trying to make sense of what had happened to him, all by himself. Presumably because, being a foster kid, he'd had no one advocating on his behalf. No one screaming at the authorities that '*this lad needs help!*'

Were things any different today? He'd like to think so. But he wasn't so sure that they were.

'You all right there?' asked Charlotte. 'You look like you're a million miles away.'

He grasped her hand and squeezed it. 'Wool gathering.'

'Not worrying?'

'Nope. Not worrying. I'm going to kick cancer's arse.'

'That's the spirit,' she replied. 'We'll do it together.'

He got up from the bench. 'Come on – let's rescue Emma from the fur kids and grab an ice cream.'

She laughed. 'She *is* a rather handy babysitter.'

He shrugged. 'You wait... that'll be us in the near future. Returning the favour.'

She patted his hand. 'Oh, stop it. You'll love it... *Gramps*.'

'Less of the Gramps.' He scowled at her. '*I'm* not even fifty yet. Remember?'

She narrowed her eyes. 'Ooh, that's below the belt, Mr Boyd.'

'Just stating facts,' he replied, ducking away as he did so.

THE END

EPILOGUE

21 August, 1993

Richard brought the tray of beers over to his friends. They were sitting outside in the pub garden around a rickety wooden picnic table, away from the other patrons. Being the eldest, even if only by a few months, he was the only one of them old enough to go to the bar, legally at least.

'Here we go,' he said, setting it down. A pint of Carlsberg for Mark and Andy, Woodpecker cider for Robin.

He dealt out the packets of crisps, then sat down, grabbed his pint of bitter and raised it solemnly. 'To the end of fucking A levels. To the end of fucking school...'

The other clinked pint glasses willingly to that.

'To the future,' he added. They clinked again and gulped their drinks.

Richard's maths exam this morning had been the last of them. He was confident he was going to get his much-needed B when the results came out. The extra maths lessons his dad had paid for had probably helped cinch it.

'What's your summer looking like, Ricky?' asked Mark.

He stretched. 'Gonna hit Glastonbury. Get pissed. Down some E's. Ian Drury and the Blockheads are on the Pyramid stage. It's gonna be fucking wicked.'

'Lucky bastitch,' muttered Andy. 'It's fifty-eight quid a ticket. All right if you're a rich kid.'

Richard shrugged. It wasn't his fault his dad was loaded. 'What about you grubby plebs, then?'

Robin tore open his packet of cheese-and-onion crisps. 'I'm going backpacking. Maybe get some holiday work abroad.'

Richard suspected Mark and Andy had no real plans to speak of, other than watching Gaby Roslin on *Big Breakfast* every morning and wanking their way through the rest of the day. He had little time for either of them. Wasters. They probably were going to pull in useless grades in September and wind up working someplace where they'd be wearing plastic nametags for the rest of their working lives. Robin, on the other hand, might make something of himself one day, he mused.

He let the chatter about plans going forward run on for a few minutes, then shut it down. They were here this afternoon to talk about the Thing that happened four years ago.

'You know why we're here,' he said, lowering his voice. 'What this is about, right?'

The others nodded.

Four years had passed, a lifetime almost, and apart from the manic exchanges between them all in the days following the Thing, and the pointing of fingers about who did what, it had settled down to become the Thing We Will Never Talk About.

'We got away with it,' he said. Andy shook his head. Richard turned to him. 'Why the head-shaking, mate?'

'*You*... got away with it.'

Richard narrowed his eyes. *Fucking moron.* 'We've been through this, shithead. You wimps may have just sat and watched... but who the fuck's ever going to believe that?' Richard smiled. 'You were all there. You watched. You laughed. You cheered me on... that makes us *all* an equal part of it. And this stays between us.' He leant forward on the creaking table. 'We're all going off to different places, doing different things.'

Although Andy probably won't... the useless twat.

'We're going to make new mates, find girlfriends, and *this* –' he looked round at them all – 'is gonna feel like a thing of the past.'

'Oh, so you're ditching us, Ricky?' said Mark. 'That's nice.'

Richard shrugged. 'The point is... we're all going our own ways and we're gonna move on, right. Meet new people, make new friends that we trust...'

Robin could see where he was going with this. 'But the... *Thing*... stays right here.'

Richard nodded. 'Exactly, Robbie. We can't tell anyone. Ever. Not in five years, not in ten years. Not on our deathbeds. Not to girlfriends. Not to wives.'

'Yeah, right!' Mark laughed. 'Like I'm ever going to let myself get shackled.'

'I'm being deadly fucking serious!' snapped Richard. 'We were all there. That means if this ever comes out, we're all guilty.'

'It won't,' said Robbie. 'The police got nothing. They've given up.'

'It won't if we all keep our mouths tightly shut,' continued Richard. 'That means no "What's the worst thing you ever done?" conversations. Even if you're pissed or stoned, or with someone who's sworn they'll never blab. Never. Ever. Okay?'

'Hey, Rick... it's all cool,' said Robin. 'We're solid. Right, lads?'

Richard watched Mark and Andy – nodding donkeys the pair of them. Robin he trusted, well, *semi*-trusted, but these two were fucking morons.

'I'm going to say this now. Just once. If I get even a whiff, from any of you, that you've had a heart-to-heart with someone about...'

What to call it? The Thing was the name they'd given it all through school, but maybe it was time to call a spade, a spade – give their dirty little secret the gravity and weight it deserved.

'... about what we did to that queer, I will fucking come for you.'

His friends – his minions, truth be told – had come out on this sunny afternoon to celebrate the end of exams. To sink some beers and have fun. But now their stupid slack-jawed faces made them look like the Three Little Pigs cowering behind a splintering wooden door.

'I will silence you,' added Richard, clenching a fist. 'And you *know* I'm capable of doing that.'

Robbie was the first to break the long, uncomfortable silence. 'And we won't, mate. Chill. Okay?'

Yes, maybe it was time to chill. He could see he'd scared them shitless. There was no way they'd tell now. He tipped his pint glass and took a long chug, nearly emptying it, then set it down on the table.

He mustered a cool, disarming smile. 'Right then, who's forking out for the next round?'

. . .

THE END

DCI BOYD RETURNS IN

THE ARCHIVE available to pre-order here

ACKNOWLEDGMENTS

This is going to be a very different note from me. During the writing of this book, two things happened. Firstly, I got bowel cancer. Secondly, I lost my dad to pneumonia. Both things blindsided me; both things hit me like a hammer. That's why this book took much longer to come out. I have the usual people I want to thank for their help, but I'll do that in a bit. First, I want to say something about those two events.

My dad... had always been my first beta reader. He'd always be the guy who got first eyes on the initial, usually awful, draft. He was always honest and forthright, but tempered that with a genuine affection for my writing style, rightly or wrongly. 'You may be my son, Al, but....' was how he always began the praise bit, but it was important for him to start with that because he wanted me to know it wasn't the usual 'oh, that's wonderful' praise a parent gives their child. He wanted me to know he was a genuine fan, and, of all the books I've written, it was the Boyd series he loved the most.

It's hard for me to write this, to be honest with you; I'm a bit weepy as I type this. I lost him sixty-eight days ago and, while I can go through a couple of days now without having an emotional moment, writing this is... well, stirring it all up. But I want to have something immortalised in print, something out there forever that is me speaking to him.

Dad, you helped me form Bill Boyd into a real person. And he's going to be around for a while yet, I promise. Some of you is in him, some of me... He's our guy, our buddy, right?

The bowel cancer hit me six months or so before Dad passed. He was so worried about it. He's never been religious. In fact, in all but name he was an atheist, but he did admit stopping by once or twice at our local church to have a quiet word with God. I'm not the religious type either, but every now and then, in quiet moments of reflection, I entertain the idea that Dad may have made the deal with God: 'For fuck's sake, take me, not my bloody son.' Who knows? As a father, you would. I know I would.

Anyway, as they often say to writers, write what you know. So, yes, Boyd is embarking on the same journey I have been on, and am still on. As the series catches up with real time, Bill and I will have gone through the same things, together. And if I make a full recovery, so will he. If I don't... well, that arsy bugger will be coming along to keep me company.

By the way, the prognosis for us both, right now, is quite promising. Not out of the woods yet, but watch this space...

Now, to wrap up this indulgent missive, I want to thank a number of people. Firstly, my wife, Debbie, who as always, puts a shine on my best writing and an editorial filter on my worst. But more so for all the emotional support she's given to me, my dad and my mum. During the crapfest of the last nine months of my life, she's been my saviour.

Also I want to thank my copy-editor, Wendy Shakespeare, who – as always – finds a way to save my bacon time and time again when it comes to continuity errors, incorrect character names and dumbass grammatical errors.

Lastly, I want to thank the wonderful people who have cared for me medically – the NHS folks who do what they do because, unlike so many others, they actually give a damn. I am so very grateful to live in a country where a random illness won't suddenly and completely bankrupt you. If you'll allow me just a little politics here... let me just say that the NHS is the one thing this nation's successive governments (sorry, not the current lot) have got right. If there's only one basic job a government should do... surely, it's to keep their people well, right?

There done. No more politics. (Slapped wrist.)

Finally, I want to thank you, dear reader, for following me through to this last page. I'd like to think that you and I and Boyd have a connection together. The Three Musketeers. The Three Amigos. And, as a result of reading this series, perhaps you have the faintest connection to a man you never met, but who has enjoyed the same thrills and spills as us... Anthony Scarrow.

Until next time, dear reader.

Alex Scarrow

ALSO BY ALEX SCARROW

DCI Boyd

SILENT TIDE

OLD BONES NEW BONES

BURNING TRUTH

THE LAST TRAIN

THE SAFE SPACE

GONE TO GROUND

ARGYLE HOUSE

THE LOCK-UP

Thrillers

LAST LIGHT

AFTERLIGHT

OCTOBER SKIES

THE CANDLEMAN

A THOUSAND SUNS

The TimeRiders series (in reading order)

TIMERIDERS

TIMERIDERS: DAY OF THE PREDATOR

TIMERIDERS: THE DOOMSDAY CODE

TIMERIDERS: THE ETERNAL WAR

TIMERIDERS: THE CITY OF SHADOWS

TIMERIDERS: THE PIRATE KINGS

TIMERIDERS: THE MAYAN PROPHECY

TIMERIDERS: THE INFINITY CAGE

The Plague Land series

PLAGUE LAND

PLAGUE NATION

PLAGUE WORLD

The Ellie Quin series

THE LEGEND OF ELLIE QUIN

THE WORLD ACCORDING TO ELLIE QUIN

ELLIE QUIN BENEATH A NEON SKY

ELLIE QUIN THROUGH THE GATEWAY

ELLIE QUIN: A GIRL REBORN

ABOUT THE AUTHOR

Over the last sixteen years, award-winning author Alex Scarrow has published seventeen novels with Penguin Random House, Orion and Pan Macmillan. A number of these have been optioned for film/TV development, including his bestselling *Last Light*.

When he is not busy writing and painting, Alex spends most of his time trying to keep Ozzie away from the food bin. He lives in the wilds of East Anglia with his wife Deborah and five, permanently muddy, dogs.

Ozzie came to live with him in January 2017. He was adopted from Spaniel Aid UK and was believed to be seven at the time. Ozzie loves food, his mum, food, his ball, food, walks and more food...

He dreams of unrestricted access to the food bin.

For up-to-date information on the DCI BOYD series, visit: www.alexscarrow.com

To see what Ozzie is up to, click on the instagram link below...

Printed in Great Britain
by Amazon